# ELEMENTAL HEIR

# Also by Rachel Morgan

RIDLEY KAYNE CHRONICLES, BOOK 3

# ELEMENTAL HEIR

## RACHEL MORGAN

ISBN 978-1-928510-29-1

www.rachel-morgan.com

# CHAPTER 1

MAGIC FUELED THE STORM that raged across the land. Ridley Kayne, wrapped in her own magic and invisible as air, looked out across the bare landscape beneath the swirling mass of clouds and imagined a city as she mentally ran through every step of the plan.

*We're going to return magic to society.*

It had been two weeks since Nathan first uttered those words to Ridley, but the idea still sent adrenaline racing through her. They were simple words, yet their meaning was staggering. World-changing. Thrilling and terrifying. And Ridley was one hundred percent on board.

The earth shuddered around her. Cracks split the ground, zigzagging away in all directions. This was step one: Break apart the arxium machines buried in the wastelands around the city. Elementals in their earth form were now charging through the ground, causing the earth to tremble and heave. All that arxium gas from the broken machines would end up in the air, and until it dissipated, magic would rampage in response. Hence the wild storm roaring above.

Step two: the fractures splitting their way through the earth raced toward a single point. They would converge upon the city. The arxium-reinforced wall would tremble and crack. It would begin to come apart.

Step three: *Burn, burn, burn.* Ridley watched as elementals morphed from the earth into racing, leaping flames. Another thrill of excitement rushed through her at the memory of the conversation she'd had with Nathan the night he explained his plan. "Arxium repels magic," Ridley had argued. "Even if we throw all the magic we have at the walls and panels, the arxium will just throw it right back at us."

Nathan had given her a bemused smile. "Ridley, you burned through a Shadow Society base outside of Lumina City. A building full of arxium. You destroyed that place. I thought you would have realized."

"Realized what?"

"Ordinary fire doesn't burn arxium. Even magical fire created by an ordinary person pulling magic from the environment can't burn through arxium. But *we* can. In our elemental fire form, we can burn through arxium."

*We can burn through arxium.*

Ridley watched as the blazing elemental flames raced toward one another, meeting up to form a giant circle. This circle would burn through the broken pieces of the city wall. The fire was captivating, mesmerizing. But Ridley didn't have long to appreciate the beauty of the flames because the storm calming above her meant that step four was about to begin. The step where she played a part.

There was a dome-like shield of arxium panels above the city, protecting everything and everyone from the magic that often raged overhead. Like the wall, those panels had to go. Ridley raced across the ground, morphed into flames, and shot into the sky as a ball of fire. Nearby, other elementals did the same.

Since there were no real arxium panels out here, several people down below used conjurations to hurl branches high into the air. Ridley's fireball self struck the nearest branch, then leaped to the next and the next and the next, setting as many ablaze as she could. Around her, other elementals did the same, until the air was filled with burning branches tumbling back toward the earth. It wasn't a competition, she knew, but when she saw that her fire form leaped faster from branch to branch than any of the others, it spurred her on to try even harder.

No, not to *try*. That had always been the problem. This wasn't about control, it was about trust. Trusting the elements to know how she wanted to direct them without having to consciously exert her will. She simply had to *let go*.

Ridley imagined a deep, long exhale of breath as she released all control. She let her elemental form drift apart while holding a single thought in her mind: *Burn*.

Her fire self blazed outward in an explosion of flames, catching on almost every remaining branch that was yet to be lit. Someone else ignited the remaining few branches, and that was it. Step four complete.

The branches continued to burn as they struck the ground

far below, but the arxium panels would be consumed by elemental fire. If all went according to plan, the end result would be this: No wall. No hovering panels. Sun shining through the scattering storm clouds because the arxium gas would have been dispersed by the raging wind, leaving the city safe. Exactly the way it was before the Cataclysm.

Ridley shifted to air and swooped down. She released her elemental form and became human shaped, feeling the grassy ground beneath her shoes. "Well done!" someone called from behind her. As other elementals stepped from the air and morphed out of the earth, Ridley turned to face Saoirse. She clutched her gray-streaked auburn hair in one hand as the last of the wind died down. "We're getting better," she said, smiling at Ridley. "*You're* getting better. I think we could actually pull this off."

"Except for the fact that we need to do this on about ten times the scale," Ridley reminded her. "Maybe more? I don't know. And the fact that Nathan wants it to be one big synchronized event for every city across the whole world, and he first has to get everyone to agree on that."

"It'll happen eventually," Saoirse said. "Some people just need a little more time to see that the life we have now isn't enough. And you know there are plenty more of us here at the reserve who will join in when we do this for real. Our target city—Lumina City—is big, but I think we can handle it."

"I know, I know. Bria said she's practiced this a dozen times, and so have many of the others. I understand they're not interested in running through it all again just because Malachi and I are new to the whole plan. But ... even with most elementals from our community joining in, do you think we'll have enough power?"

Saoirse seemed unconcerned, her gaze never wavering from Ridley's. "I believe we'll have enough power."

Ridley bit her lip. Part of her didn't want to get her hopes up, especially when she knew some people were vehemently opposed to Nathan's plan. They didn't think it was worth the risk when they were happy with the life they'd fashioned for themselves out here in the wastelands. But Saoirse knew this community and its people far better than Ridley did. If she thought some of them just needed a little more time to come around, she was probably right.

Ridley's gaze slid past Saoirse to the jagged mountain peak that rose behind her. Beyond it lay her new home, a place simply referred to by its occupants as *the reserve*. The area had once been part of an enormous national park before the Cataclysm destroyed much of the world. In a way, the piece of land served the same function it had served in pre-Cataclysm days, but instead of preserving a section of the countryside and its wildlife, it now preserved a group of people. "Shall we head back with the others?" she asked.

"Let's walk for a bit," Saoirse suggested. She strode a few paces away and bent to retrieve her knitted, rainbow-striped sweater from where she'd secured it beneath a rock. Like Ridley's favorite hooded jacket—which she'd lost inside the Shadow Society building she'd burned to the ground—this sweater seemed to be the only one Saoirse ever wore. If she lived in a city instead of out here where it was safe, Ridley would have told her to choose a different favorite sweater. This one was far too easy to spot from a distance.

"Are we having another lesson?" Ridley asked. A few days after her arrival at the reserve, Saoirse had offered to help her with her magic. Dad must have mentioned that she hadn't fully embraced her power until recently, and that using it for an extended period often resulted in horrendous headaches. Fortunately, the latter no longer happened, which probably had something to do with her being able to transform without guilt or fear and the subconscious stress that accompanied those emotions.

"No, I thought we could just talk."

"Oh, okay." Ridley directed a frown at Saoirse—not because talking was unusual for them; indeed, they'd spoken at length about all sorts of things since Ridley's arrival—but because there was something a little ... *off* in Saoirse's tone.

"Are you still practicing the meditation?" she asked, her hands kneading her bunched-up sweater.

"Yes, every morning." Saoirse had taught Ridley several meditation techniques and encouraged her to begin all their one-on-one training sessions that way. It had sounded silly to Ridley at first, but she'd played along, and soon she found that the more she did it, the easier and faster it became to let go and fragment. "I won't have to keep doing that forever, right? Sometimes it's just not practical. Sometimes—"

"Sometimes you need to transform instantly instead of sitting down, closing your eyes, and breathing deeply for several minutes?" Saoirse filled in with a smile. "Yes. I understand that. But for now, while you're learning how to access all your power, the meditation really helps you to sink into that calm, tranquil state where you can properly let go. You're very close to reaching your full potential, Ridley. Just let yourself fragment even further."

Ridley almost laughed. "My full potential?" Saoirse sounded like one of those motivational speakers she'd been forced to listen to at special assemblies at Wallace Academy. "I think I've reached that already. Did you see that explosion of flames I managed? Not sure I can do much more than that."

"Mm, perhaps." Saoirse shrugged, a quick movement of her small shoulders. "Or perhaps I'm right. There's also the fact that you're still afraid of earth."

"Oh, well that's going to remain unreached potential, I'm afraid," Ridley said quickly. She had tentatively transformed into rocks and loose sand—anything that kept her firmly above ground—but disappearing into the earth itself, the way others had done earlier to cause earthquakes, was not something she was interested in trying. What would happen if she accidentally returned to human form while still down there? Surely she'd be crushed?

"Ridley—"

"Other people can do the earthquakes," Ridley said firmly. "We don't all have to do everything, right? You keep reminding me that I'm not alone anymore. That I have other people to rely on now, not just myself. Not like when I was—" She paused. "Well, you know ... the stealing." At some point in the last two weeks, she'd told Saoirse what she used to spend her free time doing: Stealing from Lumina City's wealthiest, selling the items to a dealer, and using the money to help those in need.

"True," Saoirse admitted. "You're no longer alone, so I suppose you don't have to master earth if you're not comfortable with that. Anyway, uh ..." She stopped walking, turning the sweater bundle around and around until something fell from it and hit the ground with a heavy thud. She bent and picked it up. "Um, so, I've been meaning to give this to you. I thought of it when you first arrived, but it took me a while to find it among my things." She extended her hand toward Ridley, and on her palm sat a large stone pendant on a metal chain. It was smooth and gray with silvery veins coursing through it. Egg-sized, but flatter.

Ridley stepped forward to take a closer look. "It's pretty."

"It was your mother's."

Emotion surged through Ridley's chest. For several heartbeats, she couldn't move. Then she lifted her hand and Saoirse placed the necklace on her palm. Delicately, as if it were a fragile artifact, Ridley traced her finger along the pendant's silver veins. They lit up instantly, glowing vibrant blue. She inhaled a quiet breath, lifting her finger and watching as the lines faded to their former metallic silver. "There's magic inside here?" she asked, looking up.

"Yes." Saoirse pulled her sweater on before crouching down to tighten her shoelaces.

"So ... um ..." Ridley paused to untangle her jumbled

thoughts. "This was my mother's. How did you end up with it? From what my dad told me, you all left in a huge rush when the Shadow Society found you. I assumed none of you had time to grab any belongings."

Saoirse stood and pulled her sweater straight. "I was wearing it at the time. Your mother used to say the stone had certain healing properties. I wasn't feeling well, and she urged me to wear it for a while."

"Oh." Ridley stared at the stone again. "Thank you. I have nothing left of my mother's, so this ..." She swallowed against the emotion tightening her throat. "Well, it means a lot to me. More than I can say."

Saoirse pulled in a deep breath before letting it out slowly. "You're welcome. I ... I'm glad you have something of hers now." Ridley looked up, but the moment she met Saoirse's gaze, Saoirse looked away. "Anyway, so—"

"Is something wrong?" Ridley asked.

"What do you mean?"

Ridley tilted her head, trying once again to catch Saoirse's eye. "I don't know. I feel like you don't want to look at me."

Finally, Saoirse's soft green gaze settled on Ridley's. "I'm sorry. I just ... um ... I know it must have been so hard for you to lose your mother. I didn't want to cause you any additional pain by reminding you of your loss, but—"

"No, no, no," Ridley said. "I'm glad you gave this to me. Thank you." Ridley looped the chain over her head and let the pendant rest against her chest. The weight of it was oddly comforting.

"Okay. Well. I ... I'm just going to check if ..." Saoirse's form shifted, becoming air in the blink of an eye, then returning to normal before Ridley could finish taking her next breath. A small smile lifted her lips. "They're back."

# CHAPTER 2

"CAN YOU SENSE THEM TOO?" Saoirse asked.

Ridley turned her face toward the breeze, closing her eyes as the air and its magic caressed her skin. She let go of her form and became air, and when she thought of Archer, the unspoken answer came immediately. As always, it was a feeling rather than anything that resembled actual words in her mind. The certainty that Archer was just on the other side of that mountain. Her invisible heart beat double time at the knowledge that she would see him soon.

She thought of Dad too and felt the same gentle pull toward the reserve. Returning to her human form, she said, "The answer comes so easily when they're near." She knew now from conversations with Saoirse that the further someone was from her, the more difficult it would be to find that person. Not impossible, but it would take a lot more searching. A lot more listening to the elements, then traveling a while, then listening again.

"Let's go," Saoirse said. She gave Ridley a knowing smile and added, "I'm sure you're eager to see Archer." Before Ridley could respond, Saoirse vanished once more. Cheeks warm and chest filled with a flutter of anticipation, Ridley followed.

She'd discovered soon after arriving at the reserve that every few days someone travelled to one of the nearby cities to pick up signal to send and receive messages. Occasionally this person would enter the city to meet up with contacts and collect certain things, like medicines or other specific items that were difficult to create with conjurations. Saoirse had been the one to go the day after Ridley had arrived, and then two days ago, when it was Nathan's turn, Dad asked to go with to try to contact Grandpa. Since Dad was going, and Nathan was already slowed down by taking a non-elemental with him, Archer decided to accompany them. He had an important message that needed to be sent.

Ridley hadn't expected to miss him so much. She'd spent almost every free moment with him since arriving at the reserve, so she thought it might be good to have a bit of space and alone time. Turned out alone time was overrated and she'd had enough of it after about ten minutes. It had been two days now, and it seemed she missed Archer more with every passing minute. If her mind wasn't occupied with something else—like a training session with Saoirse or doing a trial run of Nathan's plan—it turned to Archer instead. She longed for his arms around her and his lips on her skin and their lengthy discussions about the future they both dared to dream of in which everyone was free to use magic.

It was a little ridiculous. She definitely hadn't admitted it to anyone else.

Ridley let herself fragment, traveling faster and faster on the wind, and within seconds the mountain peak had sped by beneath her and the settlement appeared far below. It seemed small from way up here, but it was larger than she'd first thought. The log cabins—which had originally been here when this spot was a campsite and had, for the most part, survived the Cataclysm—were interspersed with more modern-looking buildings, constructed since the Cataclysm through a combination of materials, labour and conjurations. Exactly the way buildings used to be built before magic was outlawed.

Ridley followed the tug of magic that pulled her toward Archer and slowed near the far side of the settlement. She felt her fragmented air self snap back together as she examined the figures moving below. It wasn't always easy to identify people from above, but Archer was definitely close by. She dropped to the ground and pulled her magic back inside herself, looking around. School was out, and a few kids ran by. Two older girls played a conjuration game as they walked. A collection of buttons hovered between them, and they took turns to add a new button, waiting to see how many they could hold in the air before—

"Ridley," a voice called, and she turned to see Nathan. He lowered a bag from his shoulder and grinned. He wasn't much younger than Dad, but his dark hair had far less gray in it. The stress of everything that had happened since the Cataclysm had prematurely aged Dad, while Nathan had abandoned the idea of living in one of the cities early on, choosing instead to build a new home out in the wastelands. Ridley had asked soon after meeting him if he had a family somewhere, but the only person he'd mentioned was an ex-wife. He hadn't said anything more about her and had changed the subject quickly.

"Hey, welcome back," Ridley said. "What's going on out there? Everyone else on board with your crazy plan yet? Or are some of the communities still divided?"

"Slow down," Nathan said with a laugh. "We've been debating this for months. Nothing's about to change overnight."

"Nothing's changed?" Saoirse asked from just behind Ridley. "Is it still those two communities in the south that are so opposed? And you, by the way," she said to Ridley as she stopped next to her, "are getting faster. You beat me here."

Ridley shrugged. "I guess I have a good teacher."

"True. So, you were saying?" she asked Nathan. "Nothing's changed?"

"Hey, would you at least let me have a shower before we do an in-depth analysis of every message from every community? We can have a meeting before dinner and I'll update all the reps on all the communication received. Sound good?"

"I suppose I can wait until then," Saoirse said. She, Nathan and a few other elected occupants of the reserve were 'in charge' around here, but they regularly met with representatives from most of the families. When it came to major decisions, everyone got a say.

"Hey, Riddles, there you are." Ridley heard her father's voice a moment before his arm swung around her shoulders. She turned toward him and hugged him.

"Hey, Dad. Everything go okay out there?"

Dad released Ridley and rubbed a hand through his thinning hair. "Yes. It was just … strange. We had to stop along the way, and I still find it weird to walk through all those abandoned areas. There's so much that evokes a sense of nostalgia. And then heartache, for the things we lost." Ridley's thoughts turned immediately to her mother. Was Dad thinking of her too? "But yes, it was fine," he finished. "No unexpected or unpleasant incidents."

"And did you contact Grandpa?"

"I tried. I told him we've left Lumina City. But I didn't hear back from him."

Ridley frowned. "I hope he's okay."

Dad toyed with the old-fashioned arxium charm on the leather bracelet around his wrist. He'd gotten rid of the amulets he'd had for years—his AI1 and AI2—when they'd fled Lumina City so the drones couldn't track him. The AI1 was protective, to prevent someone using harmful magic against him. Well, against the interior of his body, at least. If someone wanted to punch him with magic, they could. If someone wanted to boil his blood with magic, that was impossible. Now that Dad's AI1 was gone, the small, uneven lump of arxium hanging from the leather bracelet would serve the same purpose. The AI2, which had to be embedded beneath the skin and prevented someone from pulling magic from the environment, was unnecessary out here where everyone was free to use magic without fear of the law.

"I'm sure Grandpa is fine," Dad said. "He's managed to take care of himself all these years, hasn't he?"

"True. I guess with the kinds of conjurations he knows, he's far more capable of taking care of himself than most people."

Ridley's grandfather had been a historian, and his years of research had led him to discover centuries-old conjurations. Dangerous ones that most believed had been long forgotten. Dangerous enough to potentially be weaponized.

Before the Cataclysm, when magic was still part of everyday life, members of a secret government department involved in weapons development had got wind of the conjurations Grandpa knew about. They tried to force the information out of him. When he refused, they began to threaten his family. He realized they wouldn't stop as long as he was still alive.

So he had faked his death and disappeared. Drastic, but it had worked. Once he was gone, the people who'd been threatening Mom and Dad—and Ridley too, apparently—backed off.

"Yes, he definitely knows a few conjurations that can get him out of a sticky spot if necessary," Dad said. Then, with a cringe, he added, "And potentially wipe out a block or two in the process. While keeping himself completely shielded, thank goodness."

Ridley's eyebrows climbed. "Well, let's hope the old man hasn't done anything crazy."

"I'm sure it's nothing like that. He isn't always near a city, remember? He's probably having communication difficulties, the way we do now."

"Yeah, probably. It's interesting," Ridley mused. "Some things are so much easier out here, now that we can use magic

for everything. But communicating with people far away—
something I used to take for granted—is impossible."

"Still think it was worth it?"

"To be able to live without hiding who I truly am?" Ridley
let out a choked laugh. "Absolutely."

With a wry smile, Dad said, "I was joking, Riddles. Of
course it was worth it." He gave her shoulder a brief squeeze
and moved past her to greet Saoirse. The two of them walked
away together, and Ridley watched them go. To anyone else,
their conversation probably appeared casual, but Ridley noticed the tension in her father's shoulders. She hadn't missed
the numerous quiet discussions he'd had with Saoirse since
they arrived here. She mentally shoved away the conclusion
her mind always immediately jumped to. It wasn't something
she wanted to think about.

She looked around again, and finally, her eyes landed on
Archer. All thought of what may or may not be going on between her father and Saoirse scattered from her mind. Her
insides flip-flopped as Archer strode toward her. He stopped
a few paces away, a cocky grin on his lips. "Miss me?"

Fighting the smile that tried to curve her lips, Ridley
crossed her arms over her chest. Her body warmed as pure
happiness swelled in her chest until she thought it might explode from her in a starburst of light. She longed to throw
her arms around Archer, but she managed to hold her pose.
"Nope, not at all."

"Yeah, I didn't miss you either," he said, moving closer. "I
didn't dream about you, I didn't think of you first thing in the

morning, I didn't imagine lying next to you last thing at night while you tell me, yet again, how bright the stars are outside the city." He stopped right in front of her. "I didn't imagine picking you up and kissing you." He looped his arms around her waist and lifted her as she uncrossed her arms and slid them around his neck, finally giving in to the smile trying to tug her lips upward. Her hair fell around his face as she tilted her head down.

"Liar," she whispered.

"You too."

He pressed his lips to hers, and as silly as it was, everything suddenly felt like it was right again in Ridley's world. It hadn't been this way at first. She'd had so many doubts in the beginning, after they'd kissed beneath a storm in the wastelands outside Lumina City. After realizing that he meant more to her than was logical or sensible. But out here, in the safety of the reserve, she had let go. She had abandoned fear and doubt and let herself tumble head first into ... what? *Love?* Was it too soon for that? Yes. No. Yes? She had known Archer forever, even though she had only really *known* him for a few weeks. Would she even recognize love when she felt it? Was it the kind of thing that suddenly slammed into you, or did you only notice it when you'd already been steeped in it for some time?

Ridley wrapped her legs around Archer's waist as his arms tightened around her. Everything else disappeared. This moment consisted of only the two of them, lips and tongues and quickened breaths.

"Wow, would you two like to get a room?" a voice interrupted.

Ridley pulled away from Archer, face burning as she looked around for the owner of the familiar voice. Callie, one of the elementals who'd escaped Lumina City with Ridley, stood a few paces away with her arms folded over her chest. "I share my bedroom with you, remember?" Ridley said to Callie as Archer set her on her feet. "So that might be a little awkward."

"Well, things are getting awkward for everyone out here." Callie raised one hand to her golden blond hair and smoothed a few strands that had escaped the neat bun atop her head. "There are children present. You're going to scar them for life."

"They'll be fine," Archer said, his tone dismissive. "What would really scar them is the unicorn tattoo on Ridley's right butt cheek."

Ridley choked out a protest. "There is no such tattoo."

"Really? I figured you would have got a real one by now."

Ridley blinked. "I genuinely have no idea what you're talking about."

"You don't? You mean you've forgotten the fake tattoos you and Lilah stuck on each other's backsides when you were like six years—"

"You *knew* about that?"

"Of course. Nosy older brothers know everything."

Ridley crossed her arms and did her best to glare at Archer. "It was Lilah's idea."

"Suuure."

"It was!"

Archer laughed and kissed her nose. "You're adorable."

"Okay stop," Callie said, holding both hands up. "You're making me feel old and alone and depressed."

"Hey, you're not old," Ridley said. At thirty-four, Callie was double her age, but in her opinion, the word 'old' was reserved for people like Grandpa. "Neither are you alone," she added, gesturing to the people around them.

"And since I found you a cello," Archer said, pointing over his shoulder to a gigantic cello-shaped case Ridley had completely failed to notice when her eyes had zeroed in on him, "you shouldn't be depressed either."

"Ah, you found one!" Callie exclaimed, her downcast expression turning to glee in an instant. In the pre-Cataclysm days, Callie had been a popular singer. She played the guitar while song-writing and during most of her performances, but it turned out her first love was actually the cello, and she could play numerous other instruments as well. This news had spread quickly through the reserve, and she'd been here only a couple of days when she was roped into teaching music lessons at the school. She'd secretly admitted to Ridley that she was terrified, but she'd overcome her fear of little children by the end of day three and now wouldn't stop telling Ridley about her dear, sweet students and the cute single guy who was the principal of the small school.

"You're welcome, Miss Hemingway," Archer said as Callie rushed toward the cello.

Callie stopped and pointed a glare at him over her shoulder. "Don't 'Miss Hemingway' me. Didn't I just tell you I feel old?"

Archer laughed. "Sorry, couldn't resist."

"Where'd you find this anyway?" Callie asked, crouching down and running her hand lovingly across the case.

"There's a string instrument store we used to go to back when my mom was convinced that Lilah was going to be the world's greatest violinist. In one of the suburbs outside Lumina City. I convinced Nathan to stop there. The store was only half demolished, and the room at the back had a few instruments still in cases. This was one of them."

"Amazing," Callie breathed. "I mean, the strings will need to be replaced, and I'll probably need to re-hair the bow. Not that I've ever done that before, but I think I remember some conjurations that might help. I don't know ... This definitely gives me something to work on in my free time ..."

Ridley looked at Archer as Callie continued speaking. "Want to go get that room she was talking about?" Archer asked, one eyebrow raised. "Mine, perhaps?"

Ridley slipped her hand into his. "I like that idea."

Minutes later, they were climbing the stairs toward the loft inside one of the residential cabins. "Did you manage to contact someone about Christa?" Ridley asked. Christa was the woman who ran the secret bunker housing Lumina City's illegal magic users. She provided a safe home for those who wanted to live the way they used to live before the Cataclysm—with magic. Unfortunately, as it turned out, she also had a habit of handing elementals over to the Shadow Society.

"Yes." Archer pushed his door open. "I contacted one of the protectors in Lumina City. I don't know what he'll do with the information, but he'll make sure Christa won't be giving up any other elementals who happen to find their way into her bunker."

"Good." Ridley stepped through the doorway ahead of Archer, feeling a little lighter. The knowledge that Christa was still free to betray other elementals had been weighing on her mind. Hopefully it would no longer be a possibility now. "I wonder what she has against us. Elementals, I mean. She's pro-magic, but definitely not pro-elemental. And I wonder how she got mixed up with the Shadow Society. And the director himself. That guy at the base—when we were locked up—said she had some kind of agreement with him."

"Yeah, I wonder." Archer dumped his bag on the floor of his bedroom. The room was small—one third of the loft space at the top of this cabin—but big enough for a bed and a wardrobe. "I don't understand her. She hands over elementals to the director, but she didn't—" He cut himself off, looking away.

"Didn't what?" Ridley prompted.

Archer rubbed one hand over his face. "She knows I was living with an elemental community before I returned to Lumina City. I guess I just don't understand why she didn't press me for more information about them. Why didn't she try to find out exactly where they're located so she could tell the director?"

"Too much effort for her?" Ridley suggested.

"Mm. Perhaps she only bothers with those who cross her path."

"Somebody must have suspected something was going on though, if you were told not to reveal any more information about elementals to her than was necessary. You thought it might be for her safety—and for the elementals' safety—but maybe it was because someone knew elementals had disappeared after finding the bunker and didn't know who could be trusted there."

"Maybe." Archer flopped onto his back on the bed.

"Did you get any other messages while you were there?"

"Oh, um, a few. Just ... my family. I guess they want to know where I disappeared to." That was pretty much the answer Ridley was expecting, but there was something about the way Archer purposefully *didn't* look at her that made her doubt, for just a moment, that he was telling the truth. Was there someone else he might possibly have been messaging? Some other ... *girl*? But then the doubt was gone. The old Archer was the one who might have done something like that. The Archer Ridley knew only through tabloids and stories passed around by other kids at school. She knew the real Archer now, and she had chosen to trust him. There was nothing *purposeful* about the way his gaze had been turned toward the ceiling at that moment instead of focused on her.

"Anyway, the other big news is that Mayor Madson is alive," Archer continued, rolling onto his side and looking at her.

"Really? He survived the fire?" The last time Ridley had seen Lumina City's mayor, he'd been motionless on the floor inside a Shadow Society base in the wastelands. She'd sent an inferno blazing through that building, and as she sped away, she saw a few people fleeing the fiery ruin. But she'd been too far away to recognize any of them.

"Someone must have got him out before your fire brought the whole place down. Of course, the public knows nothing about that. I saw a few stories in the media about the mayor missing a public appearance due to being unwell, but that was it."

"Right." Ridley lowered herself to the edge of Archer's bed. "And even if someone did find out about elementals and the Shadow Society and a secret base out in the wastelands, I doubt anyone would actually run a story on all of that. Who would believe it?"

"They wouldn't get that far. Someone would silence them."

"Of course," Ridley muttered.

"Anyway." Archer leaned over and looped one arm around Ridley's waist. He pulled her down next to him. "You were telling me outside how much you missed me?"

"Oh was I? I thought you were telling me how much *you* missed *me*."

"I think I might have been *showing* you," he said against her lips.

She kissed him back, pressing closer and hooking one leg around his waist. He gripped her thigh, then ran his hand all the way up her back and into her hair. She sat up and straddled his waist, then leaned down to kiss him again. His jaw, his earlobe, the bare skin beneath the wound from the hasty removal of his AI2. He hadn't done a particularly neat job—he'd been in a rush at the time—but it was healing well now. Amid his heavy breaths, Archer murmured something against Ridley's mouth.

"Mm?" she asked, kissing him again.

The window rattled abruptly, startling them both. Ridley pulled back, looking toward it as a gale shrieked past and rain spattered against the pane. "Weird," she muttered, unease cooling the fire in her veins. "That's not supposed to happen here, right? It's always calm. Saoirse said ... something about living in harmony with the elemental magic and ... that keeps the weather in a good mood?"

Archer took her hand and kissed the inside of her wrist, where her pulse had been racing wildly moments before. "It must be you," he said, dead serious. "Your crazy amount of desire for me is stirring up the wild magic out—"

"Oh shut up." Ridley shoved his shoulder and rolled her eyes. "You know it doesn't work that way."

"You'll have to calm that racing heart of yours," he said, ignoring her protests. "Wouldn't want to accidentally ring the emergency bell with a whirlwind or an earth shudder."

"I doubt that'll happen." She pictured the bell Nathan had pointed out to her, an old cast iron thing hanging from a stone arch near the edge of the settlement. "Did you know they've never rung that bell before? Like ever. Which means it's probably so rusted, not even a hurricane could move it."

Archer's hands slid into her hair as he pulled her face down toward his again. "Want to test that theory?"

# CHAPTER 3

"ONIONS AND GARLIC READY?" Ridley asked Archer that evening. They were cooking dinner in the cabin Ridley lived in, waiting for Dad and anyone else who might want to join them. The meeting Nathan had mentioned with the family reps would soon be over, and Dad would fill them in on everything that had been discussed.

"Yeah, watch out," Archer answered. Ridley ducked as a cutting board soared past her head and tipped itself to the side over the pan on the stove. The sliced onions and garlic slid neatly into the pan and began sizzling in the oil. "Nice," Archer said. "I'm enjoying this food-prep-with-magic thing. So much easier than cutting vegetables by hand."

Ridley snorted. "Like you ever cut a vegetable in your life, Archer Davenport."

"Hey, I prepared plenty of food while living with those other elementals." He grabbed the cutting board out of the air as it flew back toward him. "I'll have you know I'm extremely talented in the kitchen."

Ridley's snort-laugh was even louder that time. "Sure,

whatever. And you're telling me you didn't use magic in these other kitchens you're speaking of?"

"Nope. There was this chef. Like, legit trained-at-the-world's-top-restaurant type of chef. He was convinced that food prepared by hand tasted better. No one was allowed to use magic when he was the one in charge of the meal. He would—"

"Hey, watch out!" Ridley called, looking over her shoulder in time to see Archer's knife reach the end of the celery sticks and continue off the board and onto the table.

"Oops." Archer grabbed the knife and rubbed at the marks on the wooden table. "We'll, uh, just pretend that was already there. Okay, I'm sending you the celery now."

The celery joined the onions and garlic in the pan just as the back door opened. "Well, I'm not changing my tune," a woman said. "I'm sorry, but I just can't agree with you."

With a simple one-handed conjuration, Ridley left the wooden spoon stirring the pan's contents and turned around. The person speaking was Tanika, a woman who had the room next to the one Ridley and Callie shared. She and Callie argued endlessly over their vastly different music tastes, but other than that, Tanika was fairly easy to get along with. She had taught Ridley a conjuration for scented bubbles, which Ridley now used almost every night in her bath. She also had a seemingly endless collection of vibrant scarves, which she used to tie up her thick, curly hair.

"Good meeting?" Ridley asked as Nathan and Saoirse walked in behind Tanika.

"Same meeting," Saoirse said with a sigh. "Nothing ever changes. Ooh, what are you cooking?"

"Uh, not totally sure. Some kind of veggie stir-fry type of mix."

"Smells amazing, whatever it is."

"What's amazing is having so much fresh produce to work with," Ridley said. "This stuff costs a fortune in the city. Almost everything I've eaten over the past decade has come out of a can or a box."

"And that's the world you want us to join?" Tanika said to Nathan. "The world where they only eat out of cans and boxes?"

Nathan groaned. "You know that's not the way it would be. We want to *change* the world. Make it more like the way it used to be. Once magic isn't raging across most of the wastelands anymore, there'll be plenty of space for farms and crops and all of that."

"Uh, where's my dad?" Ridley asked Saoirse.

"Oh, he and Cam and some of the others are packing chairs away after the meeting." Saoirse sat beside Archer and added, "Can I, uh, show you a slightly different conjuration? One that won't mutilate the furniture in addition to the vegetables?"

"Look, it's not that I don't *want* change," Tanika continued. "Change would be great. I just don't think we'll ever have enough power to get through that much arxium."

"Some people do," Nathan argued. "There are elementals out there who have tremendous power. They could probably single-handedly burn through all the panels over a city."

"Right, sure, these mythical elementals we've heard of. But we're not lucky enough to have anyone like that here. So while other communities might be powerful enough to liberate their nearest city, I don't think we are. The life we have now—it *works*. Why mess with that?"

"Because this isn't enough!" Nathan insisted. "Sure, life 'works' right now, but it could be *so much more*. So much fuller. Don't you want a world where children can do and be whatever they want? A world where they don't have to hide? Don't you remember what that was like?"

"No," Tanika said flatly. She plopped into the chair opposite Saoirse. "We've always lived in hiding, Nathan. Yes, we used to use magic out in the open, but no one ever knew about the magic *inside* us. No one knew about elementals. We've been hiding forever."

"And that was wrong," Nathan said. "We should be free to be who we truly are."

"I'm free right here," Tanika reminded him.

"And if the Shadow Society finds us?" Ridley asked carefully, not wanting to anger Tanika but feeling that this was a valid point. "It happened before, when I was a baby. I know you've lived here safely for a long time, but they'll probably find us eventually. Then what?"

"That's why we have a backup home," Tanika said. "We can get away and hide there. At the speed we can travel, there's no way they'll be able to follow us."

"Backup home?" Ridley asked with a frown.

"Sorry, I forgot to mention it," Nathan said. "We've been safe for so long that most of the time I forget we even have a backup. Oh! That reminds me. Has someone given you a gas mask yet?"

"A gas mask?"

"I'll check if we have spares. Everyone's supposed to have one, just in case. We've never had to use them, so—"

"Best to be prepared though," Saoirse said. "I'll check for one tomorrow."

Ridley's gaze moved between Nathan and Saoirse. "Uh, thanks."

"Yeah, anyway. The backup home," Nathan continued. "It's on the other side of those far mountains. The ones you see in the distance when you're out there practicing your magic. We spent a few years building it after we first set up home here at the reserve. We have some supplies stored there already—I made sure we wouldn't have to start over from zero—but our magic is all we really need. It would be difficult, but we'd survive."

"See?" Tanika said. "So we don't need to worry about that."

"But we *do* need to worry about all the lies the rest of the world is constantly being fed," Nathan argued. "And the rest of the communities are starting to agree with me on this. They recognize what some of us have been saying all along: that governments across the world don't actually have any plans to reintegrate magic into society. They're intentionally—"

"Oh, here we go again." Tanika pressed her fingers to her

temples and rubbed in small circles. "The conspiracy theories."

"You know I'm right," Nathan said.

"I love a good conspiracy theory," Archer said, successfully executing the conjuration Saoirse had just shown him. He sent a cutting board of red peppers and various green vegetables flying over Saoirse's head and flipped it upside down over the pan. Ridley rescued the wooden spoon from beneath the pile of vegetables and continued stirring everything together.

"It's still called a conspiracy theory even if it's true, right?" she asked. She knew what the others were referring to. Nathan had spoken to her about it the night she arrived.

"Everyone in the cities believes the magic out here will kill them," he had said. "But that's a lie. Magic is wild, but if you don't fight it, it isn't deadly. And the only reason it's wild is because people constantly cause it to retaliate. Way out here, far from any city, we're fine." Ridley might have thought he was crazy if she hadn't seen the machines buried in the wastelands. The ones that rose from the ground and sprayed arxium into the air, stirring the elemental magic into fierce storms. She'd asked Nathan *why* anyone would do something like that, but at the back of her mind, she already knew the answer.

*Control.*

There were those who never wanted magic to be part of society, and after the Cataclysm, when everyone was afraid of magic, they took advantage of that. They made sure it *remained* wild. They kept it on the other side of a wall, and they forbade anyone from using it.

"Look, a conspiracy is exactly what's happening," Nathan said as Ridley slowly stirred the sizzling vegetables, "and it's going to keep happening unless we do something to stop it. More and more elementals are recognizing this. We just need to get everyone on board and then we can all act at the same time."

"Why?" Ridley asked, looking over her shoulder. "Why does it need to happen everywhere at the same time?"

"Well, we believe that if we do this only in some cities, it'll be a warning to the Shadow Society chapters in other cities. It'll give them a chance to put further protection in place and make it even harder to liberate those cities."

"We keep saying 'liberate' like we're doing something good," Tanika said. She leaned forward and snatched up a piece of celery from the pile of excess vegetables Archer hadn't chopped. "But what if people don't want to be liberated?" She crunched on the celery. "What if they're terrified of us?"

"That's why we do the video as well," Nathan said.

"Video?" Ridley asked. She hadn't heard this bit yet.

"A recording that explains everything. The history of the elementals and the Shadow Society. The way government took advantage of the situation after the Cataclysm to take control of the cities that remained. How they continuously stir up the wild magic in the wastelands to keep people afraid. Everything. I've already written a rough draft of all the things I need to explain. I'll send the recording to all the news networks. I'm sure *someone* will broadcast it. And one of you can upload it to the social feeds."

"You're not on any of the social feeds?" Archer asked.

"You should do it," Ridley said, turning fully and pointing the wooden spoon at Archer. "I'm pretty sure at least half the surviving population of the world follows you."

"That might be a *bit* of an exaggeration."

"Actually, you know what?" she continued as an idea occurred to her, "maybe you should be the one in the video. People know who you are—in several cities, if not all of them—so they'll listen to you. When your face shows up on a giant billboard screen, people will stop and pay attention."

"That's a terrible idea. People may have a sick desire to know what underwear brands I like, and what cologne I'm wearing, and who I'm having dinner with, but they also think I'm an irresponsible trust fund brat. They may hear the words I'm saying, but they won't actually *listen* to me."

"But you'll be so different from the Archer they know. The Archer they *think* they know." Ridley turned the stove off and placed the wooden spoon into an empty mug. "You'll be genuine, telling them all about the truth you've discovered. They won't be able to help taking you seriously."

Nathan leaned on the back of a chair. "That is an idea," he mused.

"Yeah, a terrible one," Archer repeated. "How about I throw around some spectacular shielding conjurations that protect people from any falling pieces of burning arxium that aren't totally consumed before they hit the ground? Like Ridley's dad and all the others who aren't elementals."

It turned out Ridley's grandfather had shared a little of his extensive conjuration knowledge with his son, and even though Nathan's plan already included people using magic to protect those inside Lumina City, Dad was able to teach everyone a few new shielding conjurations.

"I don't know, I like this idea too," Tanika said. She grabbed another celery stick.

"I thought you were against all of this," Ridley reminded her, lifting her jacket from the back of one of the chairs. It wasn't her favorite jacket with the hood that she'd lost in a burning blaze, but Dad had conjured up something very similar. Before the Cataclysm, he'd designed and created fantastical jewelry and accessories for celebrities and anyone else who could afford his items, but his training had included garment conjurations. He was a little rusty after so many years of not using magic, which was why the right sleeve was longer than the left and the two sides of the zip didn't properly meet, but Ridley had told him not to worry about fixing it. She loved having something unique that Dad had made specifically for her. It had been years since the last time that happened.

"I'm saying *if* we were to ever go ahead with this plan," Tanika corrected. "Like I said before, I'm not against it. I just don't think we'll succeed if we try. We don't have enough power."

"Maybe we do," Saoirse said quietly. "Maybe you underestimate us."

"You think I'm underestimating us?"

"I do."

"Okay, let's play this all out again."

"Tanika—"

"No, seriously. Let's say this works. We break apart the arxium machines and the wall. Our earthquakes are targeted enough to stop right at the wall and *not* destroy any buildings on the other side."

"Or the bunker," Ridley interjected. "Don't forget about the bunker. It extends right up to the wall."

"Right. The earthquakes are somehow super targeted to hit all parts of the wall *except* that section. The arxium gas dissipates quickly enough that the magic doesn't freak out for too long and cause one epically insane storm. We burn through the wall. We burn through the hovering panels. We tell people the truth. They actually *believe* us and *accept* us. But then what about—"

"The Shadow Society," Saoirse said quietly.

"Exactly."

"This is always your final point," Nathan said, dropping into a chair with a sigh.

Saoirse looked at Ridley. "We've argued about this so many times. It's like listening to the same song on repeat. You know what lines are coming next."

"And with good reason!" Tanika said. "This will always be my final point because the Shadow Society will always be the biggest problem. They operate in secret, but their influence is far-reaching. We can't possibly hope to dismantle their entire organization. So once we reveal ourselves, it'll be easy for them to wipe us out. And I know—" she added loudly, speaking over Nathan "—you think the law will be on our side. That once we tell everyone about the existence of an organization that likes to kill elementals that that organization will be too afraid to act because of the consequences. But that won't be the case. The Shadow Society will still have influence over law enforcement, politicians, news media, everything. They'll kill us all, pass it off as a series of accidents or whatever, and even though no one will entirely believe it, they'll probably all be relieved."

Nathan paused, then said, "That isn't what I was going to say."

Tanika arched a disbelieving eyebrow. "New lyrics? This isn't the same song we sing every time?"

"We get rid of them before they get rid of us," Nathan said simply.

"Get rid of?" Ridley and Archer echoed at the same time.

"Yes. Not all of them. Just the leadership. The director, plus the chairperson of every chapter."

Silence greeted Nathan's words. Then Ridley said, "Murder? Is that what you're talking about?"

"You don't know who they are," Tanika said, "so how are you going to get rid of them?"

"Actually," Nathan said, "we now know that the mayor of Lumina City is one of them. He's the chairperson of the Lumina City chapter. Who knows, maybe he's the director too. Maybe he's running the whole show."

"Or maybe it's someone else, in some other city, on some other continent. You have no idea."

"My point," Nathan said, "is that if I get to *him*, I can get all the information I need."

"What makes you so sure he'll tell you anything?" Tanika asked.

"I'll make him."

"So now we're talking about *torture*?" Ridley demanded. "Torture and murder?" An image of the rooms in the Shadow Society's base flashed across her mind. The beds, the straps. She knew the mayor had been involved in experimenting on elementals. He'd probably *tortured* plenty of elementals. Yet the idea of doing the same to him—or anyone else—made her sick.

Nathan sighed. "This is why I didn't bring it up at the meeting."

"And this is why you probably shouldn't have brought it up now either," Saoirse added quietly. "You didn't think people would agree with you, did you?"

"Actually, this might be the first thing we do agree on," Tanika said thoughtfully.

"You can't go out and *murder* a bunch of people," Ridley said to Nathan.

"Ridley, I thought you, of all people, would be okay with this. You were captured. You were almost killed. You told me what you saw inside that Shadow Society base. You burned it to the ground. You killed whoever was left inside."

The truth sucked the air from Ridley's lungs. She *had* done that. She'd blazed through that building, not caring how many terrible Shadow Society people were left inside. How was this—what Nathan was proposing—any different? It wasn't, and yet it *felt* different to sit here coldly making plans to walk up to someone and kill them face to face. What a hypocrite she was to think that one type of murder was fine while another was not.

"I—I know," she stammered. "But ... I ... I wasn't really thinking. I was acting out of anger. Maybe I ... I should have got rid of the place and not the people. Things are different now, and we have a bigger plan. If we want the world to know the truth about everything, then all these people who've done terrible things need to be around to stand trial for what they've done. And if we want the world to know that *we're* not dangerous, then we can't go around torturing and killing people. That makes us no better than them."

"Perhaps I don't care about being better than them," Nathan said, "if it means every elemental gets to live in a world without fear."

"So you're serious," Archer said. "You're actually intending to kill people."

Nathan sighed and rubbed a hand over his face. "I don't know. Maybe. We have new information now, so maybe this is what we should be doing with it."

"Or not," Ridley said. "I can think of other things you could do with that information."

"And I think this is the end of our discussion for tonight," Nathan said, pushing up from the table. His easy smile was back in place as he headed for the stove and leaned over the pan to sniff its contents. "Saoirse was right. This smells amazing. Mind if we stay and join you for dinner?"

# CHAPTER 4

AFTER DINNER—WHICH WAS surprisingly *not* awkward, given the awkward conversation that came before it—Ridley walked with Archer to his cabin. The quiet rumble of thunder hinted at a distant storm, but here at the reserve, the night was clear, the dark sky crowded with a billion glittering pinpricks of light. Far more stars than Ridley had ever seen when she lived in the city. "The stars feel close enough to touch," she to Archer, a smile in her voice.

He slipped an arm around her back and pulled her closer. She heard the matching smile in his voice as he replied, "Stretch high enough, and maybe your magic *can* touch the stars."

She'd commented on the stars so many times since they'd left Lumina City that this had quickly become a Thing for them. A standard statement and response. It went along with the other thing that had become a Thing: lying together almost every evening on a mattress beneath the night sky, wrapped up in a cozy duvet, talking about anything and everything.

"I'm supposed to walk you to *your* door," Archer said,

leaning his head down to kiss her temple. "Not the other way around."

"Don't be sexist." Ridley snuggled against his side as weariness settled over her shoulders like a heavy blanket. Headaches might not plague her anymore, but shifting into elemental form repeatedly for several hours definitely sapped her energy. "I'll be perfectly fine walking back to my cabin on my own. But you, my non-elemental friend, might need protecting from the big, bad magic out there."

"Friend?" Archer repeated with a laugh. "I thought we were a little more than that."

"Is that the only part of that sentence that bothers you?"

"It was the most important part."

Ridley smiled. "More than a little more." They continued walking, and then, because she couldn't get the earlier conversation out of her head, she added, "I keep thinking about what Nathan said about killing the Shadow Society leadership. And I keep thinking about the people I probably killed inside that base. It seemed different at the time—probably because I didn't see them face to face, and I don't even know if any of them were left inside or if they all got out—but it's no different. It's the same as what he's planning."

Archer shook his head. "It's not the same. Maybe it still wasn't *right*, but I don't think it's the same as intentionally planning to kill specific people and then seeking out each of them and following through."

"I suppose," Ridley said slowly.

"And when it comes down to it—when Nathan's face to

face with someone—I don't know if he could really do it. I mean ... they've done terrible things, these Shadow Society people. But they're still just *people*."

"Well, they might be a little closer to *monsters* than the average person. But ... now that I'm thinking about it properly ... I don't want them all dead. They should be alive to pay for the heinous things they've done to others."

"Yeah," Archer murmured. "I think I agree. Thing is ... if we go through with this crazy plan, there are going to be casualties. It's not possible to break apart the entire city wall without coming into contact with any people. If we're going to take part in this, we need to be okay with the fact that some people won't survive it."

Ridley breathed out heavily. "I know. Anyway, as you say, that's if we even go through with this. I'm not sure it'll ever actually happen. Sometimes part of me thinks ..." she paused, feeling guilty at the idea of voicing her thoughts out loud. "Maybe Tanika's right. Maybe this is enough, the way we live now. We're safe. We have each other. I have my dad. But then I think," she rushed on before Archer could say anything, "of all the people who aren't free. The people who are living in hiding the way I did for years, constantly fearful that someone might find out what they can do. And I remember how I always wanted to end up at The Rosman Foundation after graduation, so I could help people who lost everything after the Cataclysm, like Dad and I did. And if I stay here and do nothing, then I'm helping no one. Even though sometimes all I want is to just *do nothing* and be safe and enjoy not having to hide who I am. And I know that makes me a terrible person, and *most* of the time I *do* want to get out there and change the world. It's just that sometimes the idea seems so big, so impossible." She sucked in a deep breath and let it out slowly.

After a pause, Archer asked, "Are you done?"

She thought about it, then said, "Yes. Sorry. Just emptying my brain of all its horrible thoughts."

"It's not horrible to think that life would be easier if we simply stayed here and ignored the rest of the world. That's the truth. It *would* be easier. You're not a terrible person for recognizing that, or for wanting it sometimes."

"So ... sometimes you want that too?"

"Yes." Archer kissed her cheek. "Sometimes I very, *very* much want to forget everything that's happened in the past and everything that's still happening and instead lie under the stars with you forever."

*Forever* ... Ridley almost commented on his use of the word, but that would take the conversation in a direction neither of them was probably ready for. "Anyway, I was also thinking—"

"So you haven't emptied your brain of all its thoughts yet?" he teased.

"Apparently not." She bit her lip, then said, "If it looks like things aren't going to change any time soon, then ... then I want to return to the city so I can talk to Meera. Not for long. Just to let her know I'm okay and to explain things to her. I mean, first Shen disappeared, and then me. Both of her best friends, just gone. Zero explanation. I don't want her to spend the rest of her life wondering about us."

"Okaaay," Archer said, drawing the word out slowly. "Your father would probably have heart failure if he knew you were planning this."

"I know, but I'd be careful. I'd go over the wall as air and stay in that form until I get to Meera's place. Then once I'm inside her home, the scanner drones won't be able to pick up that I don't have amulets. Her apartment block is big. I'll just be one more warm body inside a building full of warm bodies." When Ridley had lived in Lumina City, she'd worn her AI1 and AI2 on a chain around her neck. She also had illegal backup copies on an ankle bracelet. The drones flying overhead had never known the tiny pieces of metal weren't embedded beneath her skin the way they were for everyone else. But just like Dad, she'd had to get rid of them when they were escaping Lumina City, in case the drones were able to track them.

"That would probably work," Archer said. "But why not just try to get a message to her instead of actually going into the city?"

"I ... *could* do that," Ridley said hesitantly. "But there's just so much to say, you know? It would be better if I could *talk* to her. Tell her the truth about everything. Well, about me, at least. I won't give away other people's secrets if they're not mine to share. But I don't want to have to make up more lies to explain why I had to leave the city and why I won't be safe there ever again. I've told her enough lies already, and I just ... I don't want them sitting between us forever."

"I know. I understand." They had reached Archer's cabin

by now. Stopping at the foot of the stairs, Ridley detached herself from Archer's side and faced him. She laced her fingers between his. She was about to rise up on her toes to kiss him when he said, "Ridley ..." He trailed off, whatever he'd been about to say hanging invisibly in the air between them.

An odd sense of foreboding crept into the far reaches of Ridley's mind. "Yes?"

Archer's dark eyes searched her face as she tried to decipher his expression, but before she could figure it out, he smiled. It was strained at first, but then warmth reached his eyes and his lips found hers. He kissed her. A rush of butterfly wings filled her insides, and she almost forgot the hint of dread that had brushed against her thoughts. Almost.

"Sleep tight," he whispered against her lips.

"That's not what you were going to say," she replied, her eyes still closed.

"No. It wasn't."

"So what were you going to say?"

When he didn't answer immediately, she lifted her gaze and met his eyes. He asked, "Do you know how much I care about you?"

Ridley's skin heated and her stomach flipped over. Somehow, she knew that wasn't what he'd been about to say either. Her heart squeezed as it occurred to her that he might have been about to say *more*. Was it possible ... was he trying to tell her ... did Archer Davenport think he *loved* her? Was he too afraid to get the words out?

She swallowed and answered, "Far more than you ever

expected to feel about me?"

This time, when he smiled, it was genuine from the start. "That's a good way of putting it."

She shrugged and admitted, "That's how I feel."

He kissed her again, then rested his brow against hers. "I was thinking ... I can do more to help out than just a video recording. More than conjurations to protect people from falling arxium or whatever other damage we cause to the city."

Ridley's brain took a moment to switch gears. She was pretty sure this was also not what Archer had been going to say. "Um, okay." She tilted her head back so she could see his face. "What do you mean exactly?"

"I'm a Davenport. I have connections. I know the mayor. Maybe I can get more information out of him, like who else is in the Shadow Society. Without resorting to torture, the way Nathan might do it."

"Would he actually tell you anything? You said you tried to get Lawrence to tell you things—to invite you to meetings— and he wouldn't."

"I ..." Archer scrubbed a hand through his hair. "Maybe. I don't know." He looked out at the night and sighed. "It's late. Can we talk tomorrow?"

"Sure, of course." But when Ridley took a moment to think about it, she realized it wasn't that late. They stayed up much later most nights when they lay beneath the stars, talking and ... *not* talking. Still, she was tired from all her magic-use while training with Saoirse, and Archer was clearly in need of sleep too.

They said goodnight, and Ridley returned to her cabin. She climbed the porch steps with unusual slowness, exhaustion weighing her down. A chilly breeze brushed wisps of hair across her face, and she wrapped her arms around herself as she reached the front door. The air gusted, curling around her, and a sense of unease unfurled in her chest. She stopped, a frown pulling at her brow. She tried to reach out to the magic around her. Was it telling her something? She was about to shift form to better understand the magic when a loud voice nearby startled her.

"Is this a joke?" It sounded like Nathan. Ridley looked around but couldn't see him.

"Can you keep your voice down?" came a whispered response in Saoirse's distinctive accent. "And no, this isn't a joke." Ridley turned again, following the sound of their voices. They were out of sight, just around the side of the cabin.

"Why didn't you tell me as soon as we returned here with them?" Nathan hissed. "You've been holding onto this information for *two weeks*."

Ridley frowned as she stared at the floorboards. This sounded like a conversation she probably shouldn't overhear. She reached for the cabin's front door, but Saoirse's next words froze her hand in place: "Because Maverick didn't want me saying anything. You know it's going to complicate things for him."

Nathan heaved a deep sigh. "Right. Of course."

"You can understand why he doesn't want anyone to know."

"I can, but what we're working toward is so much bigger than this. We're talking about changing the world for every single elemental who's been forced into hiding. Surely Maverick has to understand—"

"He does, but he says he needs more time. He just ... he needs to figure out how to tell Ridley."

Ice shot through Ridley's veins at the mention of her name. She'd suspected there was something going on between her father and Saoirse, but she hadn't wanted to even think about it, let alone ask Dad. Because whatever it was, it couldn't be new. There had been some sort of weird vibe between them since the moment Ridley and her companions had arrived here and Dad discovered that his old friends, Saoirse and Cam and their daughter Bria, were still alive. Something must have been going on between Saoirse and Dad years ago.

When Mom was still alive.

Once again, Ridley shoved the thought aside. It made her sick to think her father could be capable of that kind of betrayal. Maybe it was something else. After all, why would Saoirse need to talk to Nathan about it? Why did it have anything to do with Nathan's big plans to return magic to society? From what Ridley could tell, Saoirse was closely involved in helping Nathan figure out the precise details of the plan. So maybe ... maybe whatever was going on with Dad was distracting her, pulling her focus away from more important work?

Ridley shivered, physically recoiling from the idea of whatever might be happening between Saoirse and Dad that was so *distracting.*

"He needs to tell her soon," Nathan said, pulling Ridley from her disturbing thoughts. "*Very* soon."

Ridley shook her head, tiptoeing away from the door. Nope, no, this was *not* something she wanted to talk to Dad about. As long as she didn't know exactly what was going on, she could continue to think the best of her father, rather than—

A floorboard creaked beneath her foot. She froze as Saoirse's words cut off.

Silence.

Then Nathan's voice: "Did you hear that?"

In an instant, Ridley became air, twisting away from the porch and up into the night sky as fast as possible, afraid Saoirse or Nathan might do the same and follow her. They would sense her if they did. They would know she'd been close enough to hear them. She shot higher and higher into the sky, faster and faster, reaching for the stars that seemed close enough to touch. It was silly to be so afraid. After all, Nathan and Saoirse were the ones having a whispered conversation about other people. If anything, *they* should be embarrassed, not Ridley. But that still didn't mean she wanted to deal with any of this—whatever *this* was.

When she'd soared so far and so high that she could barely see the lights of the settlement, she thought of Nathan and Saoirse and sensed them somewhere far below. They hadn't followed her. She headed back, swirling around to the other side of her cabin and slipping through the open window into the bedroom she shared with Callie. The room was empty;

Callie was probably hanging out with the school principal she most definitely had a crush on.

Ridley returned to human form, let out a breath, and dropped onto her bed. She pressed one hand over the stone pendant that rested against her chest. She hadn't removed the necklace since Saoirse gave it to her earlier in the day. She liked having something that was once her mother's sitting so close to her heart. *Dad loved you, Mom*, she thought. *I know that. He couldn't possibly have cheated on you.* With that final thought, she banished all thoughts of her father's possible betrayal from her mind.

# CHAPTER 5

RIDLEY DREAMED OF FIRE. She dreamed of smoke and screams and a body on the ground, limbs unmoving and eyes unseeing. She tried to look closer, to see who it was, but instead her attention snagged on the bell that stood tall and still and ageless beside the body. Suddenly she was right next to it, her hand reaching for the rope, her fingers wrapping around it, tugging it down—

Ridley jerked awake, her heart a frightened bird in her chest and silence pressing on her ears where there should have been the ringing of a bell. She took a calming breath, reminding herself it was only a dream. But the fear and urgency remained. She touched the stone pendant lying against her sweaty chest, seeking comfort from it. Her gaze moved across the room to Callie's sleeping form. Her breaths were deep, slow, peaceful, while Ridley's heart still thrashed against her ribcage. Fear wormed its way into her bones. Fear that made no sense.

A gale screamed past the window, startling Ridley as it shook the pane. For a moment, all she could think of was Archer joking about her desire for him stirring up the elements. But she knew magic didn't work that way. Something wasn't right. She wasn't sure *what*, precisely, but the longer she sat in bed, her heart still racing, the sicker she felt.

She shut her eyes, breathed out slowly, and let her human form vanish into air. Immediately, her terror intensified.

*THEY'RE COMING!*

The thought pressed in on her from all sides, so *loud*, despite there being no words, no sound. Her mind flooded with knowledge: The Shadow Society was coming. They were almost here. They would kill everyone.

*FLEE!*

Magic screamed in Ridley's mind as lightning split the sky and rain thrashed against the window. The sense of urgent motion was so overpowering that even though she hung in the still air of her bedroom, she imagined she could feel a swift current dragging her away.

Callie stirred and mumbled, "Is that ... a storm?"

Ridley's attention turned to Callie as she lifted her head and squinted at the window through one half-open eye. Abruptly, Ridley was human again. "They're coming," she said. "We have to go!" There was no time to explain further. She rushed to the window and opened it.

"Hey!" Callie yelped. "What are you—" But the rest of her words were lost as Ridley dove headlong into the stormy night, her air form tangling with the gale-force wind. She thought of the emergency bell a moment before realizing the wind was already carrying her that way. Cabins rushed by beneath her, then trees, a playground area, the school, and then she was whirling down toward the stone arch where the weatherworn bell hung.

Someone was already there.

Ridley released her magic, and her feet, clad in nothing but socks, stumbled across the uneven ground. Rain pummeled her from every direction, drenching her almost immediately. "Saoirse?" she gasped, her heart pounding as if she'd run all the way here.

Saoirse stopped, her hand inches from the rope. Her expression puckered, confusion and fear flashing across her face. "Ridley?"

Ridley's words tumbled from her mouth: "The Shadow Society is coming. Magic told me. Did you hear the warning too?"

"I—yes." Saoirse blinked through the rain beading her eyelashes and streaking down her face. "It—it told you too?"

"Yes. We have to tell everyone. Wake everyone. We have to ring the bell. Now!" She rushed forward, launching past Saoirse for the rope because it seemed the older woman had frozen. She grabbed the rope and tugged downward. For a second all she could think of was telling Archer that this bell was probably too rusty to move. But it did move. A loud clang issued forth. She tugged again and again—*clang, clang, clang*—while all around her, the gusting air let out a sigh as it stilled. The thrashing rain slowed to a drizzle, and the repeated flashes of lightning became distant flickers.

But the urgency thrumming through Ridley's veins remained. She dropped the rope and turned back to Saoirse. "The backup home. That's where we have to go, right?" Behind her, the metal clapper knocked once more against the inside of the bell. Then again, quieter. Then ... silence.

"Yes. Grab whatever you can. Grab *whoever* you can. Anyone who isn't elemental. Most of us know where to go, so you can—"

"Sense where you are and follow you. I know."

With a single nod, Saoirse vanished, leaving a small whirlwind of leaves in her wake. A second later, Ridley did the same. As she raced on the breeze back to her cabin, she heard shouts and spotted movement below. People running. Flurries of leaves as others vanished into the air.

The bell had done its job.

She spun back down toward her bedroom window and slipped inside. Releasing her magic, she skidded across the floor just as Callie straightened from tugging on a pair of shoes. "Oh, it's just you," she gasped, pressing a hand to her chest. "What's happening? That bell was a warning, right? We have to—"

"Run. We have to run." Ridley was soaked, but there was no time to change out of her wet pajamas. She grabbed her hooded jacket from the small wardrobe in the corner and shoved her arms into the sleeves. "I mean fly. As air. Go!" she added a little more forcefully, when Callie did nothing but stare at her with wide eyes. "Follow the others. Tanika, Saoirse, whoever. They know where to go. I'm going to get Archer." She snatched a pair of sneakers from the floor, tugged them on, then raced toward the window, becoming air between one step and the next.

Within moments, she'd reached Archer's cabin. She blew through the tiny loft space that belonged to him, but it was empty. She was so sure he would still be here—barely any time had passed since she'd rung the bell—that she hadn't even thought to reach out and ask the magic around her where he was. She turned back toward the window, casting her thoughts out.

But she couldn't sense him.

A sound caught her attention, and she swirled around, her first thought that it must be Archer. But it wasn't him. The man's face was cast in shadow, so Ridley couldn't tell whether she recognized him, but the fact that he was inside some type of hazmat suit was a good indication he wasn't on her side. There was also the fact that he held a canister in one hand and a gun in the other. He swung both hands up—

Ridley spun around and shot away through the gap at the top of the window, hearing first the spray of the canister and then, as she whirled up into the night, the crack of a gunshot. She knew the man hadn't seen her, but perhaps the curtains had billowed or the sheets had rippled as she spun around, giving away her presence.

The night air, which had been so crisp and clear earlier, was now heavy with arxium. Ridley struggled to hold onto her elemental form, wishing someone had given her that gas mask Nathan had been talking about earlier. Too late now.

*Where are you, where are you?* she thought as she pictured

Archer again. He had to be close by, so why couldn't she sense him? She thought of Dad instead, and the answer came back almost immediately. She whirled down toward him as he ran between two cabins.

"Oh, Ridley, thank goodness," he gasped the moment she materialized. He grabbed her hand. "We have to go *now*. They've—"

"Have you seen Archer?"

"Uh, I saw him a few moments ago, coming out of your cabin."

"I can't sense him. That's weird, right? What if he's—"

"He must be gone already if you can't sense him."

"But then—"

"Some of the others can move really fast. He's probably beyond your reach already."

"But he wouldn't have let someone else take him if he didn't know whether I was—"

"Ridley, we have to *go*!" Dad insisted. "Someone probably just swooped by and took Archer without stopping to have a conversation about it."

"Okay, okay." Ridley didn't want to leave without knowing for sure, but she had to get Dad out of here, and he was probably right about Archer. She took a deep breath—then coughed and retched. Had these monsters brought one of their arxium machines with them? Was that why the suffocating particles were filling the air so quickly? Thunder growled overhead, and rain drops began to spatter the ground.

"This way," Dad said, tugging her between the cabins.

"Hurry. We need to get away from the arxium. The river, maybe? Water should be easier for you. Hopefully it isn't full of arxium like the air."

They rounded the corner of a cabin—and stopped mere inches from tripping over a body on the ground. Ridley saw the colorful scarf first, then the pool of blood, then Tanika's lifeless gaze.

Horror crashed into her. "No," she whispered. "No. How is this ... this isn't supposed to be *happening*!"

"Keep moving," Dad said, steering her past Tanika. "We have to keep moving. Just keep moving. Just—" His voice caught, but not before Ridley heard the intense emotion in his words.

She followed him blindly. Suffocating smoke and the flickering orange glow of flames filled the air. Rain pattered down in fat droplets, but it wasn't enough yet to quench the fires. They seemed to burn brighter with every passing moment, sending more and more smoke into the air. It was just like her dream. How many other bodies were lying in pools of blood, hidden by smoke, about to be consumed by flames? What if Archer—

"There it is," Dad said, tugging her forward a little faster. She blinked and looked ahead. He was talking about the river. "Can you shift? Is there less arxium here?"

"I ... um ..." She tried to push aside the image of Archer lying dead somewhere and instead pushed her magic outward. It made her feel ill, but not so terrible that she couldn't handle it. *Water*, she thought as they reached the river bank. *Water,*

*water, water, water—*

She felt herself fall, heard herself splash. A moment later, she released the magic, rising fluidly back into her human form. A muffled shout met her ears, but before she could look behind her, Dad said, "Quickly! Now, Ridley!" He threw his arms around her just as she moved to throw herself around him. They became water together, slipping easily into the river and racing away on the current.

Once Ridley judged they'd put some distance between them and the reserve, she arced out of the water in a stream of droplets and became air instead. Her mind reached out for Nathan. Sensing the general direction he'd gone in, she followed.

Time lost meaning as she flew over hills, ravines, lakes, and then finally, the mountains she'd seen in the distance every time she and Saoirse went out to practice magic together. She dove downward, listening to the magic around her, reaching out toward Nathan.

And suddenly, there it was. An enormous structure of stone and glass jutting out from the side of the mountain. A great many conjurations must have assisted in the construction of this building, which was situated far above the ground and was at least ten stories tall. Simply getting all the materials up here must have involved a lot of magic. Ridley could see how it would be extremely difficult for anyone without magic to access this place. At the same time, it was probably a terrifying home for anyone who had a fear of heights.

Ridley spotted a wide opening on the lowest level. Heading closer, she could see a large, high-ceilinged space filled with people. She swooped inside a few moments later, reaching out with her mind toward Archer once more. As had been the case the whole way here, her question went unanswered.

She pulled her magic back inside herself and let go of Dad, feeling panic begin to tighten her chest and steal her breath. Archer couldn't be ... *dead*. There had to be another explanation. Maybe ... maybe the arxium she'd breathed in earlier had muddled her senses. Maybe some of it was still in her system, so her magic wasn't functioning properly. He had to be here *somewhere*.

She began pushing her way through the crowded space, her eyes scanning the area for anyone male and tall and dark-haired. It seemed almost everyone from the reserve was squished into this entrance room. Clearly no one knew where to go yet.

She passed Nathan and Cam, Saoirse's husband. "... didn't make it," Cam was saying to Nathan.

"That makes three so far," Nathan replied. "That we know of for sure. *Dammit*. We've been safe for so long. How did this happen?"

Ridley continued past them. Right now, it didn't matter *how* this had happened. All that mattered was figuring out who was left. Her damp pajama bottoms flapped around her ankles as she went. Hopefully the supplies Nathan had referred to included clothing, since she'd brought nothing aside from her jacket and shoes with her. But she could worry about that once she'd found Archer.

She saw Saoirse next, sitting on the floor near the edge of the room with her daughter Bria. Bria spoke quietly to Saoirse as she wrapped an arm around her mother's shoulders.

"Saoirse!" Ridley hurried over.

"Oh, what a relief," Saoirse said on an exhale. "I was supposed to get you a mask, and I didn't, and with all the arxium gas in the air, I was so worried maybe you'd—"

"Hey, I'm okay." Ridley took Saoirse's hand and squeezed it. "I'm glad you're okay too." She was about to move on when Bria glanced up with fear-filled eyes. Ridley paused. "*Is* she okay?" she asked Bria, nodding toward Saoirse.

"I think she's having a panic attack," Bria said, her voice high-pitched.

"No, no, no," Saoirse said. "I'm—I'm fine. It's just ..." She took a deep breath. "It was like before. The smoke and the flames ... I didn't realize it would be the same." She shook her head. "I mean I—I used to have nightmares. After the last time they found us. This was like the nightmare."

Ridley almost said it was like her nightmare too, but that wouldn't have helped. She crouched down in front of Saoirse. "But we got away. Magic warned us they were coming, and we got away. Well, most of us."

"I know, but people *died*, Ridley." Saoirse wiped moisture from beneath her eyes. "We should all have been able to get away in time, but we didn't."

Ridley nodded, tears pooling in her own eyes as she pictured Tanika. Then she pictured Archer in exactly the same position—and immediately wiped the image from her mind.

*Don't think like that*, she instructed herself. "It could have been worse," she whispered. "It could have been so much worse. If magic hadn't warned us."

Saoirse took another deep breath and nodded, straightening a little. "I have to keep telling myself that."

"Wait, magic *warned* you?" Bria asked as Ridley was about to stand.

"Um ... yes," Saoirse answered.

"Oh. I didn't know ... Why didn't it do that before? The last time the Shadow Society found us."

Saoirse shook her head as she stared at the ground, her brow furrowed and her gaze far away. "I don't know. I didn't realize until tonight that it could communicate so clearly with—with us. Maybe ... we were too deeply asleep that night? The last time, I mean, when we had no warning. I don't know. I ..." She inhaled shakily, wringing her hands together.

"Are you sure you're okay?" Ridley asked.

"Yes, yes, I'll be fine."

"Okay." Ridley stood, glancing to the side and spotting Malachi a little further away. Relief eased a tiny fraction of her anxiety. "I really need to look for Archer."

"Yes, of course. I think I saw him ..." Saoirse looked around. "No, I'm sorry, I can't remember."

The flame of hope that had flickered briefly to life died a quick death. Ridley turned around just as someone almost barreled into her. "Callie?"

"Ridley, I've been looking everywhere for you." Callie swiped her tangled hair out of her face. "I ... I saw Archer."

Ridley's heart sped up. "Where?"

"I saw someone tackle him back at the reserve. They knocked him out. A man and woman were forcing him into one of those hazmat suit things, and I was going to try to be fire, to attack them and stop them, and then there was so much arxium in the air I almost passed out. I was on my knees, and I couldn't see him anywhere, and then someone else grabbed my hand and suddenly we were air, and then we were—Ridley, wait!"

But Ridley had spun around and begun forcing her way back through the crowd toward—toward what? Who? Who would be able to help her if the Shadow Society already had Archer? Fear gripped her. The same fear that had stolen her breath when magic snatched Archer away in the wastelands outside Lumina City. Only now it was worse. This wasn't a confused, undefined feeling of not wanting to lose him. Now she *knew* just how much she cared for him.

She had to go back. She had to find out if he was truly gone or if he'd managed to escape and was waiting for her—

"Ridley?" Someone caught her arm and pulled her to a stop. She tugged free—a little too forcefully—before realizing it was Dad.

"They took Archer," she said in a single breath.

Dad frowned. "Are you sure he isn't just—"

"He's not here, Dad. Callie saw someone take him. I have to go back and—"

"No, no, no." Dad took hold of both her arms.

"I have to!"

"Stop, Ridley. Just ... just wait. You can't go racing off without a plan. You have to think."

"I don't have time to think, Dad. If he's not an elemental, then they don't care about him. They might be about to ... to *kill* him." She could barely get the words out.

"If he's not an elemental," Dad said, his steady gaze holding hers, "he's more likely to survive. It's your kind they want to kill, not people like Archer and me. He's a Davenport. He'll be fine."

"What does being a Davenport have to do with it?" Ridley demanded, her voice shrill.

"Because that name *means* something. He can negotiate with it. Offer them a small fortune in exchange for his freedom. Even the Shadow Society needs money, right? Or contacts, or favors. Maybe that's why they took him—because they recognized who he is."

"But—he—" Ridley shook her head. "That makes no sense. The Shadow Society already has influence over ... I don't know, pretty much *everything*, right? The *mayor* of Lumina City is one of them, for goodness' sake. They *have* contacts already."

"Okay, but maybe ... maybe they want to bribe Alastair Davenport. He does control almost all the arxium in the world, so—"

"Dad, stop. You're only saying these things because you don't want me looking for Archer and putting myself in danger."

Dad pressed his lips together before answering again.

"Yes. But what I'm saying could very well be the truth anyway. I'm not letting you go."

"You can't stop—"

"Just *think*." Still holding onto her—probably so she wouldn't be able to shift form without taking him along with her—Dad reminded her of the danger she'd be putting everyone else in. He pointed out that the Shadow Society might catch her and torture the new location out of her. They may have invented some way to follow her back here while she was in her elemental form.

Then he dragged her to Nathan, who freaked out almost as much as Dad had about the idea of her returning and putting everyone in danger. Nathan promised that within an hour or two, a small, select team of elementals would return to the reserve and covertly check things out.

An *hour* or two.

There was a not insignificant part of Ridley that wanted to scream. But knowing that there were more lives at stake than just Archer's, she managed to keep herself from racing off immediately. That didn't mean she had to be *still*, though. She changed into the dry clothes Callie brought her at some point, then started pacing.

The giant receiving room slowly emptied of people, and she continued to pace.

As the moon inched across the sky, she paced.

After the team of elementals left—a team Nathan flat-out refused to allow her to be part of—she finally grew too exhausted to continue pacing and sat down against the wall.

With every passing moment, her insides wound tighter.

The sun was rising as the group returned. Ridley had half fallen asleep with her head tilted back against the wall, but she forced her eyelids open at the sound of voices. Dad, sitting beside her, had properly fallen asleep. Ridley stood, daring to hope that Nathan would deliver good news. But the expression on his face—and the fact that there was no Archer among the group of people who'd just returned—was answer enough.

Nathan sighed and shook his head. "He wasn't there."

# CHAPTER 6

RIDLEY SLIPPED AWAY A LITTLE after dawn. She'd known from the moment Callie told her what happened that she would go after Archer. The only thing that might have stopped her was confirmation that he was no longer alive.

The supplies Nathan had mentioned to Ridley included not only shelves and shelves of canned food, but a collection of gas masks as well. As Ridley hastily dropped a mask and a few cans into a backpack she'd 'borrowed' without permission, she heard Malachi's voice in her mind: *Don't those things last forever?* It had been only a couple of weeks ago, but that conversation felt as if it had taken place in another lifetime. That was the day they'd taken refuge in an old hotel in the wastelands near Lumina City. The day Ridley had finally given herself over to the magic in the elements, desperate to find Archer after he'd vanished. Magic had helped her then and it would help her now. She would find him again.

Dad would be furious once he realized she was gone, but she doubted he'd be surprised. Hopefully, when he stopped to think about it, he would understand. Nathan, who was turning out to be a bit of a dictator, would be irate too. He had actually used the words 'I forbid you to leave.' Ridley and her father had raised equally stunned eyebrows at that. She'd almost responded with 'You're not my father,' and if Dad had been given the chance to say anything before someone else tugged on Nathan's arm, demanding his attention, he probably would have pointed out the same thing.

This community of fugitives that Ridley was now part of might make major decisions together, but anyone was free to leave if they wanted to. Free to seek out other elementals hiding in the wastelands. Free to return to whatever city they'd fled or attempt to start over in a different one. There was nothing stopping Ridley from doing the same thing.

Nathan had promised that someone 'more experienced' would go after Archer, but there was no one who knew Lumina City better than Ridley. She'd been sneaking through its streets and inside its buildings for years. Of course, this advantage would mean nothing if Archer had been taken somewhere else by a different Shadow Society chapter, but Ridley had no way of knowing yet if that was the case. Besides, she doubted anyone else felt the same sense of urgency she did. Four bodies had been found when Nathan and his team returned to the reserve, and everyone else was now accounted for. Archer was the only one who'd been taken. It seemed Dad may have been right about him being recognized. It was this that gave Ridley real hope he was still alive.

Once she was soaring amid the air currents above the mountains, she let herself fragment and gave herself over to the wind, letting it sense the urgency in her heart and the desperate need to go faster, faster, *faster*. The kind of speed she could never have reached if she had Dad or another non-elemental with her.

She cast her mind out repeatedly but received no hint of Archer's whereabouts in return. That in itself was an answer: He was most likely within a city, blocked from magic's reach by a multitude of arxium-reinforced buildings. Lumina City? Or one of the others? It didn't matter. All her pacing earlier had given her time to come up with a plan. If she couldn't sense exactly where Archer was, she would get an answer from a Shadow Society member.

The only one she knew of was Lumina City's mayor, but she was nervous to confront him directly, even with a gas mask on. Not just for her own safety, but for the safety of the community she'd left behind. She didn't *plan* to give up their location, but the mayor might somehow get it out of her anyway.

No, the safer option was to get information from a distance and without Mayor Madson knowing about it. If Ridley could remotely access his devices, she could see his calendar, his text messages, his emails. Perhaps she could even listen in on his calls. She didn't know. But there was someone who *did* know. Someone who would happily break the law for Archer. Someone who had the kind of influence and contacts that might help her to get valuable information even if the device-hacking plan didn't work out.

Lilah Davenport.

* * *

It was twilight when Ridley became aware of Lumina City nearby, but whether it was the first night or the second, she couldn't be sure. She'd lost all concept of time and place while in her fragmented form, speeding too quickly above the earth to make sense of anything. She hadn't stopped for rest or food. She hadn't felt the need for either.

As easily as the last time she'd done it, she swooped through Aura Tower's main entrance, up an elevator shaft, and into the apartment below the penthouse. The Davenports' front door was lined with arxium, but, as Ridley had pointed out to Archer, their floor was not. A conjuration that might possibly have been illegal—even in the days when magic was permitted—easily created a hole for her to access the penthouse.

No one was home. Invisible, Ridley made her way to Lilah's bedroom, only wondering now what she would do if Lilah didn't come home for hours. How long was she willing to wait? Without a clear answer in mind, she slipped into the walk-in closet and allowed herself to become visible. The sudden weight pulling down on her shoulders reminded her of the bag she'd completely forgotten about. Without removing it, she sat on the floor and practiced some of the deep, slow breathing Saoirse had taught her. When she was a little calmer, she pressed her hand over the place where her mother's pendant lay beneath her clothing. Its presence made her feel a little less alone. *I'll find him*, she told herself again. *Every-*

*thing's going to be okay.*

She thought of the last time she'd hidden inside this closet and how different things were now. She wasn't here to steal, for one thing, and for another, her view of her own magic had changed. She used to limit herself as much as possible, afraid of the intense headaches that would inevitably come with too much magic use. It seemed silly now that she'd disabled the penthouse security system last time so she could walk around in human form without setting off alarms. It was silly that she'd run and hidden in this bedroom when Lilah returned home earlier than expected. Silly that she'd been afraid to use even a little more magic in case it cost her later when she had to sneak out. The entire operation would have been far less stressful if she'd been air the entire time.

An indistinct beep reached Ridley's ears. The front door. Someone was home. She rose silently to her feet, listening intently, wondering if she was too far away to hear the soothing tones of the smart home system's voice as it greeted—

*"Good evening, Delilah."*

Adrenaline pushed Ridley's heart rate higher. The computerized voice was muffled, but she'd definitely heard it. Next came the *click, click* of hard shoes against the tiled floor, growing louder, then disappearing as Lilah stepped onto the carpeted floor of her bedroom. The sight of her in her perfectly pressed Wallace Academy school uniform almost punched the air from Ridley's chest. Wallace Academy, Lumina City's most prestigious private school, was where Ridley herself had been a student until she'd fled the city after accidentally revealing her magic. She ached inside at the thought of everything she'd lost. The future she would never have. Unless ...

*Unless we change the world.*

Lilah crossed the room, dumped her designer satchel on the floor, and perched on the edge of her bed as she scrolled through something on her commscreen.

*Archer first*, Ridley told herself. *Then we can change the world together.*

She slid the closet door open and stepped out. A quiet gasp escaped Lilah as her gaze shot up. Her body tensed briefly, but other than that, she concealed her surprise well. "Ridley," she said. Without breaking eye contact, she lowered her commscreen to the bed. "What excellent timing you have."

Ridley wasn't sure what Lilah meant by that, but since she hadn't had to wait long for her, and Mr. and Mrs. Davenport weren't home, Ridley considered it good timing too. "I need help," she said. "*Archer* needs help." Now wasn't the time to explain all the details of elementals and the Shadow Society. That could come later. First, she needed to secure Lilah's assistance. "He's been taken. You have to help me find him. Please."

Confusion puckered Lilah's features. Then her gaze turned pitying. "Oh, Ridley," she said, her tone bordering on patronizing. "I almost feel sorry for you."

"You—what?"

"I warned you not to throw yourself at my brother's feet like every other pathetic girl who's ever pined after him."

"Um ... I don't you think you did, actually. You told me I

*was* like every other girl who's ever done that."

"Right. Sorry. It was already too late for you. Now you're the has-been while he moves on to the next girl."

"Lilah, that is not what's happening right now! He's gone, and we need to find him."

"Sure," Lilah said, slow and sarcastic as she nodded.

"Lilah! This is not a joke. I know we stopped being friends a long time ago. I know I messed up your fancy celebrity party when I used magic—"

"Used magic? You didn't just *use* magic, Ridley."

Ridley's words caught in her throat before she could get the rest of them out. What had Lilah seen that night? What had she been told? Did she know the magic Ridley had used came from within her own body? Had she seen Ridley vanish, taking Callie with her? Or did she think Ridley was just one more criminal who'd removed her AI2 and pulled magic from the environment?

Ridley's pulse throbbed. Her fingers twitched. But she managed to hide the tremor in her voice when she said, "What I did that night doesn't matter right now."

"Of course it does. It's the only thing that matters now. Because I—" Lilah's voice faltered. She cleared her throat, and when she spoke again, her voice was smaller, quieter. "I thought I knew you, Ridley."

Ridley stared at the girl who'd once been her best friend. Lilah's fierce, dark gaze swam with something else now. Hurt? Betrayal? Gently, Ridley said, "I'm the same person I've always been."

"Exactly." Lilah shook her head, inhaling deeply through her nose. "I almost wish I didn't have to do this." Then she reached swiftly past the lamp on her nightstand and slammed her palm over a small white button on the wall. Ridley tensed, expecting an alarm to blare out. But in the silence that followed, all she heard was Lilah's voice: "They're going to catch you."

# CHAPTER 7

FEELING ODDLY BETRAYED, Ridley turned and raced from Lilah's room. Clearly she had never fully grasped just how much Lilah disliked her. Perhaps her hostility had intensified after she'd seen Ridley's use of magic at one of her parties. The Davenports had always been big supporters of the anti-magic laws. Ridley told herself it wasn't personal that Lilah hoped the cops would catch her. Still, that didn't stop it from *feeling* as personal as if Lilah had physically attacked Ridley herself.

She dove around the corner into the open living space and became air before her human form could hit the floor. The siren wail she'd expected was still absent, but Lilah had clearly alerted *someone*. Aura Tower security, most likely. That button was probably her hotline to the building's security control room. *Emergency in the penthouse!* she imagined someone yelling. *Fair Delilah is in trouble! All knights to her rescue!*

She would have rolled her nonexistent eyes if not for the sickening lurch somewhere in the region of her nonexistent stomach. *Arxium*, she thought just as she fell from the air and stumbled into a glass table displaying a small ballerina sculpture and a vase of fresh flowers. The vase wobbled, fell, and shattered. "Dammit," Ridley hissed, gripping the arm of a couch as her head spun. Mayor Madson must have gifted his good friend Alastair Davenport some of his special 'air freshener' and now Ridley was suffering the consequences because her gas mask was sitting useless in her backpack instead of on her face.

She held her breath as the frightening sensation of her throat beginning to close threatened to overwhelm her. Her thoughts spun wildly. With the precious moments she had left before Aura Tower security arrived, should she get the gas mask out of her bag and put it on, or should she continue holding her breath and see if she could perform a conjuration without passing out?

*Conjuration*, she decided, lifting her hands. The quicker she got out of here the better. She clawed hastily at the air, pulling magic from it instead of using her own. As Malachi had discovered in the wastelands after they'd woken on the wrong side of the wall, arxium didn't affect their ability to pull magic from the environment, probably because that magic didn't come from within them. Normal conjurations were still possible.

Still holding her breath, Ridley let go of the couch and slid to the floor beside the broken glass and damp flowers. She began the conjuration. Dizziness made her hands swim oddly in front of her, but she managed to keep her fingers moving correctly. It was a precise and detailed dance through the magic that hung in front of her, a series of movements that required a level of concentration she could barely sustain. But then it was done, and she hadn't passed out, and she was hurriedly pushing the magic at the floor as her lungs screamed louder and louder for air.

A crack appeared in the floor. The tiles folded swiftly down and back in on themselves—as did every other layer of material between this apartment and the one below it—creating a roughly square-shaped hole. With lungs threatening to explode, Ridley skidded forward on her butt and dropped into it.

She hit the floor feet first, then staggered sideways and landed clumsily, painfully, on her right side, narrowly missing the corner of a dining room table. She sucked in a great gasp of fresh air. Well, not fresh, but arxium-free, which felt like the same thing right now. She looked up, her chest heaving. The ceiling unfolded itself and melded back into place, and the last thing Ridley saw of the Aura Tower penthouse was Lilah's shocked face peering down at her.

"Crap," Ridley whispered. She had no time to breathe through her remaining nausea. No time to steady her spinning head. No time to decide on her next move. Lilah was probably racing to tell security which way she'd gone right at this moment. At the very least, though, Ridley had to stop and get the gas mask on. It was useless sitting in her backpack.

Sick and sweaty and dizzy, she fought with the zip until she managed to get it open and retrieve the mask. With shaking fingers, she pulled it on, fumbling with the straps until she managed to click them together at the back of her head. She took a breath, hoping she'd put the mask on correctly. She pulled the backpack onto her shoulders once more and began the conjuration again.

By the time she'd dropped down another two floors—terrifying two children in a playroom on one of them—she was feeling steady enough to use her own magic. She let it rise from her skin and managed to become air again. The weight of her backpack and the discomfort of the mask vanished instantly. She swooped away, beneath a door, past an elevator—which had just opened to allow two people out and another three in—through a gap to the stairs no one in their right mind ever used, and then plunging down the center of the stairwell all the way to the ground floor.

She aimed for the grand entrance and flew straight toward it. She wouldn't have noticed the people she sped past if some quiet yet insistent voice-that-wasn't-a-voice hadn't seemed to say, *Look now. Look now, look NOW!* She whirled back around, the swirling air in her wake lifting the edge of a man's coat as he strode past her with a slight limp. It was Mayor Madson.

Aside from the limp, Jude Madson appeared to have recovered from the injuries he'd sustained a few weeks before when Malachi hurled multiple fireballs at him. Without a second's hesitation, Ridley followed him. Lilah wasn't going to help, so she'd have to get a whole lot closer to the mayor to discover anything useful. Even if he didn't personally know Archer's whereabouts, there was a good chance that he would, at some point, meet up with or contact someone who did.

If Ridley followed him for a few hours, she might discover enough to find Archer. Failing that, she could to turn to riskier methods.

She hovered nearby as the mayor signed in at the security desk—a process Ridley generally skipped, seeing as how she usually entered this building unseen—and then waited as the man behind the desk placed a call. He nodded politely at the mayor, whose grumpy expression didn't change a fraction as he strode past the desk and through the retractable glass turnstile. Ridley flew over it.

She followed the mayor into an elevator, her nerves a little on edge once the doors closed and she was inside the small space alone with him. She missed which button he pressed, so she was surprised when the elevator began to move down instead of up. After several painfully slow moments of listening to the mayor's heavy breathing, the elevator doors slid open again.

The mayor walked as briskly as his limp would allow, and Ridley followed at a distance of several paces. This was a part of Aura Tower she had never known existed: A maze of passages and office doors and something that might have been the security control room she'd imagined earlier.

She was trying to imagine who Mayor Madson could possibly be meeting down here when he stopped in front of a closed door with a keypad set into the wall beside it. He poked the numbers aggressively with one pudgy finger. Ridley heard a quiet *click*, then the mayor turned the handle and pushed the door open. He limped forward, stopped at the head of a large rectangular table, and gripped the back of the chair. The rooms' occupants—some standing, some sitting—grew quiet. "Where is he?" the mayor growled.

Ridley's insides lurched in hopeful anticipation. He couldn't possibly be asking about Archer, could he? No way was life ever that easy.

A woman sitting a few seats away said, "Late. Something came up. But he said he'll be here soon."

Not Archer then. As the door began to swing closed, Ridley's invisible heart beat out an agitated rhythm. She'd planned to follow the mayor inside, but instinct made her hesitate. If this was a meeting of the Shadow Society—and it was entirely possible, of course, that it wasn't—then there would probably be some form of anti-elemental security. Arxium in the air, perhaps. She had a gas mask on, but would it work properly if it was invisible just like the rest of her? Probably, since the rest of her still seemed to work the same, and it wasn't as though anything else she wore disappeared when she became air. And most of the elementals at the reserve had escaped wearing gas masks. Still, she hadn't tested this one, and she wasn't keen to do so in the midst of a possible Shadow Society meeting.

The door clicked shut, cutting off the mayor's irritated response. Still in her air form, Ridley spun around, looking for a panel on the wall or ceiling that might lead to a ventilation duct. *Bingo*, she thought, spotting a metal grille above her. Surely the room the mayor had disappeared into would have a similar air vent she could spy through. There were no windows below ground, so there had to be some way to ventilate the rooms down here.

Her air form slid easily through the gaps in the grille and into the metal duct. It was large enough that she could have squirmed through it in human form if she had to, but remaining invisible was both easier and safer. She followed the sound of voices and came to a stop in front of another grille. Peering through the gaps, she confirmed she'd found the correct room.

Mayor Madson, chairman of the Lumina City chapter of the Shadow Society—and possibly the director of the entire organization, if Nathan's guess was anything to go by—remained at the head of the table, glaring down at a man who was saying, "... complete disaster. They all got away. Every single group. It's like they were all warned ahead of time. And the director's latest experiments didn't even make it there, so that was extremely disappointing."

Ridley became as still as possible, intent on catching every single word. No one had said 'elementals,' but unless it was a major coincidence, that's who this man was talking about. And he'd spoken about *multiple* groups, meaning the reserve wasn't the only community of elementals they'd found.

"Seems your information wasn't reliable," the man continued.

"If you thought my informant couldn't be trusted," the mayor said icily, "you shouldn't have voted yes when we decided to act." He paused, then added, "I think we all know who warned them."

The man he'd been speaking to chuckled as he leaned back in his seat and crossed his arms. "Why don't you tell the director about your suspicions? The rest of us will sit back and watch the show."

*So it's not him*, Ridley thought, and at the same moment, a hiss loud enough to have been scarily close to the air vent startled her. She wasn't the only one surprised by it. In the room below, one of the women pressed a hand to her chest.

"That stupid thing gives me a fright every time," she said.

"Stupid but necessary," the mayor snapped at her. "And don't start going on again about how it makes you feel faint. All the research says that's nonsense. It passes through our bodies without any side effects. It's only elementals who react to it."

Finally. Confirmation, just in case Ridley still had any doubts, that this was indeed a meeting of the Shadow Society. She waited anxiously for the effects of the arxium particles to hit her. But there was no nausea, no dizziness. It seemed the gas mask worked after all.

In the room below, the lock on the door clicked and the handle turned. The murmurs quietened, and all heads turned toward the door as it swung open. Without consciously deciding to, Ridley held her breath.

"Good evening," the newcomer said from the doorway. "Sorry to keep you waiting."

*That voice*, Ridley thought as a chill crept across her skin and fear clamped a fist around her throat. The mayor moved out of her line of sight, away from the head of the table, and the newcomer stepped into the room.

Alastair Davenport.

Ridley almost stopped breathing at the sight of him, but it was the person who strode in behind him who stole her breath away entirely.

Archer.

# CHAPTER 8

"NO," RIDLEY WHISPERED. Something solid and cold pressed in around her. The ventilation duct. She was human again, though she hadn't consciously let go of her magical form. "Nonononono." Her face was hot. Cold sweat dampened her palms. Her thoughts stalled, rammed into one another, like cars in a pileup. This didn't make sense. *Nothing* made sense. Archer was on her side. He had helped her escape the city. Helped her escape the Shadow Society's base. He had *lived with* elementals for months.

Her mind raced back to everything that had happened, every incident that proved Archer couldn't possibly be part of the Shadow Society, but everything was becoming too tangled for her to clearly examine.

"This isn't happening," she whispered, pressing her cold hands against her cheeks. They had spent hours—hours upon hours upon hours—talking, daydreaming, kissing, planning. He cared about her. She *knew* it. She'd felt it in the depths of her being. And yet there he was, dropping casually into a seat right beside the director of the organization that wanted to slaughter her kind, his dark gaze utterly devoid of the gentle warmth she'd become accustomed to seeing whenever his eyes found hers.

He was supposed to be on her side! But he had somehow avoided capture when she, Callie and Malachi ended up inside a cell in the Shadow Society's base. He was the only one who'd been 'taken' when the Shadow Society attacked the reserve. An attack that happened *now*, mere weeks after Archer had joined them, when their location had remained hidden for years.

Ridley's wild thoughts stilled, leaving a cold, empty space for the horrible truth to finally settle into place. She had always known what an excellent act Archer Davenport could put on. But somehow, she'd been foolish enough to fall for it anyway.

*I warned you not to throw yourself at my brother's feet.*

"First," Alastair Davenport said to the room, "there's something I need to address."

*What excellent timing you have.*

"A question of loyalty."

*They're going to catch you.*

Lilah had not been talking about the cops. She knew what Ridley was. She knew about elementals and the Shadow Society. The whole Davenport family obviously knew. It made sense now that the button Lilah pressed had produced no sound. It probably wasn't an alarm. She wouldn't have wanted to alert security. She didn't want the *cops* to catch Ridley. She wanted the Shadow Society to catch her. That button was probably what had released arxium into the air.

"My *son's* loyalty, to be specific," Alastair Davenport continued. "Some of you have been spreading rumors about betrayal—" his hard gaze fell on Jude Madson for a moment "—but Archer has proven himself time and again. He has remained close to the elemental girl who revealed herself at a party several weeks ago. Pretended to assist in her escape so he could travel with her to one of the elemental communities further north. You *fools* already screwed things up once when you went after them in the wastelands after you were told to let them go—"

"That was because *my* son discovered—"

"—and now you've further messed things up," Alastair said loudly, speaking over the mayor as if he were a child, "by convincing us to act too soon. If you want to talk about betrayal, Jude, then perhaps we should be looking at *you*."

The mayor's face reddened. "How dare you."

"Well, either your informant fed you misinformation, or you're secretly acting against us. Which is it?"

"My loyalty lies with the society," the mayor growled.

"As does Archer's," Alastair replied. "But you seem to have forgotten that while he's been busy with his *long-term* undercover operation. This isn't about finding a handful of communities and getting rid of them. This is about learning their plans to fight back and taking them *all* out before—"

"Information your son was taking far too long to pass on," the mayor interrupted. "If I hadn't heard from that other—"

"You're aware communication is a little difficult when

there are *no networks* out in the wastelands, Jude," Archer said to the mayor, speaking up for the first time. Part of Ridley had been desperate to hear his voice, but now his disrespectful drawl sent another crack running through her barely held-together composure.

"Clearly not impossible, since I heard from someone else," Jude Madson answered.

"Forgive me for waiting until I had *all* the information we required before acting. You convinced the rest of the society to attack all those communities, and where did that get us? Nowhere. Clearly someone warned them what was coming, and most of them got away. You should have let me go too. Now you have no one on the inside."

"Because I believed you had betrayed us. I *still* think you've turned. You were certainly *convincing*," the mayor sneered, "when you broke into our base, attacked your fellow society members, and freed those elementals."

"Of course I was convincing. That was the point. And I'm ready to be convincing again if I have to be."

The mayor shook his head. "I don't buy it. Lawrence gathered plenty of evidence of your betrayal before he was murdered. That evidence was mysteriously destroyed soon afterwards, but my wife will happily sit here and tell you all about it. Lawrence told her—"

"The evidence that all points to the fact that I was *doing what I was asked to do?*" Archer demanded, leaning forward as he raised his voice. "We want to wipe them out, don't we? *All* of them—and their disgusting, unnatural magic. If a few of us end up as casualties along the way, so be it."

Ridley physically recoiled from his words, almost banging her head on the ventilation duct surface just above her. Archer was so callous, so cold. So full of *hate*. How had he hidden this from her? How had she been so blind?

Something seemed to tighten around her throat, making it harder to breathe. She felt smothered, suffocated. The gas mask was too uncomfortable. The backpack was too heavy. The metal tunnel she hunched inside was too small.

She couldn't do this. She couldn't stay and listen. Couldn't be still. Couldn't be silent. She had to move, had to get out, had to get OUT! She managed to focus enough to become air once more, and then, in a desperate rush, she was gone.

# CHAPTER 9

RIDLEY SOARED TO THE VERY top of Aura Tower. The moment she was human shaped again, she tugged the mask free and screamed into the buffeting wind. How could she have been so, so, *so* stupid? How could she have fallen for Archer Davenport and all his lies? She should have listened to her head and not her ridiculous heart.

She thought of their first kiss beneath a stormy sky in the wastelands. Of Archer saying that her magic was beautiful. Of the way he'd held her gaze when she asked him to confirm he wasn't part of the Shadow Society. *That is the absolute truth*, he'd said.

She screamed into the wind again.

Then she became air once more, let herself fragment, and whirled, directionless, amid the shimmering skyscrapers of Lumina City's Opal Quarter. Waiting, waiting, waiting. Archer was hidden within an arxium cloud in a secret room below ground, but eventually, he would come out. Magic would find him and magic would tell her.

An indeterminate amount of time later, as a fine mist of

rain began to fall, that's exactly what happened.

Ridley was near enough that she sensed Archer's presence somewhere in the lower part of Aura Tower. She sped back, rushed through the open doors, and spotted him waiting in front of the private elevator reserved for the penthouse level. His father stood beside him, speaking into a commscreen, but Ridley didn't care. She soared past security, wrapped her air form swiftly and tightly around Archer, and whisked him away. Whether or not Alastair Davenport noticed his son's sudden disappearance—whether *anyone* in the Aura Tower foyer noticed—didn't concern Ridley. She was beyond caring what anyone else knew or saw.

Archer fought back instantly, struggling and cursing. Ridley tightened her magical grasp on him and let him continue, the city lights becoming a blur around them as she spun around and around. She slowed near the top of a building where a lush rooftop garden was illuminated by low, hidden lighting and the nighttime glow of the city. The Boards24 Building, from which Lumina City's vast network of billboard screens was controlled. *Probably run by a Shadow Society member*, Ridley thought bitterly. Someone who could make sure all the lies about the wild wasteland magic were continually spread to everyone.

She dropped Archer in the middle of the garden, letting go a moment sooner than necessary so that he staggered forward as he landed and took a few clumsy steps before catching his balance. She lowered herself a few paces away and released her magic.

Archer started, then blinked. "Ridley." He let out a long breath and moved toward her. "You—you're okay. Thank goodness. When did you—"

"I always knew you could put on a great act," she said, stepping quickly out of his reach, "but I had no idea you were this good."

His brow furrowed. "What are you talking about? What's wrong?" He reached for her again, but she snatched her arm away. A wisp of magic detached itself from her hand, and with barely a thought, it snapped tight and lashed out, striking him across the face.

"Don't touch me."

Eyes wide and one hand pressed over his cheek, Archer said, "Ridley, what the—"

"How could you lie to me like this?" she shouted, hating the way her voice cracked before she finished speaking. Tears burned behind her eyes. This wasn't the way this conversation was supposed to go. She was supposed to show no emotion. Hide how deeply he'd hurt her. Never let him see the kind of power she'd allowed him to have over her.

"What are you—"

"You're one of *them*!" she spat. "I saw you, sitting there with your father. The *director*. All this time, Archer—*all. this. time*—you've been going on about protecting elementals when you're actually one of the people who hunts us down and kills us."

Archer was silent, barely moving except for the rising and falling of his chest. Then a whispered curse fell from his lips.

Ridley let her eyes slide shut for a moment as the terrible truth caved in on her all over again. It wasn't as though he could deny it, but the fact that he didn't even try somehow made this worse. "Yeah," she said. Her face was wet now, not with tears but from the fine droplets of rain in the air.

"It was you," Archer said quietly, lowering his hand, and Ridley was perversely pleased to see the angry welt on his cheek. "In our apartment earlier. Lilah sent an alert, but she didn't say who—"

"Did she tell you I was *worried* about you? That I came to her for help? That I thought you'd been *taken*?"

"Ridley—"

"Actually, you know what? I've changed my mind. I don't want to have this conversation after all." She turned and started walking away. "I don't want to hear anything from you ever again."

"Wait, stop. Ridley. Stop, stop, stop." When she didn't listen, Archer shouted, "Stop! *Please!* I'm not one of them anymore! I was, but not now. I've been pretending for months. Please just *listen* to me!"

Ridley paused but didn't look back. She focused on the giant red blossom crowning the top of a leafy plant that reached almost to her shoulders. If not for the whine of a siren and the nearby buzz of a scanner drone, it was possible to imagine she wasn't in the center of a city.

"Please don't leave without hearing me out," Archer begged. "*Please.* I don't want you believing a lie."

At that, Ridley swung around. "Are you kidding? You've

been letting me believe a lie since the moment this all began."

"I know! But it's—it's part of my past. Of course I wasn't going to tell you about it in the beginning. And since then, since we got closer, I've ..." He pushed a hand through his hair. "I knew I had to tell you. I've been trying—"

"Oh, right," she sneered. "You haven't been trying very hard." Though he *had* tried—sort of—to tell her something the last evening they'd spent together. Stupidly, she'd thought he might have been about to confess that he *loved* her. A pang radiated through her chest as she realized *this* was what he'd been trying to say instead.

"I know. I'm sorry. I'm so, so sorry. I knew it would hurt you, and I didn't want ..." He took a deep breath. "I told you I wanted you to know everything, and I meant it. I knew it would probably ruin things between us, but I also knew we couldn't have a solid future together with all these lies piling up between us. I've just ... I've been trying to find a good moment, and there hasn't been one."

"There was never going to be a good moment for something like this, Archer."

"I know. I know. That's why I kept putting it off. I wanted just one more day with you before everything fell apart between us. And then one more, and one more."

Ridley shook her head and settled her gaze somewhere over his shoulder. On the purple bell-shaped flowers. On the plant with spiny leaves and blossoms like large pink sea urchins. Anywhere but directly on Archer's pleading, desperate face. Part of her wanted him to be able to explain everything away, while part of her flat-out refused to fall for anything he said ever again. Still … could she really walk away without hearing the full story? If she was going to hate him, it would be because of *everything* he'd done, and not just part of it.

"Fine," she said, removing the backpack and lowering it to the paved pathway between the plants. She folded her arms and met his gaze. "This is your chance. Tell me everything."

He hesitated. "Here? We could go back to—"

"Yes, here, Archer. In the cold. In the rain. We're not going anywhere near your Shadow Society friends."

He sighed. "That's not what I meant, Ridley. I just—I thought you'd be more comfortable if—never mind." He took a deep breath and wiped the sheen of moisture from his face. "My family has always been part of the Shadow Society. My father has been director for over a decade. My mother was once a member too, but she got bored of all the meetings and the politics, and Lilah was never that interested in being part of the official proceedings either. But my father made sure I was part of it all from a young age.

"He always told us elementals were … unnatural. Twisted and perverted by the magic that constantly lived inside them. Intent on taking over and ruling the people who had no magic. It was our noble purpose to rid the world of them."

Ridley clenched her shaking fingers into fists. "So many lies," she hissed.

"I know. But back then, I believed him because … well, why wouldn't I? Why would my father lie to me? I still don't understand why he lied. Why he *still* lies. Sometimes I wonder if ... if maybe he actually believes the things he's always told me. It's what the Shadow Society has taught its members for so long."

"So when you saw me all those years ago when we were children and I accidentally used my magic while in your home, you thought I was one of these twisted, evil people?"

"No," Archer said immediately. "*No.* That was the moment that planted the first seed of doubt in my mind. It was one thing when elementals were faceless evil people that the world would be better off without. It was entirely another when it was *you*, a person I knew. You were Lilah's best friend, not some evil, inhumane being. So even though I knew I was supposed to tell my father, I didn't. I told no one."

Ridley held his gaze as she nodded slowly. This, at least, she could believe. If Archer had told someone, the Shadow Society would have killed her years ago. "So you started doubting," she said, "but that was years ago, and your father still seems to think you're a loyal member of the Shadow Society. Clearly you never confronted him about the horrendous things he does to elementals."

Archer's jaw tightened as his gaze slid away from hers. "It was just ... it was easier to go along with things. Easier not to question. I thought maybe you were an anomaly. That I could put you into a separate category while still hating the rest of those faceless elementals." He pressed one fisted hand to his mouth before continuing. "It's terrible, I know. Horrible, shameful."

"Yes," Ridley said harshly. "It is."

Archer nodded. His gaze had settled somewhere in the region of her chin. Or perhaps her shoulder or neck. Somewhere that wasn't her eyes. "So when I finished school and went to France, it wasn't just to take a year off and have fun. I didn't *accidentally* discover that elemental community while hiking La Tournette. I was sent there when my father discovered it. To infiltrate, to gather information."

"Yeah, I figured," Ridley muttered. "A *long-term undercover operation*, as your father reminded everyone earlier."

"Yes," Archer answered quietly. "But I wasn't lying when I told you that I started to change there. It just ... it wasn't in the way you assumed I meant. My father had warned me that elementals were master deceivers, but the more time I spent with them, the harder it was to believe. It seemed that everything he'd ever told me was untrue. And yet ... how could my own father be so wrong? How could he have told me so many lies? I couldn't quite believe that either, so I existed in this conflicted space for months.

"When I returned to the city the first time, with that flash drive of information that I was supposed to pass on to one of the protectors, I was still planning to give it to my father instead. I may have spent most of my youth disregarding every rule my parents set, wasting their money, and generally making an art form out of caring as little as possible about anything, but when it came to Shadow Society stuff ... yeah, disobeying my father wasn't an option. It just wasn't.

"So even though I felt awful about what I was planning to do, I hadn't yet realized that I could choose not to. My loyalty was to my family and to the Shadow Society, and that was just the way it was."

Archer finally met Ridley's eyes. "So you went all that time without telling your father about me," she said, "but then you were going to give him a flash drive that had my name on it."

Archer shook his head. "I removed your name. And Serena's, and one other. I removed the names I recognized."

Ridley felt a jolt of surprise, then reminded herself once again that most of what came out of Archer Davenport's mouth was a lie, so he might very well be lying about this too. "Great, so a few of us would have been safe, but you were happy for the others to die."

"Not happy, no. But yes, I was going to give up those other names. Because I was—I am—a terrible person. I didn't think I had a choice. But then ..." Archer's eyes slid down once more, seeming to look *through* Ridley. "I was standing inside my own home, waiting for Dad to return from work, and it just ... it didn't feel like *home* anymore. And it suddenly hit me that every experience I'd had out there in the wastelands with people I was supposed to hate was genuine, real, full of hope. And I just couldn't do it. I couldn't betray them like that. It was a terrifying decision, Rid, but it was such a relief." He ran a hand through his hair, almost smiling for a brief moment. "But I was still too afraid to go against my father. Too afraid to confront him. I decided to pretend I'd never been there.

"I had just made the decision when two men arrived at the apartment, responding to some security alarm I must have unknowingly set off. I suppose I could have let them see it was me. Told them nothing was wrong. Told them to leave. But ... everything was still so confused inside my head. I had no plan. So that's when I hid the flash drive—just in case they caught me—and ran."

"And that's when my father helped hide you," Ridley said.

"Yes. I lied, just as I did to you, about how I'd accidentally found an elemental community. But everything else was the truth. After I left, when I eventually made contact with my father, it seemed he thought it was an elemental who'd broken into our home. So I went with that. Told him one of them had followed me, that I was risking blowing my cover, that I'd ended up losing the flash drive along the way. He told me to return to the elementals and continue gathering more information.

"As the months went by, I had limited contact with him, and I made excuses about why I couldn't return or why I couldn't access certain information and send it to him. But eventually he became impatient and insisted I return home. I had to concoct a story about how my true intentions had been discovered just before I left, and how I'd had to fight my way out with magic and hadn't been able to steal any information. I told him they had never fully regained their trust in me after I was unable to deliver the flash drive to the intended recipient in Lumina City."

"And of course he believed you," Ridley said quietly, bitterly, "because everyone believes the lies Archer Davenport tells."

"Ridley—"

"We stood in my living room and I asked you point-blank if you were part of the Shadow Society. Remember that, Archer? Do you remember how you denied it? Do you remember using the words 'absolute truth'?"

"It *was* the truth," he insisted. "It just wasn't the whole story."

"Right. And why exactly did you decide to keep the whole story to yourself when you could very easily have it explained it all right then and there?"

"I just ... I was ashamed, okay? You trusted me. Your father trusted me. So because of my stupid pride, I didn't want to admit that I used to be one of them. And I was leaving it all behind anyway. I had planned to leave the city and my family and the society forever. They would never be part of my life again, and there would never be a reason for me to tell you what had happened in the past. Especially since you and I weren't that close yet. I mean, I ... I knew I cared about you. More than I had expected to. But I didn't know it would turn into anything. I didn't know how close we would become. And I certainly didn't know someone would discover the location of multiple elemental groups and tell the Shadow Society. I didn't know I would be captured and dragged back to Lumina City."

"Where you're still lying your way through everything."

"Yes. I don't know where Jude Madson got his information from or how much more he knows, but I can't exactly find out anything about future Shadow Society plans if they know he's right about me betraying them all. I swear, Ridley.

*They're* the ones I'm lying to, not you. Please, please believe me. Even if—if you never ... *forgive* me for everything I've kept from you ... at least believe me."

Ridley shook her head and looked away. She wasn't saying no. She wasn't sure what she was saying except that everything hurt and whether she believed him or not, whether she forgave him or not, that didn't change. In a small voice, she said, "Disgusting and unnatural."

After a moment of hesitation, Archer asked, "What?"

"In the meeting. That's what you said about our magic. *My* magic. You want to get rid of us and our disgusting, unnatural magic."

"Ridley—"

"It wasn't that long ago that you told me you thought it was beautiful."

"I *do* think that." He moved toward her, and once again, she stepped out of his reach. "Rid, I was just telling them what they wanted to hear. Repeating their own words back to them."

"And when you used the word 'beautiful,' were you just telling me what you thought *I* wanted to hear?"

"No. In fact, I figured you *didn't* want to hear something like that—especially from me—but it was the truth and it slipped out."

Ridley released a long sigh and shut her eyes. "You're such a great actor, Archer Davenport."

"This isn't an act, Ridley, I promise. *Nothing* with you is an act."

His anguished tone was so genuine, Ridley struggled not to believe it. Perhaps this *was* the truth. The fact that he wasn't currently knocking her out with arxium and dragging her back home to the director of the Shadow Society was a good sign. She opened her eyes again, thinking vaguely about the fact that putting the gas mask back on for this confrontation would have been a good idea. It hadn't even crossed her mind until now.

"I want to believe you," she told him as she met his desperate gaze once more. "I really do."

"Please, Rid—"

"And I think I actually do." She pushed her hands through her damp hair. "Despite my better judgement, I think I do believe you."

"Thank you, Ridley. Thank—"

"Which probably just makes me really stupid."

Archer shook his head, holding her gaze. "Every moment we've spent together recently was genuine. Every time I told you how I feel about you, it was real. You must know that."

Ridley wanted to look away, but she couldn't. She wanted to cry, but she refused. "It doesn't really matter. Even if everything you've told me is the truth—and even if I believe you—it doesn't matter. Because I'm returning to the elementals and you're not. This is the end for us."

Archer turned his gaze down. He clenched his jaw, then nodded slowly. "I hope you at least understand why I put off telling you the truth for so long. I knew it would be the end for us, and even though it was wrong, I wanted to delay that for as long as possible."

Ridley let out a frustrated sound. "You don't know that, Archer. If you'd been truthful from the start, maybe it wouldn't have gone this way." She lifted the backpack, shoved her arms through the straps, and tugged it onto her shoulders. Turning her back to him, she let her magic rise from her skin as she prepared to become air. "But like I said," she added, "it doesn't matter now."

"I do know, Rid. I know because I haven't finished telling you everything."

She hesitated, her back still to Archer.

"There's more," he said, and it sounded a little as though his voice broke on the word 'more.'

"More?" she asked, looking over her shoulder at him.

"I have to tell you … everything." He tugged at his hair with both hands. "I should have told you long ago, but—" He inhaled sharply, blinking furiously. "I didn't want you to hate me," he finished, his voice hoarse.

Ridley let out a heavy sigh. She wanted to hate him. She wanted it so badly. She could even try to pretend that this sickening ache eating away at her core was hatred, but she knew it wasn't. It was pain because of how much she'd come to care for him. It was shame because she'd been stupid enough to fall for him when she knew—she *knew*—she shouldn't have. "I don't hate you," she said quietly, wearily. "I may never like you again, but I don't *hate* you."

He couldn't look at her as he said, "You will. Once you've heard everything."

"What's worse than you betraying my trust and being part of a secret organization that wants to kill me?"

He swallowed. His breaths grew shallower. His eyes glistened, and he blinked furiously again, then pressed a fist over his mouth. *This is an act*, Ridley reminded herself. *A damn good one, but still an act. It isn't real. He's just trying to—*

"The Cataclysm wasn't an accident."

Ice-cold shock flooded Ridley's body.

A moment passed.

Then another.

Another.

"E-excuse me?"

"The GSMC was meant to be the end of the energy crisis," Archer said in a shaky voice, "but the Shadow Society—my *father*—saw an opportunity to change the world. To cripple it. To *control* it. To decimate the population and ensure the survivors would always fear magic."

Ridley opened her mouth, but no sound came out.

"The Shadow Society selected certain cities around the world. They convinced those in power that something *might* someday go wrong. They planted the idea of hovering arxium panels. The right people liked that idea. The arxium panels were slowly put in place. More panels were discreetly embedded in the ground around these cities. And as the event itself—the GSMC—grew closer and closer, my father made sure that the complement of magicists for every group conjuration that would take place that day included at least one Shadow Society member. A person who would make very slight adjustments to the conjuration they performed. Adjustments that rendered all the other energy conjurations useless.

"Near every group conjuration, Shadow Society chapters gathered in secret. They had all been taught an ancient conjuration my father discovered. A conjuration people used to do to … *cleanse* small areas of land for renewal and regrowth. A conjuration that stirs up the magic in the elements until it reaches a point where it reacts violently, wiping out everything in that area."

Ridley's body was shaking now, but still she couldn't utter a word.

"It was only ever meant to be done by one person on a small scale," Archer continued, his voice still shuddery, broken. "Not in groups. Not attached to the kind of amplification conjurations that were going on because of the GSMC. But I … I didn't know that. I didn't know anything back then except what my father told me: We were aiding the GSMC. We were clearing the world of all the bad in it. Elementals and their magic. *All* dangerous magic. He said the world would be a better place afterwards. And I—" Archer breathed in a ragged breath "—I believed him. I was young. I thought my father knew everything. If he said this was how we would save the world, then I figured he must be right.

"So when he—" Archer broke off, blinking again as he cleared his throat. "When he took my hand and pulled me into the circle along with my mother and everyone else, I didn't stop him. I …" Archer shook his head, leaned forward with his hands pressed to his knees, and breathed in shakily. His voice was strained and oddly high-pitched as he said, "I watched my father start the conjuration that ended the world, and I didn't do anything to stop him."

Ridley shook her head, tears fracturing her vision. "My mom ..."

"Your mom," Archer whispered. "And billions of other people—" He broke off as he straightened, turned away, tugged at his hair yet again. "All dead," he managed to say. "And afterwards, when I saw what had happened, saw how many people had been wiped out, I felt so ... so sick. I couldn't believe he—*we*—had done that. I thought I might die from the guilt. So I told myself to never think about it. That was the only way I could survive. It was the only way I wouldn't ... *implode*."

He turned back to face her, but his red-rimmed eyes and contorted expression were blurred by her own tears. "So when I told Lilah it wasn't appropriate for her to be your friend anymore, it was because of my own guilt. It was because I couldn't stand to look at you knowing what I'd done to you."

A sob clawed its way up Ridley's throat as her heart cracked open. A shuddering breath passed her lips. She whirled around and pushed blindly through the flowers and bushes until she came to the edge of the roof. She grabbed the railing that ran atop the wall and pulled herself up. She stepped over the railing.

And she let herself fall.

Down, down, down, glittering glass panes flashing by and the road rushing toward her, until finally, with a heartrending cry, she pushed her magic out and vanished.

# CHAPTER 10

*IT WASN'T AN ACCIDENT.*

Ridley fled the city upon the gusts of a windstorm and kept going until she was too weak to continue. Which wasn't particularly long. The wind slowed to a persistent breeze as she collapsed on a crumbling street of a storm-ravaged waste-land suburban area, her body sick and shaky. Part of it was the shocking knowledge that the entire world had fallen apart because of a small group of power-hungry people. Part of it was simply hunger.

*It wasn't an accident.*

Ridley had no idea how much time had passed since her last meal, and she didn't *feel* like eating, but she knew her body needed something. Somewhere far above her, the constant flicker of magic and lightning illuminated the dark night as she let the backpack slide off her shoulders. With trembling fingers, she opened it and removed a can of soup.

*It wasn't an accident.*

Mom had died. Billions of people had died. And it was all because someone had planned it. Archer's deceit was still a shard of ice wedged into her heart, but *this*—the revelation that the Cataclysm had been a carefully orchestrated event—was monumental in comparison. The weight of it was crushing her.

She clutched the unopened can with one hand while pressing the other over the stone pendant lying against her chest. She squeezed her eyes shut and let hot tears drip down her cheeks. How could individuals take it upon themselves to decide the fate of the world? It was so heinous, so utterly unjust. Everything inside Ridley screamed to fight back. To make them pay. She wanted desperately, fiercely, to destroy all their wicked arxium and bring about the future Nathan envisioned. The future she and Archer—the ice shard pierced a little deeper—had discussed so often over the past couple of weeks.

But hopelessness draped its heavy self over her fighting spirit. The Shadow Society controlled far more than she'd ever imagined. If they wanted the world to stay as it was now, what could she and a bunch of elementals do?

Ridley wiped her wet cheeks with the back of one hand. The breeze that had curled around her when she first landed here had vanished, leaving a strange stillness in its wake. She swallowed, sniffed, and peeled back the lid of the soup can. She thought of fire, and the resulting flames dancing across her palm quickly heated the can's contents. She forced herself to eat. Then she summoned just enough energy to blow a few warm gusts of air around herself, partially drying her damp clothes and hair.

*It wasn't an accident.*

She had to get back to Dad and the others. She had to tell them the truth about what had really wiped out most of the earth. She had to warn them that the Shadow Society might—if Archer had been lying about everything and was still loyal to them—know where their new home was.

But she was so tired. So, so tired. When last had she slept? It didn't feel that long ago, but it must have been ... days? When she'd been racing toward Lumina City to find Archer, it had seemed like she could keep going forever while in elemental form. Well, if not forever, then at least far longer than anyone could last in human form. But now, she doubted she had the energy to even *become* one of the elements, let alone remain that way for any decent length of time.

She lay down, right there on the road, with her backpack as a pillow and a clump of weeds cushioning her shoulder. *Just for a little while*, she thought. *A storm will start up again soon. It won't be long before it's raining again. Then I'll wake up. Then I'll ...*

\* \* \*

It didn't start raining again. Ridley woke up to the sort of dim, gray light and cloud-obscured sky that meant it was impossible to tell what time of day it was. She had no idea how long she'd been asleep. A night, a day, a night *and* a day? It took a moment, and then the pain of Archer's betrayal pierced her chest again, followed closely by the unbearable weight of the

Cataclysm truth. Then the physical ache of a body forced to sleep on a solid surface quickly made itself known.

*It wasn't an accident.*

She had to get back and tell everyone that they probably needed to find a new home. Archer didn't know exactly where the mountainside building was, but Nathan had shared enough information that Archer could probably find it. Her pulse thrummed with renewed urgency, but she took the time to quickly eat a can of something pretending to be a fruit salad. She needed the energy if she was hoping to push her elemental form to its limits and return to the mountains as quickly as she had made it to Lumina City. She stood, wincing at the ache in her stiff joints. But the discomfort would be gone once she was …

Her thoughts slipped away like smoke on a breeze as something whispered at the edge of her mind. Something … Dad? She was about to change form and question the magic more closely when a gust of wind blew her hair away from her face. It vanished, and two human forms appeared out of thin air a few paces away.

Nathan. And Dad.

Ridley was hit by the overwhelming urge to run to her father, fall into his arms, and sob her heart out. But the expression on his face kept her feet rooted to the spot. "For the love of all that's magical," Dad said, striding toward Ridley. "You have *got* to stop racing off on your own and putting yourself in danger." Up close, Ridley could see the relief mixed in with his frustration. He swept her into a hug.

"How did you find me?" she asked, her voice small.

"We headed for Lumina City and listened to the elements as we went. Well, Nathan listened," Dad corrected as he released Ridley. "I suppose I was just a passenger."

"A passenger I could have gone much faster without," Nathan growled.

Ridley decided to ignore him. "You didn't have to come after me, Dad. I was on my way back—"

"You should have taken someone with you. I know I can't stop you from doing this sort of thing, but did you have to do it *alone*?"

"Oh, so I should have waited around until someone else decided they had time to come with me?" Ridley snapped, her tone harsher than she'd intended it to be. The tide of hurt she was trying to keep at bay battered against her defenses, leaking into her voice and curling her hands into fists. "People were a little preoccupied with other things, Dad. We had all just fled for our lives. Everyone else was busy with their own family and friends and—and people they care about." She broke off as the ache in her chest intensified. Archer was someone *she* cared about. She hated how true that still was, despite all the lies he'd told her.

"Ugh, none of this is important right now," she continued, blinking her tears away. "There are things I need to tell you. Archer is ..." She took a deep breath. "He's part of the Shadow Society. Or he was, but isn't anymore. I don't know. He says he's changed and that he's on our side now, that he's lying to them and not to us, but who knows. So we probably need to move our entire community all over again, because he knows roughly where it is and it's possible he's told his father. Who is the director of the entire Shadow Society, by the way. And the Cataclysm ..." She sucked in another deep breath. "The Cataclysm wasn't an accident. The Shadow Society planned for it to happen. They messed with the conjurations the energy magicists were doing, while also doing their own conjurations that provoked the elements into reacting violently on a massive scale. It was all intentional."

Dad and Nathan simply stared at her.

"Yeah," Ridley said quietly, finally unclenching her hands at her sides. "It's kind of a lot to take in."

"The ... it ... what?" Dad stammered.

"That ... actually ..." Nathan frowned as he stared past Ridley, one hand rising to slowly scratch his chin. "Makes a lot of sense," he finished. "All the things the public doesn't know ... the wild magic that isn't actually deadly, and the arxium they spray into the atmosphere to keep the violent storms going ... I always assumed it was the government—or the Shadow Society, or both—taking advantage of the Cataclysm after it happened. But they actually *caused* it in the first place."

"This is unbelievable," Dad murmured. His eyes glistened with unshed tears, and Ridley knew he was thinking of Mom. "What a waste," he whispered. "What an utter waste of everything beautiful in the world."

"I know," Ridley said quietly.

"And ... Alastair Davenport? *He's* the director?" Dad shook his head. "I can't believe it. We were ... *friends*. Well, sort of.

Not close friends, but more than acquaintances. You were Lilah's friend. You were at their home all the time, and I just—it never crossed my mind that you might not be safe there. But he would have killed you if he'd known what you are."

"I know," Ridley repeated, even quieter now.

"We need to leave," Nathan interrupted. "Warn everyone we might not be safe in the mountains. Then we can discuss all of this in detail and figure out if it changes any of our plans. It would be a lot quicker," he added with a glare in Dad's direction, "if we could fragment. Instead we have to take a non-elemental with us."

"So you go ahead then," Ridley told him, unable to keep the irritation from her voice. Nathan being pissed off at Dad was pissing her off. "You can fragment and travel faster. I'll bring my dad."

Nathan shook his head. "I'm not letting you out of my sight again. Well, my magical sight, if not my actual sight. I can't trust you not to do something stupid and irresponsible again."

"Hey, can you stop with the whole over-protective father act? If I decide to risk my own life, it has nothing to do with you."

"It has everything to do with every elemental. We can't afford to lose you."

"Nathan," Dad warned.

"I'm just one elemental!" Ridley exclaimed. "If I leave and never come back, it'll make zero difference to your big plan."

"It will make *all* the difference," Nathan said. "You're not like the rest of us."

"*Nathan*," Dad growled, a threat in his voice.

"No, I'm sorry, Maverick. It's time to tell her. If you won't, I will."

A sick feeling coalesced in Ridley's stomach. "Tell me what?"

Nathan looked at Dad, gestured as if to say *Go ahead*, and waited. Dad gripped Ridley's arm. "We're leaving."

Ridley stood her ground. She almost repeated herself, but then she thought of Saoirse. If this secret was about the two of them, did she really want to know it? But ... it couldn't be. If something had happened years ago between Dad and Saoirse—and even if there was a possibility it was happening again now—how could that affect Nathan's plans for returning the world to the way it used to be?

"Long ago," Nathan said, "there were certain elemental families far more powerful than the rest."

"Nathan—"

"According to the stories, they were the rulers of their time. Their children were born just as powerful. Even more so if their magic was inherited from both sides and not just one parent."

"This is not for you to—"

"These elementals were the first to be killed when those without magic decided to turn on our kind. They had the power to fight back, but they were taken by surprise with various forms of arxium. We thought they were all gone, but it turns out—"

"Nathan!" Dad shouted, his expression furious now. He turned to Ridley, and in a gentler tone, he said, "You're one of them. You're one of these powerful elementals Nathan is talking about."

Ridley stared at Dad. Then at Nathan. Then at Dad. "What?"

"You have no idea how much power you truly possess," Nathan told her. "You've never pushed yourself far enough because you didn't know you could. Ridley ..." He watched her intently. "You could probably single-handedly bring down the arxium panels over Lumina City. And the wall. You could burn through all of it."

"Um ... I don't think so."

"I know so," Nathan argued.

"But ... then ..." Ridley shook her head. "Does this magic skip generations? Because Dad doesn't have magic, and neither did my mom. And my grandfather doesn't have magic either."

Dad took a breath, but no words left his tongue as he exhaled. Quietly, Nathan said, "No. It doesn't skip generations."

"But then ..." Ridley raised both eyebrows, wondering why the flaw in Nathan's logic wasn't as clear to him as it was to her. "Obviously I'm not one of them."

"You are," Nathan said. "Of that there is no doubt. The stone—your family heirloom—recognized you. Saoirse told me how it lit up at your touch."

Ridley's gaze returned slowly to her father. The truth shoved up against a door in her mind. A door she was trying desperately to hold closed because once it opened, there would be no bottling up what was on the other side. But the truth was unrelenting, and it seeped through the cracks around the door, sinking slowly into Ridley's being until finally she gave in and stopped trying to hold it back.

The truth flooded her mind.

A faint ringing filled her ears.

Her body felt shivery and hot and numb all at the same time.

"You're not my father," she whispered.

"Ridley—"

"And Mom. She's not ... she wasn't ..."

"I can explain all of this."

"Have you ever told me the truth about *anything*?"

"I love you," Dad said fiercely, his blue eyes piercing into hers. "That is the first and last truth. The only truth that matters."

Tears prickled at the corners of Ridley's eyes. She swallowed. "And what is the rest of the truth?"

Dad inhaled deeply, his expression tortured. "Your parents, Sarah and Karl Ohlson, were our closest friends. They were elementals. Very powerful. *Both* of them. With so few of their kind left, it was highly unlikely two of them would ever come across each other, let alone end up together. But they did.

"When the Shadow Society discovered us, they were killed. We—Claudia and I—managed to get to their house and we ... found them." His voice shuddered on those last two words, hinting at the horror of whatever state he'd discovered his friends in. "We heard you crying and so ... we didn't think, we just took you and ran.

"We reached Lumina City and Grandpa. We tried to find out if you had any surviving family, but we already knew your biological grandparents were no longer alive. The Shadow Society made sure of that years ago. And we could find no trace of your aunt—your mother's sister. So ... we decided to raise you as our own. We already loved you as much as if you were, so it wasn't a difficult decision. We had all the necessary documents forged. We remained in Lumina City, building a life for ourselves there and never reaching out to any other elementals. It was ... safer that way."

He trailed off, watching Ridley closely. Somehow, she was still standing, which was surprising because it felt as if the ground had been tugged from beneath her feet like a table-cloth trick. Except there was no table underneath. There was nothing, and she should have been falling.

Fat raindrops began to spatter the crumbling road around her. She pressed her palms against her cheeks, vaguely aware that Nathan was standing some distance away now, giving her and Dad a small amount of privacy. She didn't remember him moving.

"So this," she whispered, her hands still pressed to her face, "is why you've been having whispered conversations with Saorise. She knows all this. Of course she knows. You all used to live together. The last time she saw you, when I was a baby, I wasn't *yours*. I belonged to someone else."

Dad nodded. "Yes."

"And that's why she was saying that I ... I haven't reached my full potential. Because she knows my parents were super powerful. And when she gave me the stone pendant and told me it was my mother's, I was picturing Mom—Claudia—but the whole time, she knew it was actually—" Ridley's voice cracked as it hit her yet again that the mother she'd lost was never actually her mother, and that she *still* had nothing special of hers. It was a stupid, small thing to focus on, but she couldn't help it. The stone that hung heavy against her chest belonged to a woman she didn't even know.

"Ridley, I'm so sorry. I asked Saoirse not to say—"

"Were you *ever* planning to tell me?"

Dad swallowed. Paused for too long. "I ..."

Ridley lowered her hands to her sides. "So that's a no."

"It's ... it's probably a no," Dad admitted, his eyes pleading with her to understand. "Your mother and I ... we always spoke about telling you one day. But without her, I just ... I didn't know how. And you and I have always had a good relationship. I know you don't tell me everything, and clearly I haven't always told you everything either, but we've still been close. For a teenage girl and her father, we ... well, it always seemed to me we had a pretty good relationship. I didn't want to ruin that."

"But you had the chance to tell me just a few weeks ago! When I got that letter and you and Mrs. Lin told me all about the elementals. And Grandpa made it seem like there was something else you needed to tell me and—oh." Another truth rammed into her. "He knows. Obviously he knows. That's what you guys were disagreeing about. He wanted you to tell me, and you wouldn't."

"Ridley—"

"This is the real reason you didn't want us to ever join any group of elementals. You were afraid the truth would come out, and you didn't want that."

Dad clenched his jaw before saying, "Yes. That's the truth."

Ridley looked at him as if seeing him for the first time.

Dad. Who was not her dad.

She suddenly saw what everyone else could see: that they looked nothing alike. Aside from their shared eye color—a tiny coincidence—there was no family resemblance. "You're a coward, Maverick Kayne," she whispered. The name felt wrong, like her tongue couldn't properly wrap itself around the shape of it when the shape had always been *Dad*. "Why couldn't you just *tell* me any of this?"

"Because I love you as desperately and fiercely as if you were my own, and I didn't want you to think of me as anything but your father."

"But you never even gave me the chance!" Her breaths came erratically. Her heart thudded miserably. Around them, heavy raindrops smacked the road with increasing intensity. Dark clouds swirled above. It had been so still—unnaturally still—after she arrived here and while she slept. But now the storm clouds were churning and the air was whipping itself into gusts and lightning flickered overhead. Was it because of *her*? Was she unintentionally influencing the elements? Or was the wild wasteland magic simply doing what it did best: being wild.

It didn't matter. None of it changed the horrible truths that swept repeatedly over Ridley like waves crashing relentlessly on a weatherworn shore.

Archer had lied.

The Cataclysm was not an accident.

Dad was not her dad.

"I need to go," she said faintly. "I just ... need to go."

"Wait, Ridley, please don't leave."

She shook her head, stepping backward, repeating simply, "I need to go."

# CHAPTER 11

THE PAIN INSIDE RIDLEY was too big, too blinding. She fragmented, every particle of her elemental being becoming every particle of the violent tempest that now raged across the wastelands. Her tears were the monsoon rains that gushed from above. Her breaking heart was the crack of lightning as it split the sky. She raged and sobbed and groaned, and the storm poured everything out over the broken landscape.

If Archer hadn't broken her heart, she would have run to him now. She would have told him that Dad wasn't her dad and Mom wasn't her mom and her real parents were people she would never remember. She had no family left and no idea who she really was. She would have cried until she was empty, and he would have held her the entire time.

But there was no one to go to. No one who—

*Meera*, she thought suddenly. *I still have Meera. My best friend.*

Ridley sensed a change in the storm's direction. Or at least, a direction where previously there had been none. The storm had spread out further and further, and Ridley had been everywhere at once, but now she felt almost ... pulled together and hurled toward something. Toward Lumina City, hopefully, if the magic around her was correctly reading her intent. She was vaguely aware of the speed at which the landscape raced by beneath her, and it seemed the landforms and ruined towns slid by faster than before. Though perhaps it was only her imagination now that she knew she was supposed to be some kind of super-powered elemental.

Just like her parents.

People she would never know.

Thunder echoed across the wastelands as pain spread through every particle of her being. It was so huge, this hurt. How had it not broken her completely?

She sensed Lumina City on the horizon. Wrapped in a storm, she hurtled toward it. Details she hadn't bothered to think of before rose to mind. What time of day was it? What day of the week? Would Meera be at school?

The city wall slid by beneath her, and soon she was traveling above her old district and toward Meera's building. She entered Meera's bedroom via the narrow gap where the upper edge of the window didn't properly meet the window frame. The gap Meera complained about whenever it was windy. Ridley's feet touched the worn pink rug as her human form materialized. She wrapped her arms tightly around herself. The room was so familiar it hurt. The wrinkle-free bedspread, the neatly organized desk, Meera's precious print books stacked neatly on a small bookshelf. Ridley had spent countless hours in here with Meera, studying, talking, laughing. Would there one day be a world in which that could happen again? Not that she could imagine herself laughing. Everything hurt too much for that.

"Yeah, okay, just give me a minute and I'll help you with that."

Ridley looked up, her breath catching at the sound of Meera's voice. And then, without another moment's warning, Meera was there, in the open doorway, her eyes growing almost as large as her enormous glasses. "Ridley!" she gasped.

"Um, hi," Ridley answered uncertainly. Now that she was here, she didn't know where to start. She was saved from having to come up with something immediately when Meera launched across the room and enveloped Ridley in a hug.

"Ohmygoshohmygoshohmygosh," she said into Ridley's hair. "You're okay. You're not dead. Oh thank goodness. What a relief."

Ridley brought her arms up around Meera's back and squeezed tight. Tighter and longer than she'd ever clung to her friend before. "I missed you," she whispered, mainly because her voice couldn't go any louder without breaking.

"I missed you too." Then Meera pulled back and slapped Ridley's arm. "Where have you *been*? Do you have any idea how worried I've been? You and your dad both just *vanished*. What happened?"

Ridley stepped past her and quietly shut the door. It was probably a weekend, given that Meera wasn't in her school uniform, and Ridley wasn't sure how many of her family members might also be home. She didn't need them all running in here while she struggled to get through the secrets she needed to share. "I ... there's ..." She inhaled a shuddering breath, her fingers absently playing with the zip of her jacket. The jacket that Dad—*not my dad*—had conjured for her. "There's a lot I need to tell you, Meera. I'm ... my dad ..." Emotion stuck in her throat, making it hard to speak.

"Oh no, what happened?" Meera raised both hands to her mouth. "Is he okay?"

"Yes. Yes, he's okay. But ..." Ridley couldn't bring herself to say it. The words wouldn't leave her lips. "Um, I have to tell you something about me," she said instead.

"O-okay."

"I ... uh ... I'm not like you."

A frown line formed above the bridge of Meera's glasses. "Okaaaaay."

Ridley let out a rush of breath and said, "There's magic inside me. Like, *inside my body*. I was born that way. I don't have amulets beneath my skin—neither an AI1 nor AI2—and I don't have to pull magic from the environment the way other people do. Or *used* to do, before it was banned. I can just use the magic from inside me to do conjurations."

Unmoving, Meera stared at Ridley. Then she grabbed her commscreen from the desk and shoved it beneath her pillow. "Ridley, you can't say things like that! You don't know who might be listening."

Ridley sighed, wondering if the meaning of her words had actually reached Meera's brain, or if she'd got stuck on the fact that Ridley was talking about something illegal. "Don't worry.

I'm the one saying these things, not you, and I'm already a wanted criminal."

"You—you are?"

"Yes. Because of this." A demonstration was probably simpler than trying to explain things to Meera. Ridley pushed her sleeves up and extended her arms as glowing threads of blue pulsed beneath her skin. Wisps of magic drifted into the air. Ridley did a quick one-handed conjuration and flicked the magic toward her own head. Her hair swiftly pulled itself into a ponytail. It was a conjuration her mom—*not my mom*—had done often for her when she was little.

Meera blinked. Blinked again. Then she shook her head as if waking from a daze. "Ridley!" she hissed, her eyes darting furtively around as if she might find some member of law enforcement lurking in the shadows of her own home. "What the—are you *crazy*? You can't do that here!"

"I'm sorry, but you didn't seem to be getting what I was telling you. This isn't a law I *chose* to break. This is the way I am. And I managed to keep this a secret—even from you—until the night I went to that party with Archer. Something went wrong there, and I had to use magic to get away quickly, but there were cops there and they saw me, and then Dad and I had to run."

"You ..." Meera was still staring at Ridley's hands. "You just used magic," she whispered. "In my house."

Again, it seemed like Meera might be missing the point. "Meera, I'm trying to tell you all the things I've always had to keep from you. All the secrets. The reason that man was killed outside my home, and me being able to sneak around the city to steal things so I can help the people who really need it, and Lawrence Madson and his father trying to kill me, and Shen leaving without saying goodbye, and ... it all comes down to this. There are people in the world called elementals, and I'm one of them."

Meera was gaping at her, which was probably to be expected after the number of secrets that had tumbled from Ridley's mouth in a single breath. "There are people who want to kill me because of what I can do, Meera. Because of the magic inside me. Because I can do things like this." She became water in an instant, splashing to the floor and then leaping into the air as a sparking rush of flames before whooshing up to the ceiling as air, causing the curtains to billow. It all took place within a matter of seconds before she returned to her human form.

Her feet had barely touched the floor when Meera stumbled backward and smacked into the wardrobe. Her palms flattened against its doors. "Stop," she whispered. Then louder: "Stop. Stop, stop, stop." She covered her ears with her hands and squeezed her eyes shut. "I don't want to know any more. Please don't tell me anything else, don't show me anything else."

"What? But ..." Ridley's heart floundered painfully. "I thought you'd want to know the truth."

"Nope. No. Not this truth." Meera lowered her hands and shook her head repeatedly. Her eyes were open again, pointed at the floor somewhere near Ridley's feet. "There were times when it seemed like you were keeping things from me, and I always hoped you'd eventually be honest, but I didn't realize you were keeping *these* kinds of secrets. Illegal secrets. Like, death sentence-worthy secrets."

"Meera, just—"

"I don't want to know!" Meera repeated, her eyes wide and desperate. "Please leave me out of this. I don't want to end up in prison. I don't want to ..." She shook her head again as she edged past Ridley, keeping as much distance between the two of them as possible in this tiny room. "Please, Ridley, I love you and I'm so happy you're okay, but ... you have to go. I can't be involved in this. My family can't be involved. Please don't get us into trouble. Please just ... go." She pulled the door open and rushed into the hallway, then stopped and looked back. "I'm sorry." Her eyes met Ridley's, her gaze pleading with Ridley to understand. "I'm so sorry. You're my best friend and I love you, but ... I'm not brave like you. I can't do this." She hurried away, her shoes swiping swiftly down the hall.

Stunned, lost for words or thoughts or any feeling other than the ache radiating from the center of her being, Ridley stared at the empty doorway. "What's going on?" Meera's sister Anika asked from the living room. "I thought you were coming to help me with—"

"We're going for a walk," Meera interrupted.

"What, now? But—"

"Now. Grab your coat. We'll finish lunch and your history homework when we get back." There was the scuffle of shoes and the mumble of voices and then the front door banged shut.

Ridley was alone.

# CHAPTER 12

RIDLEY WAS FOLDED INTO the corner of a couch, her arms wrapped around her legs, her body enveloped by familiar, frayed cushions. Dull orange light from a street lamp seeped through the gauzy curtains, and the only sound filling her ears was the tapping of raindrops against the window and the rustle of the flimsy plastic taped across the hole in the window's center. She was in the tiny living room of the apartment above Kayne's Antiques.

She was home.

She had imagined returning here many times over the past few weeks, but in her mind, it hadn't been like this. It hadn't been so dark, so cold, so drenched in pain. Part of her wondered if she was even here. She didn't remember planning to come. She had let the wind take her, and perhaps it had sensed she needed somewhere to feel safe. To pause. To breathe. To process.

Archer.

The Cataclysm.

Dad.

And now Meera.

Ridley needed her best friend, but her best friend had quite literally run away from her. She supposed it was what she deserved, after keeping so many secrets from Meera. They *were* life-threatening secrets, as Meera had pointed out, and Ridley shouldn't have put the Singhs in danger by trying to share those secrets. She should have kept her distance.

*I am alone.*

She stared across the room at a framed wedding photo of her parents on the wall. Golden and glowing and looking absolutely nothing like Ridley. *Maverick and Claudia Kayne*, she reminded herself. *Not my parents.* Sarah and Karl Ohlson were her parents. She was not Ridley Kayne, she was Ridley Ohlson. The name felt foreign in her thoughts. "Ridley Ohlson," she whispered, then shivered. Saying it out loud was even worse.

She covered her face with her hands and released a long breath. Dad loved her—she knew that without a doubt—yet she felt betrayed in a way she couldn't make sense of. Some logical corner of her mind knew that none of this should make a difference to who she truly was. Dad had raised her. He had been her father—was *still* her father—even though they shared no genetic material. But she was left with the horrible feeling of being ... set loose. Of not belonging anywhere. Somehow she was both the same person and not the same person at all. The same person ... reframed.

She lowered her hands and whispered, "I am alone."

*You are not alone.*

It wasn't a voice. It wasn't words. It was a feeling, the distinct sense of being comforted. Magic, Ridley realized. This was the way it always communicated with her, though she was usually in elemental form when she 'heard' it. Although ... was that true? She'd been human when she first sensed magic trying to warn her that the Shadow Society was coming to attack the reserve. First in the afternoon when she'd been with Archer, and then later that evening as she'd returned to her cabin, before she'd been distracted by Nathan and Saoirse's conversation. And then magic had warned her in her dream. She hadn't been in elemental form then.

*You are not alone*, came the feeling once again, accompanied by the sense of being held. Of course, technically, she was being held by the couch. Embraced by the cushions. But it was more than that.

*Or perhaps I'm losing my mind*, Ridley thought. She shifted sideways and lay down, burrowing into that quiet, unwavering promise that she was not alone. Her fingers searched near her feet until they found the edge of a blanket. She pulled it up over her head. She knew it wasn't safe to stay here long. Somehow, the apartment hadn't been broken into in the weeks it had stood empty—which Ridley had put down to the ever-present stigma of Dad being a former magicist—but that didn't mean it would continue to be safe. A thief might decide to take a chance, hoping there were no illegal conjurations protecting the place. A drone might fly overhead and detect Ridley's presence along with her lack of AI1 and AI2.

But she couldn't bring herself to move right now. She

wanted to ignore the rest of the world. Ignore Nathan's plans for the future. Ignore the possibility that she might be as powerful as he suggested. Ignore the difficult conversation she would have to have with Dad when she saw him again. She wanted to simply ... lie here and fall asleep and not feel.

*Run.*

Ridley's eyes popped open, seeing nothing but darkness beneath the blanket. The quiet sense of comfort that had promised to lull her to sleep was gone in an instant. Panic took its place. *Run!* it told her. *Go! Now! Hide!*

She threw the blanket off and bolted upright—just as an odd tearing sound reached her ears and a shadow of movement behind the curtain caught her eye. She launched to her feet, her magic already swirling around her. *Air*, she thought, but in the blink between human form and invisibility, yellow light flickered behind her, and then everything—

# CHAPTER 13

RIDLEY WOKE SLOWLY, becoming gradually aware of the tight discomfort at her wrists and ankles. She blinked. Blinked again. Her stomach turned, but a deep breath kept her from vomiting. She was lying on a bed, her head resting on dark gray sheets and her hands bound in front of her with a cable tie. She tried to pull one leg up, but pain bit into her ankles. Her legs were also bound together.

*Stupid*, she thought. *Stupid, stupid, stupid.* She should never have gone back home. Especially after revealing herself to Lilah at the Davenports' apartment yesterday—or whenever it had been. Days and nights had begun to blend together ever since the attack on the reserve.

Ridley pushed herself up and swung her bound legs over the edge of the bed as she looked around. Of all the rooms she'd woken in after being unexpectedly knocked out, this was by far the nicest. A thick cream carpet concealed the floor, and the walls were covered in interlocking geometric panels of dark gray. In the far corner stood a modern bucket-style armchair beside a pair of small, round nesting tables with gleaming brass legs and marble tops. There were no windows. No other furnishings. There was, however, a door near the armchair.

*Locked*, Ridley thought. *It must surely be locked.* Still, she had to at least investigate. She stood. Her head spun lazily and the desire to throw up increased several notches. She took another few moments to breathe, managing to keep her body upright and the limited contents of her stomach where they belonged. When she was certain she wasn't about to fall over, she began to hop.

She made it about halfway across the room before something shocked her cheek, her hand, her knee. She recoiled, stepping back instinctively. Which was impossible with two feet tied together, so instead she toppled over and landed hard on the carpeted floor. Her stomach heaved, and she was convinced she really would vomit this time, but after a moment of retching, she recovered.

With a shaky breath and a groan, she squinted up at the diamond-shaped mesh-like layer that had appeared, dividing the room in half. An orange glow rippled across it, originating from the spot she'd walked into. The glow faded. The silvery diamond shapes vanished. Ridley narrowed her eyes. Whatever it was, she had no doubt it was still there.

She scooted back to the bed, pushed herself up, and sat. Her pulse drummed a dull, throbbing ache across her head, and something a little like panic rose up to mingle with the nausea. Every crushing revelation from the past day or two— Archer, the Cataclysm, Dad, Meera—receded in her mind as the primal need to survive took precedence over everything else.

*Don't. Panic*, she reminded herself. *Breathe in. Breathe out. This is not the—*

A beep sounded from the direction of the door. It swung open, and in strode Alastair Davenport. "Ridley," he said, his tone businesslike. He glanced up from his commpad as the door swung shut behind him. "You'll be moved soon, but since you're awake, I thought we could have a brief chat." He swiped at the screen of the commpad, then placed it on the larger of the two side tables as he sat in the armchair. He leaned back and crossed one leg over the other, comfortable and composed in his perfectly tailored suit. The man who orchestrated the end of the world. The man who would kill her.

Ridley sat utterly still, frozen by the two opposing forces pulling her in opposite directions: fear and fury. The instinct to bolt, and the desire to inflict as much pain on this man as he'd inflicted on the rest of the world. On *her.*

"So," he said. "Ridley Kayne. Turns out you're not human. Turns out you're also not a Kayne."

Like a puzzle piece fitted neatly into place, it hit Ridley with immediate and satisfying clarity that she *was.* Face to face with her death—because that was surely what was soon to happen—the only thing she wanted to do was throw her arms around Dad and tell him she loved him. Who the hell cared whether they were related by blood or not?

She blinked and exhaled. Fear and fury eased their grip on her. With an odd sort of relief, she said, "I am. In all the ways that matter."

"Actually," Alastair Davenport replied, "in the *only* way that matters, you are not. You're descended from an extraordinarily powerful elemental. You're one of the *heirs* we hear whispers about. One of the only elementals who may be a true threat to us. And you were right here under my nose, all those years you were Lilah's friend. I could so easily have snuffed you out of existence and made it look like a tragic accident."

A shiver crawled across Ridley's skin. He'd known ever since the party that she was an elemental, but how did he know she was one of these *heirs* Nathan had told her about? "Who told you?"

He gave her a look that clearly communicated how little he thought of her intelligence. "No one had to *tell* me. The stone pendant you were wearing made it obvious."

*Were* wearing. Ridley had forgotten about the stone, but she realized now that the comforting weight of it sitting against her chest was gone.

Alastair lifted his commpad and tapped the screen. "I have a few simple questions for you. First, which of your parents was the powerful one?"

"Like I'm really going to tell you." If he didn't know that her power came from *both* her parents, she wasn't about to share that information.

"Hmm." Alastair made a note on his commpad. "And do you have any biological siblings?"

Ridley's heart raced a little faster. She hadn't even considered the possibility. But Dad would surely have mentioned it if Sarah and Karl Ohlson had another children. "No," she answered. Whether it was true or not, Alastair Davenport didn't need to know.

"I see," he murmured, making another note. "And how many other heirs do you know of?"

"None." Her tone was firm, her gaze unblinking.

Alastair returned the commpad to the side table with a sigh. "Ridley. You are mildly intelligent, are you not? Lilah told me you're a scholarship student at Wallace Academy. I thought you might have realized that being unhelpful will only make things more unpleasant for you in the long run."

"The long run?" Ridley frowned. "Not that I *want* to die, but I kinda thought you'd get rid of me as quickly as possible. That seems to be what you guys do with elementals."

"Oh, in general, yes. But you're different. The fact that you're an heir makes you more valuable to me alive. There are certain ... *developments* that have taken place in recent years that mean it would be a tragic waste if I killed you now."

"Developments?"

"I would elaborate, but the details will most likely distress you."

"And you're so concerned about my mental state."

"Well, it isn't my *top* priority, but I've been informed that the subjects' mental and emotional wellbeing do play a certain role. Too many stress hormones in the blood produce subpar results."

Ridley's insides tightened at the word 'subject,' sending what was most likely a very *subpar* amount of stress hormone shooting through her body. She pictured the rooms she'd seen as she fled the Shadow Society's base. The rooms with operating equipment and beds with restraints. The laboratory. "So," she said, trying to keep the shiver from her voice. "Too many details will *distress* me, but one or two vague details that suggest you're going to *experiment* on me are sure to put my mind at ease."

Alastair lifted his commpad and stood. "Well, this discussion has been less than fruitful. I think we should leave it at that." He turned toward the door. "Someone will be here soon to—"

"I know the truth about the Cataclysm," Ridley interrupted. "I know what you did."

Alastair paused. He looked back at her. His cold gaze was unreadable. "Somebody told you," he said quietly, thoughtfully, as if he were pondering the words as he spoke them.

"You turned the GSMC into an apocalyptic event."

"I did," he replied calmly. "It was the perfect opportunity. We couldn't waste it. Thousands of magicists gathering together around the world. Energy conjurations plus amplification conjurations. It wasn't difficult to get Shadow Society members positioned in the right places at the right times. Having dozens of politicians in my pocket was a great help. Jude Madson wasn't mayor yet, but he had enough influence to pull some strings for us. And our good friend the Secretary-General *is* actually a good friend of mine."

"The *SG* is part of the Shadow Society?" Ridley asked, despair dragging her heart down to the tips of her toes. She knew the Shadow Society's influence went high up, but if the man who'd been elected to govern the entire world was part of it, there really was no hope for a future in which elementals could be free.

"No," Alastair answered. "He knows nothing of the Shadow Society. But he's easily manipulated, like many others. In fact, if I was to explain everything to him, he'd probably agree with me that it all worked out beautifully. We placed people into key positions on the day of the GSMC, and then all we had to do was cancel out the energy conjurations, allow the amplification ones to continue, and do our own provocation ones. We pressured magic into reacting, the amplification conjurations multiplied the effect, and the whole world went boom. Devastating, but perfect. Overpopulation? Solved. Magic? Confined to the wastelands. And that's where it will stay for the rest of time."

"Boom," Ridley repeated quietly, feeling sick to her core. "I thought you might feel *some* remorse over causing such catastrophic destruction, but I guess not."

He gave her a puzzled look. "Of course not. Remorse would imply I regret what we did. Don't you understand, Ridley? We *saved* the planet."

"You killed billions of people!" Ridley shouted.

Alastair remained irritatingly unruffled. "To save everyone else. Ridley, do you think I *liked* doing what I did? Do you think I *wanted* to kill all those people? Destroy so much of the world? Of course I didn't. No one *wants* to live with that much death on their conscience. But someone had to step up and make the hard decision. No one else was doing it, so it had to be me. I will endure that burden for the rest of my days because nobody else could bear it."

"Wait. Are you saying … do you actually expect me to feel *sorry* for you?"

"No." He held his commpad near the door and it beeped before opening. "You're an elemental. I don't expect you to feel anything the same way humans do."

"Is that how you justify all the heinous acts you commit against my kind? Because you think we don't *feel* anything?"

"Well, the person who lived with you in that little nature reserve campsite clearly felt nothing when betraying the rest of you."

Ridley froze, her next breath caught somewhere between her mouth and her lungs. "Who?" she whispered.

Alastair looked over his shoulder. "Apparently someone got tired of living in hiding. Living with the constant fear of being found. Someone wanted to trade up, to live the good life, to have wealth and security. Someone offered us the location of multiple elemental communities in exchange."

"Who?" Ridley repeated, her stomach churning.

"Honestly, I can't remember the name. Jude Madson was the one who dealt with and then got rid of this person after we acquired the information we needed." He paused again, watching Ridley's reaction, then added, "We don't make deals with people like you." He glanced at his commpad, then tapped the screen. "Time for my next meeting." And with that, he walked out and pulled the door shut.

# CHAPTER 14

RIDLEY WANTED TO PACE. All the nervous energy building inside her needed to go *somewhere*, but her feet were still bound, and hopping seemed a little too ridiculous. The heavy fog of grief she'd been wading through over the past few days had mostly cleared, leaving a dull, continuous ache and several plain truths in its wake: She had to get back to Dad. She had to get back to the elementals. They had to rid the world of the Shadow Society and its influence.

Hatred burned through her veins. Hatred for Alastair Davenport. For everyone else who had brought the world to its knees and was firmly keeping it there. They had to be stopped, and Ridley was more than willing to do her part to make sure that happened.

*Beep.*

Ridley looked up, her heart jolting at the unexpected sound. The diamond mesh layer that divided the room in half flashed into existence and then disappeared. Was it actually gone this time?

*Beep.*

The door opened and a man walked in. He stopped in the doorway. "Oh, you're awake. That's unfortunate." At first glance, he was a copy of Alastair Davenport. Perfect hair, perfect suit, an unpleasant smile revealing perfect teeth. But he was younger and the suit was ill-fitting, and there was something lacking in his posture. He was a cheap imitation. A knockoff.

"Your precious director didn't tell you?" Ridley asked.

Mr. Knockoff walked to the armchair and reached toward the wall behind it. "Mr. Davenport is a busy man."

"I guess I'm special then, if he took the time to come and have a chat with me."

"Very special indeed," he said drily as he pressed his fingers to the wall. A square of paneling swung open, revealing a small compartment in the wall. "It's the only thing keeping you alive right now."

"Lucky me."

Mr. Knockoff opened a small container, removed something, and snapped the container shut. When he turned to face Ridley, she saw he held a syringe.

"Whoa, hey, what's that?" She scooted backward across the bed.

Mr. Knockoff raised an eyebrow as he crossed the room. "Needle phobia?"

"No, asshat, I don't want you sticking foreign substances into me."

"Seriously? You realize you were injected with foreign substances before arriving here, right?"

A shiver coursed through Ridley's body. "What substances?"

"Nothing too exciting. Yet. Just arxium and a sedative. Oh, and that was after we stuck a needle in you to get a blood sample."

"My *blood*?"

"Doc doesn't like it to be contaminated with arxium. We had to knock you out the old-fashioned way, get the blood sample immediately—just in case you escape before we get you to the lab—and then inject the arxium and sedative. Clearly I didn't give you enough." He leaned over her. She shoved her elbow upward, but he grabbed her arm and pressed his weight down on her as he aimed the needle at her neck. "So I'll make sure to give you enough this time, and then we'll get you transferred out of—"

Ridley drew her knees up and kicked as hard as she could. Mr. Knockoff fell backward off the bed, grunting out a string of curses as he hit the floor. Ridley scrambled up in time to see the syringe rolling away from him. She wriggled to the edge of the bed. Chances were slim she could get to the syringe before he could, but she had to at least—

"Need some help in here?"

Ridley froze at the sound of the familiar voice. Her traitorous heart leaped hopefully, even as the pain of betrayal rushed hotly through her veins once more.

"Yeah, can you get that damn syringe?" Mr. Knockoff said to Archer as he climbed to his feet. "I'll hold her down."

"Sure." Archer walked in and reached for the fallen syringe. "You shouldn't have come in here on your own." His gaze—as dark and cold as his father's—settled on Ridley as he straightened. "She's feisty."

Mr. Knockoff chuckled as he approached Ridley again. "You would know, wouldn't you."

Archer's impassive expression morphed into a wicked grin. "I would." Then he jabbed the needle into the man's neck.

"Hey! You ... what ..." Mr. Knockoff launched away from Ridley and threw himself at Archer. There was a brief scuffle, and then Mr. Knockoff slid to the floor. He didn't move.

Ridley breathed out slowly, her heart still hammering against her chest. "For a moment there," she said to Archer, "I wasn't sure who you were going to stab with that thing."

Archer's features tightened. "I guess I deserve that." He stepped over Mr. Knockoff, pulling magic from the air with one hand. "May I?" He pointed to her wrists. She nodded, watching from the corner of her eye as he did a quick conjuration to transform the glowing wisps of magic into a spark that would slice through the cable tie. Quietly, he said, "I will always be on your side, Ridley. Whether you trust me or not."

Instead of acknowledging his words, she asked, "Why isn't the arxium in the air interfering with your conjuration?"

"There isn't any in the air." He crouched down and did the same conjuration for the cable tie around her ankles. "Well, not just floating around everywhere. It somehow travels along the tiny beams of light positioned to create that dividing layer across the room. I think the arxium particles just hang around in gaps in the walls when that thing is switched off. Oh, and there's arxium in your body from when they injected you earlier," he added as he stood. "I think this form of arxium takes longer to work through your system than breathing it in. Anyway, come on." He reached for her hand as she stood, a gesture that must have been automatic because a moment later he clenched the hand into a fist and lowered it. "Um, sorry. Let's go."

They crossed the room, and Archer stuck his head through the doorway before saying, "All clear."

They hurried into a hallway lined with the same geometric gray panels as the room they'd just left. Ridley said, "This doesn't mean I forgive you."

"Rid, can we talk once we're out of here?"

"Sure. But talking isn't going to change anything."

They stopped in front of a closed door at the end of the hallway, and Archer held his commscreen against a plain black pad on the wall. A click sounded from within the door. Archer grasped the handle and pulled the door open.

"Are we below ground?" Ridley asked as they left the hallway behind and entered … a living room? It was a larger space with two comfortable couches, a television screen, and some random, abstract art on canvases. There also appeared to be an automatic coffee machine built into one of the walls.

"No. We're pretty much as far from the ground as you can get."

They crossed the room to the door on the other side and hurried into another passageway. This one, however, was made entirely of glass on one side. Ridley almost stumbled to a halt when she looked out and saw the tops of skyscrapers. "Wait, are we—is this Aura Tower? Are we in your *home*?"

"Close enough. We're five floors down from the penthouse. My father likes the *convenience* of being able to interrogate people without having to go too far. Anyone who catches his interest is brought here instead of being immediately disposed of or carted off to some other facility like the one in the wastelands that you destroyed."

"I guess I should be honored to have been chosen," Ridley said with as much sarcasm as she could muster. They entered a smaller room, this one with nothing but an orchid sitting on a table against a wall on the left, and a door straight ahead.

"To be honest," Archer said as they aimed for the door, "I'm just relieved. We're supposed to kill elementals if we happen to come across them. Unless—"

"Stop right there."

The voice came from behind them. Familiar and feminine, it sent another sickening lurch through Ridley's stomach.

"Lilah," Archer said as he and Ridley turned slowly. Then: "Whoa!"

Because Lilah Davenport had a shotgun pointed at them. She gripped the weapon in both hands, pressing the butt of it into her shoulder as she eyed Ridley and Archer along the length of it. Ridley had to admit she looked kind of badass.

"Lilah, where did you get that?" Archer asked as he raised both hands. Ridley did the same.

"Does it matter when it's pointing at you?" Lilah replied.

"Do you even know how to use it?"

Lilah's eyes narrowed ever so slightly. "Don't patronize me, Archer. Is it so hard to believe there might be things you don't know about me? Clearly there's plenty I don't know about you. Like the fact that your amulets are gone and you can pull magic. Like the fact that you're on *their* side—" she jabbed the gun toward Ridley "—and not ours."

"Lilah, I have always been on your—"

"I was in the surveillance room when you went in to get her," Lilah snapped. "I heard everything you said. I saw everything you did."

"Why don't you stop pointing the weapon at us and we can talk about this," Archer suggested.

"How could you betray us?" Lilah demanded, making no move to lower the gun. "How could you turn on your own family?"

"You don't know what Dad's done. You don't know about—"

"I do know. I know all of Dad's secrets. I know secrets even you don't know, Archer."

"I ..." Ridley didn't have to look at Archer to know he was confused. It was evident in his voice.

A short, bitter laugh escaped Lilah. "That look on your face? That hurt you're feeling? The sting of betrayal because you think Dad confided in *me* and not you? That's how I've felt for years. Dad left me out of everything. He only ever chose you to be part of his grand plans."

"Because you weren't interested. You didn't want to be part of it."

"No, *Mom* decided she was bored and didn't want to be part of it, and everyone just assumed I felt the same way, so I was left on the outside."

"Okay, well what does that matter now? You seem to be on the inside again, with Dad sharing his secrets with you."

Lilah rolled her eyes. The gun twitched, which sent Ridley's heart rate through the roof. She didn't want to die by accidental gunshot while Archer and Lilah argued about which of them their father favored more. She examined her level of nausea—still very much present—and wondered if it was worth trying to change form. Would she have enough time to push her magic out and become air, concealing Archer along with her, or would Lilah pull the trigger the instant she saw a wisp of magic?

"I'm not on the inside," Lilah said to Archer. "Dad would never trust me with any of his secrets. He didn't *tell* me anything. I have my own ways of finding out what he's up to."

"So you know about the Cataclysm then."

A loud but slow *beep, beep, beep* began to whine repeatedly from somewhere nearby. Lilah's perfectly shaped eyebrows lowered a fraction further, though whether it was because of the alarm or because of Archer's statement, Ridley couldn't tell. "The Cataclysm?" she repeated. "What does that have to do with Dad and his secrets?"

"Everything." Archer shook his head. "What secrets are *you* talking about?"

"Um, Archer?" Ridley interrupted. "I really think we should go."

"Not happening," Lilah snapped at her.

"Come with us," Archer said.

Lilah let out an incredulous laugh. She even lowered the gun a few inches, though Ridley figured she probably didn't know she was doing it. "You must be joking."

"We were wrong," Archer said quickly. "*I* was wrong. Elementals are not what we've always believed them to be. Just think, Ly. *Think!* You've known Ridley for years. Is she really the cold, soulless person we always imagined whenever Dad told us what elementals are like?"

Lilah pressed her lips together as she took a deep breath. "That doesn't matter. I'm not turning on this family the way you have."

"Lilah—"

"Family comes first. Family has *always* come first."

"*I'm* your family too," Archer said fiercely.

There was a pause as Lilah's expression became steely. She raised her weapon. "Not any—"

Ridley shoved Archer to the side, launching herself in the opposite direction. Her skin glowed with magic, and a second later, she hit the floor in the form of water—just as a gunshot cracked the air. She barely had time for the thought *Lilah actually shot at me* to take hold in her mind before she realized she was human again. She couldn't hold her elemental form with arxium still in her blood.

She rolled over as Archer lunged across the floor at Lilah's legs. Lilah fell with a shriek, the shotgun clattering heavily beside her. She pummeled her brother with her fists before he managed to get hold of her wrists and force her arms down. "I don't want to hurt you," he grunted, just as Lilah kicked hard enough to shove him away.

"I will," Ridley gasped, already rolling wisps of magic into a ball between her palms. She hurled the ball at Lilah's head. The force of the magic knocked her flat onto her back, and when the glow disappeared, she lay motionless, a swollen, red mark on her forehead.

Archer looked up at Ridley, aghast. Breathless, Ridley said, "She tried to *shoot* me. All I did was knock her out. There was no conjuration there, just force."

Archer climbed to his feet, muttering, "This is not the way I thought any of this was going to go."

"Yeah, welcome to the club. Can we go now?"

Archer looked down at his sister. "I can't leave her."

Exasperated, nauseous, and starting to go a little crazy from the continued *beep, beep, beep*, Ridley pressed her fingers to her temples. "You can. She doesn't want to come with us. *You're* the one who can't stay here now that you've freed me. You won't be able to lie your way out of this one."

"Ridley, she doesn't know the truth. The Cataclysm, the magic out in the wastelands ... She's as deluded as I was before I—"

"Fine. Whatever. I guess this could all be another elaborate ruse to get me to trust you and I'm not falling for that again. So you're on your own now. And I'm taking this," she added, crouching and lifting the gun. It was heavier than she'd expected. She wasn't sure how to use it, but since her magic wouldn't be much help getting her out of here, she hoped the oversized firearm at least made her *look* threatening.

Archer groaned. "Give me that before you hurt yourself."

"Wow. No wonder Lilah gets so pissed off at you. What makes you think I don't know how to use this?"

"Do you?"

She glared at him. "Do *you*?"

The lock of the door they'd been aiming for clicked. They both swung their heads toward it. Ridley had about half a moment to be furious with Archer because of all the time he'd wasted arguing with Lilah. Then the door flew open and two men barreled out.

Archer grabbed the shotgun from Ridley and swung it up to point at the newcomers. Apparently he did know what he was doing, and apparently he looked almost as badass as Lilah while doing it. Ridley found this immensely annoying, though she was relieved to see the men stop in their tracks at the sight of the firearm. "You probably don't want to come any closer," Archer told them.

The older one's expression darkened. "Gotta be kidding me. Jude was right about you."

Archer grinned. "Yep. You should have listened to him. Too late now." He motioned sideways with the gun. "You know those rooms you guys like to lock people in? That's where you're going. Keep your hands up and don't make any sudden moves. I might accidentally shoot you."

# CHAPTER 15

RIDLEY AND ARCHER descended Aura Tower in one of the lesser used elevators, then exited the building through a back entrance Ridley knew nothing about but Archer seemed comfortably familiar with. She pulled her hood over her head and wrapped her arms around herself as she looked up and around. Dark clouds gathered ominously above the glittering skyscrapers, and in the grayish light it was once again impossible to tell the time of day. The nausea was slowly subsiding, but Ridley's heart still pattered out an anxious rhythm. She felt dangerously exposed in human form. She needed to find somewhere to hide until the arxium had worked its way through her system.

"This way," Archer said, reaching for her arm as he gestured to the right. "There's—"

"No." Ridley stepped out of his reach, then began walking in the opposite direction, hugging herself a little tighter. "I'm not going anywhere with you."

"Ridley—"

"Seriously, Archer, can you blame me for not trusting

you?" She tossed the words over her shoulder as Archer hurried after her. "I mean, sure, you just freed me from some weird residential interrogation center, but how do I know you won't be crawling back there tomorrow to tell them it was all ... I don't know. Part of your plan to get close to me again so you can find out where everyone's living now after the attack on the reserve."

"That would make no sense," Archer said as he caught up to her, "since I already know where everyone went. Well, I mean, I know roughly where the new location is, based on what Nathan told us. And no, I didn't tell my father. Also no: I won't ever be crawling back to the Shadow Society. As you accurately pointed out, I can't lie my way out of things anymore. Look, Ridley, this—can you just stop?" He grabbed her arm and pulled her around, letting go as soon as she faced him. "Please just come with me. We need to get somewhere safe and then we can argue about this all you want."

"I'll find somewhere safe on my own," Ridley retorted, pointing her gaze over his shoulder. "Without you."

He sighed. "Ridley, please. You have no amulets, and you can't currently shift into elemental form. You probably won't make it a block before a drone detects you. I at least still have mine on me, even if one of them isn't under my skin anymore."

Ridley lowered her arms, then tightened them around herself again. The nausea was lessening, but she was beginning to feel dizzy. "No," she said, with not nearly as much force as she would have liked.

"Plus you're shaking. When last did you eat?"

"I'm not shaking," she lied. "And stop acting like you care."

"Oh, come on." Archer threw his arms up in a frustrated gesture. "I know I kept things from you. I *know*. And the—the Cataclysm—your mom—"

"I don't want to talk about that." Ridley turned her back to him again, the pain of the reopened wound slicing through her once more. She stepped off the sidewalk, glancing briefly both ways down the street. Her brain registered belatedly that numerous vehicles were moving toward her. *Stop*, she told herself, but the street was tilting, and her body was reeling, and—

"Jeez, Ridley!" Archer tugged her back onto the sidewalk.

"I'm *fine*," she insisted, blinking a few times. The dizziness wasn't *that* bad. She'd just turned around a little too quickly, that was all.

"I know I lied about so many things," Archer said again, a little quieter now. "But you can't possibly believe I don't care about you."

Ridley's hands clenched into fists. Her jaw tightened. She looked up, finally meeting Archer's gaze. "Do you remember arguing with me? In Christa's bunker, when we were locked up together. The first time we ever spoke about my magic. Do you remember *defending* the way your family responded after the Cataclysm? You told me that we needed protection, that our resources had to go into building the wall and adding more panels over the city. And all the while you *knew* it was never an accident! That you had actually played a role in the whole damn thing! And now you want me to believe the things you tell me? I'm sorry, but no. I can't."

Archer's dark eyes were glistening now, full of pain, but he didn't look away. "I do remember that," he said quietly. "And it was ..." He shook his head. "For so long, that was the only way I could stand to live with myself. I forced the truth of the Cataclysm into a dark corner in my mind and pretended I had nothing to do with it. Pretended I wasn't to blame. So I argued with you because that's what I've always done to keep the guilt from devouring me. It wasn't right—I *know* it wasn't right—and I'm sorry. I'm so sorry."

Ridley let out a long breath and closed her eyes. She felt her body swaying. Maybe she was dizzier than she thought after all. "I still think," she said faintly, "we should go our separate ways now."

The buzz of a scanner drone reached her ears. She opened her eyes as Archer glanced up. "I'm not going to leave you to pass out on a sidewalk and end up in a police cell." He put an arm around her, and it felt so familiar, so *right*, so comforting after the past few horrible days. A sob fought its way up Ridley's throat. She hated her body for betraying her like this. Didn't it know that Archer couldn't be trusted anymore? "It's heading the other way," he said as he led Ridley down the street, "but there are always more drones. I think if we stick close together, they'll detect us as a single person."

"Wonderful," Ridley murmured. Archer was the last person she should be *sticking* with, but it was possible she might fall over if he let go of her. So for the moment, while there

were no other options, she would trust him to hold her upright. Any more than that …

No. There would never be any more than that.

"I know the drones are a problem," she said, "but you'll
have to get rid of your amulets soon. If you really are on my
side and you've just revealed to your family that you've betrayed them, your dad might try to track you down. I imagine
he could make it happen pretty quickly."

"I know. And my commscreen. It might be fine if I just
switch it off, but I'm not sure. Problem is, my AI1 is still beneath my skin. I can't just stop on the side of the road and cut
it out. We need to get somewhere safe indoors. A building
with other people around."

"The Lins," Ridley said, thinking of Shen's family. They
lived across the road from Kayne's Antiques and had been
looking out for Ridley for years without her knowing it. At
least she knew for sure they were on her side—unlike Archer.

"Too far. We should avoid public transport, and it'll take
too long if we walk."

"Where, then? I don't know if I trust anyone in this part
of the city."

Archer paused at the corner of the block and looked right
and left. Traffic lights blinked and changed color. He held Ridley a little tighter as they crossed the street. "Do you trust
elementals?"

"Logic tells me I should."

"Remember Serena Adams?"

Serena Adams. The girl who *hadn't* blown herself up with

magic, as Ridley had recently discovered. She'd been killed by the Shadow Society for being an elemental. "Yes," she answered.

Archer pointed at the gleaming glass and tapering shape of the building on the next block over. "That's where her mom lives."

* * *

Days of the week didn't hold much meaning for Ridley anymore, but here in the real world, it was apparently Sunday morning. This was fortunate because it meant Serena's mother wasn't at work. Equally fortunate was the fact that she wasn't out somewhere else. The part that was *un*fortunate was when she slammed the door in Archer's face.

Archer paused a moment before knocking again. Mrs. Adams paused a moment before reopening the door. This time, the gap was barely wide enough to see half her face. "I'd like to remind you, Archer, that you're not welcome here unless it's an emergency of life and death proportions."

Ridley raised her eyebrows. Archer definitely hadn't mentioned that part when he'd assured her they would be safe with Serena's mom. "I know," Archer answered immediately. "This is Ridley. She's like Serena. I just helped her escape the Shadow Society. We need somewhere to hide for a bit while she recovers from the arxium they gave her. So ... it is kind of an emergency."

Mrs. Adams, whose firm expression hadn't changed a

bit, paused another moment. Her gaze slid to Ridley. Then she stepped back and opened the door fully. "Come inside. Quickly."

"Thank you," Ridley said as Archer hastily steered her through the doorway. His arm was still around her, keeping her unsteady body from toppling over.

Mrs. Adams shut the door swiftly and turned to face them, tucking smooth, strawberry blond hair behind one ear. Long-limbed and graceful, she looked like an older version of Serena. It struck Ridley once again that there had never been any resemblance between herself and Claudia Kayne. Why hadn't she ever wondered about that? And what had her real parents looked like? If she stood beside them today, would other people look at them and know they belonged together?

"Are you hurt?" Mrs. Adams asked. Her face was etched with concern now, the initial hardness gone.

"No, just ... dizzy," Ridley answered. "From the arxium. And maybe ... lack of food? I'm still a little nauseous, but I could probably eat something."

"Let me heat up some food for you." Mrs. Adams stepped briskly past them. "You can sit in there," she added, gesturing to a small dining room. "And there's a bathroom down the hall, first door on the right, if you need it."

They sat in the dining room, and Archer quietly explained that Serena's mother had always thought him a terrible influence on her daughter. She'd told Serena to stay away from 'that Davenport boy,' though it sounded like Serena hadn't always listened. Even after Archer visited Mrs. Adams upon returning to Lumina City to express his condolences for Serena's death and explain his ties to the elementals, she'd essentially told him to get lost. Ridley decided she was liking Mrs. Adams more and more.

She finished off the leftover meal Mrs. Adams had heated up—good old fashioned mac and cheese, made with genuine ingredients, from what Ridley could tell—without too much difficulty. It was awkward, sitting there eating while Mrs. Adams and Archer watched her and made stilted conversation, but she tried to focus on the food and not the uncomfortable atmosphere.

"Do you need to rest?" Mrs. Adams asked when she was done.

"I don't actually feel that tired," Ridley said. "Apparently someone injected me with a sedative, so I probably slept for a while. I think it was the aftereffects of that, plus the arxium and lack of food, that was making me feel so crappy. I'm definitely starting to feel better. But, uh, I definitely think I could use a shower." She didn't want to say it out loud, but she was fairly certain the unpleasant odor of sweat hanging in the air was coming from her.

"Of course," Mrs. Adams said. "You're welcome to take a shower. And your clothes ..." She hesitated, uncertain. "I could wash and dry them, but the machine will take a while."

"Oh, don't worry about it. I can take care of them with a few conjurations."

"I'm sorry, I'd offer to do it for you," Mrs. Adams said, "but I haven't used my magic in years. I just ... prefer not to."

She showed Ridley to the bathroom and produced a clean towel for her.

Ridley spent longer than necessary beneath the cascade of warm water, breathing in the scent of the bubbles produced by Tanika's conjuration and letting her tears mingle with the warm water streaking down her face. So much had happened since the attack on the reserve that she'd barely processed the fact that Tanika was gone. *I should have listened harder*, Ridley thought, squeezing her eyes shut. Magic had tried to tell her earlier in the day that there was a threat coming, but she hadn't realized it.

She did another bubble conjuration, watching the way the light caught on the bubbles' soapy surface, producing shimmering rainbow colors. She thought of Tanika's many colorful scarves. She thought of the one that had been wrapped around Tanika's hair as she lay still on the ground in her own blood. Ridley squeezed her eyes shut again.

When she was done with the shower and the conjurations that cleaned and dried her clothes, her nausea and lightheadedness were gone. She left the bathroom, glancing across the hall at the opposite room. She wasn't intentionally snooping, but the door was ajar and she couldn't help catching a glimpse of the room beyond. She stopped as she caught sight of a Wallace Academy blazer. The room must have been Serena's.

Though she knew she shouldn't, Ridley pushed the door open a little wider and looked inside. Her eyes traveled across the room's contents: A dresser covered in makeup and hair products. Candles in varying shades of blue and purple arranged among the books on a shelf. Trophies from dance competitions lining the top shelf. The school blazer hanging on the closet door. A black jacket draped over—

Surprise surged through Ridley's chest. She knew that black jacket with the popular cartoon demon-cat embroidered on the back. It was Shen's. Unless, of course, Serena owned the exact same one. But given that it didn't fit in with the rest of the girly items in this room, and that Shen had admitted before disappearing that he'd been in love with Serena, the jacket was very likely his.

*Where are you, Shen?* Ridley thought, gently pulling the door back to its original position. Shen had accidentally killed an elemental man outside Ridley's home. Then he'd tried to kill Lawrence Madson and Archer—succeeding in the case of Lawrence. He'd been convinced they were both part of the Shadow Society and were at least partly responsible for Serena's death. Ridley had insisted he was wrong about Archer. A sick feeling that had nothing to do with arxium twisted her gut. Turned out she was the fool, not Shen.

She left Serena's bedroom behind and found Archer and Mrs. Adams in the living room. As expected for an apartment in the heart of the Opal Quarter, it looked like it came straight from an interior design showroom. But it also looked a little more lived in than the Davenports' penthouse home. There were far more framed photographs—Serena's face was everywhere—plus a couple of dirty coffee mugs, a wrinkled blanket on one of the couches, and a half-finished plate of fresh fruit on the coffee table.

Archer looked up, his expression brightening when he saw Ridley in the doorway. She quickly averted her eyes, hating the way her stomach flipped over when he looked at her like that, as if she were suddenly the only important thing in the room. Her body clearly hadn't received the memo yet that she and Archer were no longer a thing.

"Feeling better?" Mrs. Adams asked.

Ridley thought of saying something about the jacket. Or saying something about Shen, at least, since she didn't want to admit to looking into Serena's room. She wanted to let Mrs. Adams know the two of them shared a connection. One of Ridley's best friends had loved Mrs. Adams' daughter. But she wasn't sure if Mrs. Adams even knew about her daughter's relationship with a guy who lived in what could almost be considered a slum in comparison to the Opal Quarter. And even if she was aware of it, bringing up anything that had to do with Serena would probably only cause her pain.

"Yes, thank you," Ridley answered, stepping into the room. "Um ... are you two getting along any better than when I went to shower?" Her eyes moved to Archer's ear, and she could just make out the edge of a small patch of gauze stuck behind it. "I see you managed to remove Archer's AI1 without leaving any major wounds, so that's a positive sign."

"Archer and I had a long chat. He told me quite the story."

Ridley sat opposite Archer, tucking one leg beneath her. "Is that the story about how his family's part of the Shadow Society, but he's apparently turned his back on everything they believe and has been helping elementals for months now?"

"Yes."

"Okay. Just checking we were both given the same story."

"You don't believe him?"

Ridley looked at Archer, holding his gaze this time. "I want to. I just don't know if that's wise."

Mrs. Adams nodded. "I know what you mean. He told me a similar story several weeks ago when he'd just returned to Lumina City. Not the Shadow Society part, but that he knew about elementals, and that his time overseas had changed him. I wasn't sure I believed him and I—I didn't want to talk about Serena." Her voice hitched slightly before she continued. "It didn't matter to me that Archer Davenport suddenly cared about her death and wanted to pass on his condolences."

"But you did tell me," Archer said, "before pushing me out the front door and slamming it closed, that if I was ever desperate and in need of somewhere to hide, I could come here. You said you wished," he added in a quieter tone, "that Serena had had somewhere to hide when she was trying to get away from them."

Mrs. Adams inhaled deeply. She looked at Ridley. "I did say that. And now ... well, him being part of the Shadow Society for so long was a fact that was bound to only make me hate him more. So the fact that he told me anyway makes me think it's probably the truth."

"Or he told you because I already know, so I probably would have told you by now if he hadn't."

Mrs. Adams appraised Ridley with a slight tilt of her head. "You are a skeptical one, aren't you. Did he break your heart?

Is that why you think it unwise to trust anything he has to say now?"

"Uh, should I perhaps leave the room so you two can continue talking about me as if I'm not here?" Archer asked.

"Yes," Ridley said, but she was answering Mrs. Adams, not Archer. "That is what happened."

Mrs. Adams nodded. "Smart. I'd probably feel the same way if I were you."

"Good. Anyway ... so ..." Ridley looked at Archer again. "Both your amulets are gone? And your commscreen?"

He nodded. "Put them all into a brown paper bag, opened a window, and sent the bag flying as far as possible on a conjuration."

"Magic? How daring."

"Mrs. A said she didn't mind."

Mrs. Adams frowned. "I did say that, but I think I might object to being called Mrs. A."

"Sorry." Archer smiled apologetically. "Too familiar?"

"Too ... old."

"Old?"

"Um, anyway," Ridley interrupted. "I can use my own magic again, so we can leave any time. Like now, before Archer becomes too annoying and you throw us out. We should probably—"

The sound of something falling in one of the other rooms cut through Ridley's words. She paused, lips parted, her eyes darting to Mrs. Adams. She had also frozen.

"Does someone else live here?" Archer asked quietly.

Mrs. Adams shook her head, rising silently from the couch. She padded over to a bookshelf, extended her hand toward a book with a wide spine, and slid it from the shelf. She flipped the book open. It had no pages, only a compartment with a small black object Ridley couldn't properly see but was fairly certain was a gun. Mrs. Adams slipped her hand around it.

Beside Ridley, Archer sucked in a quick breath and said, "Saoirse?"

# CHAPTER 16

RIDLEY'S GAZE SHOT TOWARD the doorway she'd walked through barely a few minutes before just as Archer said Saoirse's name. A slight figure was standing there. Wrapped in her favorite rainbow sweater, her gray-streaked auburn hair scraped back into a tight ponytail, it was most certainly Saoirse.

Ridley let out a heavy breath as she stood, her hammering pulse still pumping adrenaline through her system. "Saoirse, what are you—you can't just *do* that! You almost gave us heart failure. Mrs. Adams was about to ... I don't know, shoot you or something." Even as the words left her mouth, she remembered appearing in Meera's bedroom in much the same fashion. And in Lilah's bedroom not long before that. In fact, Ridley had entered a great many homes in exactly the way Saoirse had just appeared. With a twinge of both guilt and annoyance, she forced the reminder away.

"I wasn't very well about to knock on the front door when I had no idea what kind of situation you were in," Saoirse said, crossing the room. A bag hung from one shoulder, and she didn't remove it as she pulled Ridley into a brief hug. "You might have been a prisoner in here. Would have been silly to announce my arrival in that case."

"I'm guessing I can put this away?" Mrs. Adams said, holding up the book. It was closed now, hiding the weapon that lay within it.

"Yes," Archer answered, standing. "Mrs. Adams, this is Saoirse. Elemental, as you've no doubt gathered. Saoirse, this is ..." He looked at Mrs. Adams. "I'm sorry, I don't actually know your first name."

"Blair." Mrs. Adams slid the book back onto the shelf before moving toward Saoirse, her hand extended. "Blair Adams." The two women shook hands. It struck Ridley that they probably weren't too far apart in age, but Mrs. Adams looked decades younger with her perfectly dyed hair and expertly applied makeup.

"Sorry for intruding," Saoirse said. "But we've all been very worried about Ridley."

"We?" Ridley echoed. "Who else ... I mean, where did you just come from? Have you seen—my dad?" She stumbled over that last bit, and Saoirse must have noticed because her eyes filled with sympathy.

"You have seen him," Ridley said quietly. "You know that I know."

To her side, she noticed Archer looking between the two of them. "Know ... what?"

Ridley cleared her throat and turned to Mrs. Adams. "Uh, we can go now and continue all of this elsewhere. I don't want

to intrude on your hospitality any longer. But I'm very grateful for the meal and the shower and ... and a safe place to hide
for a bit. Thank you."

Mrs. Adams sighed through her nose. "No rush. This isn't
what I'd planned for my Sunday morning, but you're all here
now, so you may as well stay longer if you need to. I meant
what I said when I told Archer I wished Serena had had somewhere safe to hide." She looked around. "Anyone want some
tea?"

Archer seemed uncertain. Saoirse looked at Ridley as if
Ridley held the answer. All Ridley could say was, "Um ..."

"I'll put the kettle on anyway." Mrs. Adams left the room.
Ridley and Archer hesitantly sat down. Saoirse followed, not
bothering to remove the bag from her shoulder.

"So ... magic led you here?" Ridley asked Saoirse. "To me,
I mean?"

"Yes. Sorry, before I say anything else ... do we trust him?"
She jerked her head toward Archer. "Nathan told me about his
ties to the Shadow Society. About his father being the director." Her brows lowered in disappointment as she focused on
Archer. "I don't know you that well, but I have to admit it was
a shock to discover this."

"Saoirse, I'm on your side," Archer insisted. "I swear. Before reaching the reserve, I had planned to never see my family or any other Shadow Society member ever again. It's true
that I once bought into everything my father told me—or at
least, it was just easier not to question things—but I made my
own mind up months ago."

Saoirse looked at Ridley. "You know him better than I do. What do you think?"

Ridley sighed. "I don't know. Everything's become so tangled in my head. If I look back, I can see evidence to support his story, but I can also see times where things conveniently worked out in his favor. It just seems safer not to trust him."

"I agree." Saoirse's magic drifted around her hands. She pulled it together between her palms, then manipulated it with a sweep and curve of her hands and repetitive flutters of her fingers.

"What are you doing?" Ridley asked.

Saorise spread her arms wide, then smacked the magic together between her palms before throwing it at Archer. It hit his chest and vanished like a puff of dust. His wide eyes shot up. "What did you do to me?"

"You can't pull magic now. It's basically the same effect as an AI2. I'm sorry, but I need to be sure Ridley and I have the upper hand here. You can only use your own physical strength now if you want to attack us, and our magic should help us get away from you or restrain you, should the need arise."

Archer looked horrified. "I would never attack either of you."

"Why do you know a conjuration like that?" Ridley asked, frowning.

"People who use magic—elemental or not—aren't always good people. I've learned that the hard way. Sometimes this is the easiest method of disarming someone who's trying to hurt you."

"Permanently?" Archer demanded.

"Oh, no. Sorry, I should have mentioned that. It's not permanent. There's another conjuration to remove the effects of the one I just did."

"So, what? I earn your trust back, and you'll return me to normal?"

"I suppose so."

Ridley was still frowning. This was probably the best thing to do, given that they had no way of knowing if anything coming out of Archer's mouth was the truth. But there was still something about it that made her feel uncomfortable. There was little difference between this and the government deciding that by law, everyone would have an AI2. But this was one person deciding for another person that they shouldn't be allowed to use magic, and that seemed a bit more like a violation of a basic human right. Or perhaps this was just Ridley's silly heart caring more about Archer than she should. She needed to work on that.

"Back when magic was legal," Archer said, "I assume this kind of conjuration was *illegal*?"

"Yes. But you've probably done plenty of illegal things in service of the Shadow Society, so illegal conjurations shouldn't bother you." Without giving him a chance to respond, Saoirse turned to Ridley. "What happened yesterday? After you left Nathan and your father—well, your ... you know." She looked uncomfortable. "I had the vague sense that you were somewhere in or near Lumina City, and then the feeling simply vanished. I thought something terrible may have happened to you."

Ridley leaned back and folded her arms over her chest. It was just hitting her again that Saoirse had known the truth all along. Throughout every conversation, every training session—even the first moment they'd met, when it had been clear Ridley believed Dad was her father—the truth had hung there between them without Ridley being aware of it. "You knew," she said, an accusatory edge to her voice. "And you let me believe a lie."

Saoirse shifted her position slightly on the couch, unable to meet Ridley's gaze now. "It wasn't my place to say anything. I tried to convince Maverick, but he kept saying he needed more time."

Archer leaned forward. "I think I've missed something. What are you talking about?"

"You've missed a lot," Ridley snapped. "That's what happens when you turn out to be part of the enemy organization. We stop telling you things."

Archer let out a frustrated huff of breath. "I am not the enemy."

Ridley ignored him and faced Saoirse again. "Okay. So you didn't tell me. Fine. I guess I understand that you didn't feel it was your place. Though you did tell Nathan, and you must have known he wasn't going to keep it to himself."

"I'm sorry about that. I was trying to explain to him that I have real hope for our plans, and I suppose I must have come across far more excited than I have in recent months, so he wanted to know what changed. I told him about you. And, Ridley—" she gripped both of Ridley's hands in her own "—I *do* have real hope now. Having you with us changes everything. The rest of us could probably sit back and watch while you burn through all the arxium around Lumina City on your own."

Ridley shook her head as a shiver raised the hairs on her arms. "I don't know about that."

"Well, if you had *both* your family stones you probably could. But your father's was lost several generations ago."

"The stones? Why would it make a difference if I had both of them?"

"As I understand it, the magic within them helps to focus your power. You know how when you fragment, you sort of ... lose touch with time and place? You feel as though you're everywhere at once? It's very ... instinctive. You give yourself over to the elements, and magic senses what you want and need. But when you're wearing the stone I gave you—at least this is how your mother explained it to me—you're able to focus more sharply. You're everywhere at once, and also distinctly *aware* of everything at once, so you're able to direct it more easily. Essentially, it makes you even stronger than you already are."

"Hmm," Ridley mused. "Is that why magic was able to warn me that we were about to be attacked? Did I have, like, a stronger connection to it because I was wearing the stone then?"

"You already have a stronger connection than the rest of us because of who you are. You can just about have a *conversation* with magic if that's what you want. You can ask it for things and it will understand you in a way it will never understand the rest of us. But yes, even more so when you're wearing the stone, I think."

"But magic warned you too. It didn't warn anyone else—at least, not that I gathered—but it did warn you. Wait, are you also one?"

"Oh, no, I ..." Saoirse stumbled over her words as she shook her head. "With much patience and meditation over many years, I've honed my connection to the elements. But it's still not as easy for me as it is for you. The warning I got wasn't very clear."

"Oh. So, is this why ..." Ridley played absently with the ends of her hair, wondering if she should voice this part out loud. She'd wanted to ask Saoirse about it before, but it seemed too silly, like something she'd probably imagined. "The first time I fragmented, it felt to me as though magic said it ... *knew* me. And then after I burned through that building in the wastelands, I got the sense that it was pleased with me. I thought either I'd imagined it or ... I don't know, that maybe all elementals feel like magic is telling them it recognizes them."

"Amazing," Saoirse murmured. "No, I don't think magic says that to all of us. At least, I don't remember getting that sense myself, and no one else has ever mentioned it to me. There must be something recognizable about the magic you've inherited. Some signature to it that's passed along with each generation."

"Maybe," Ridley murmured.

On the other side of the coffee table, Archer swore beneath his breath. Ridley had almost forgotten he was there, but now she looked at him. "You're one of them," he said softly. "You're an heir. You must have inherited it from your ..." He trailed off, frowning as he looked at Saoirse. "But you said *both*. And Ridley's father isn't ..." His eyes slid away, focusing on something in the distance, and Ridley could almost see his mind working. Then his gaze snapped up to hers again, and there was something like pity in his eyes. He'd figured it out. And he'd accepted it immediately, not arguing about it the way she had. Not saying that it was impossible, that Saoirse must have got it wrong. He was probably thinking it made a lot of sense. He was probably thinking, *So that's why she looks nothing like her father.*

"Ridley ..." he said slowly.

"Don't," she said tightly. "Whatever you're going to say, just don't. And actually—" she tilted her head to the side "—now that I think about it, if you know about these so-called heirs, then you should have already figured out that I'm one of them. I showed you the pendant Saoirse gave me."

"The ... oh. That's the family stone."

Ridley rolled her eyes. "Yes, Archer. Your father recognized it, so I assume you would too. Maybe you're the one who told him what I am. Maybe that's the reason he told his guys to bring me back to him instead of just killing me."

Archer shook his head. "If someone told him, it wasn't me. I've heard of elemental heirs, and I know about the family heirloom stones that are passed down from generation to generation. I've heard stories of siblings and cousins killing each other over the single stone passed down from their ancestors. But I don't remember anyone ever telling me what they look like. Honestly, it never even crossed my mind that that's what it might be when you showed it to me. Didn't you say it was a healing stone or something?"

Ridley looked at Saoirse. "You mentioned healing properties. I'm guessing that was a lie?"

"Your mother did actually mention that she could draw power from the stone and use it to heal herself."

"Oh. But you didn't just happen to be wearing it when your community was discovered."

"No, that part was a lie." Saoirse looked appropriately contrite. "I'm sorry. When the Shadow Society found us ..." She swallowed and took a deep breath. "Cam had taken Bria to the park nearby. I went to your parents' home first, as it was the closest. But they were already ... they were dead. You weren't with them, but I hoped you were in the nursery. I knew about the stone pendant being part of your heritage and linked to your power, so I took it off your mother's neck. I intended to search the house for you, hoping I would find you alive. But by then there was so much arxium in the air. I was so dizzy and sick, and I'd barely made it through the next room when someone returned. It took everything in me to change to air and flee.

"By the time I found Cam and Bria, fire was already raging through everything. I don't know who started it—perhaps it was one of us, fighting back, or perhaps it was them. But everything was burning, and there was so much arxium, and we had to get out of there."

Ridley tried not to imagine the scene. She tried not to imagine her parents' dead bodies. "Why did you wait two weeks to give me the stone?" she asked quietly. "You could have given it to me as soon as I arrived at the reserve."

"I thought ... well, I don't know exactly how it works. You're supposed to be immensely powerful to start off with, and then the stone amplifies that even more. But when you arrived at the reserve, you had only just begun to embrace your own magic without restraint. I thought perhaps you needed to first stretch yourself, to discover the potential of your own natural magic, before adding a magical booster to your power."

Ridley nodded slowly. "You wanted me to be strong on my own first, so I could then become even stronger."

"Yes."

"And you're telling me that with this stone, I should have enough power to burn through the entire wall around the city and all the panels overhead?"

"I think so, yes."

Ridley hesitated, then said, "You're going to be rather upset when I tell you I don't have the stone anymore."

A heartbeat of silence passed through the room. Then another. Saoirse shook her head. "Sorry ... *what?* Why? What happened to it?"

"I'm pretty sure Archer's father has it. I was wearing it when someone discovered me back at my old apartment, but when I woke up, it was gone. Alastair Davenport told me that's how he knew what I was."

"He definitely would have taken it," Archer said. "He's been hoping to find an elemental heir for years. Not that it was a top priority of his, but he mentioned it every now and then, how it would be useful to find one."

"And I'm the lucky one he eventually found," Ridley muttered.

"Okay, so this explains why whoever caught you at your apartment didn't just kill you," Archer continued. "They probably saw the stone and, unlike me, they recognized it. I thought maybe my father was hoping to get other information out of you, but it's obviously because you're an heir."

"Well, I guess I really am lucky then," Ridley said, no sarcasm this time. "I'd be dead if I was just a regular old elemental."

Saoirse leaned forward, rubbed her fingers against her temples, and groaned. "It would really help us if we could get that stone back."

"You know, if it's so vitally important, you probably should have told me to be more careful with it. I thought it was just jewelry with a bit of magic in it."

"I told you it was your *mother's*. I thought that would make it important enough to you."

Ridley bristled at the accusatory edge to Saoirse's voice. "That *did* make it important. But if you'd added, 'Oh, and we need it in order to save civilization,' then maybe I could have hidden it somewhere on myself."

"Then we'd be back to you being dead," Archer said quietly, "because if no one saw it, they would have killed you."

"Look, it's not that we *need* it in order to return the world to the way it used to be," Saoirse said to Ridley. "After all, we've been planning this for a long time without an heir. But I think we have a much higher chance of succeeding with you on our side. With you *and* your family stone. There's so much arxium around the city, and so many of those panels in the sky. We just don't know how much power it'll take to burn through them all. The more we have, the better."

"Okay, so I'll get it back then. I've stolen things before—I'm pretty good at it, actually—so if we need it, then I'll get it. I *want* this plan to work. I don't want the Shadow Society controlling things anymore."

"Don't be foolish," Archer said. "You don't know where my father is keeping it, and even if you did, it's too dangerous to try to get it back. This isn't like breaking into some random apartment. If he catches you again, he'll make sure you can't get away."

Ridley pinned Archer with a level gaze. "*You* probably know where the stone is."

He sighed. "If I knew—"

"Or, if you don't, you at least have a good idea of where he might be hiding it."

"Sure, I know of all the places we could look for it, but that doesn't make it any safer. And what if he has it *on* him?"

"Well then I guess I'll just have to get it *off* him. If I have magic and a gas mask, I'll be fine. I'll get him on his own somehow, and—"

An ear-splitting crack tore through Ridley's remaining words. Saoirse's hand shot out and landed on Ridley's leg as a bolt of magic flashed outside and thunder reverberated through the building. "Just another storm," Ridley said, though her own heart raced from the shock of the abrupt weather change. Rain began to shower against the windows.

Saoirse stood and crossed the room, raising one hand to the window pane. "We're out of time," she said, her quiet voice barely reaching Ridley over the sound of the rain.

"No, it's normal here," Ridley said. "That was maybe a little angrier and more out-of-the-blue than usual—and magic itself doesn't often make its way past the panels—but storms are common over the cities. Not like out there at the reserve where magic has learned to be calm around elementals. You're probably not used to it."

Saoirse shook her head. "This isn't an ordinary magical storm. The attack has begun."

It took a moment for the words to settle into Ridley's brain. Then she stood abruptly. "Attack? What attack? Like ... Nathan's plan? Elementals destroying the arxium around the city?"

Saoirse turned and met Ridley's eyes. "Yes."

"But ... *now*? Since when?"

"Since we were attacked and everyone decided to retaliate without waiting any longer. Since ..." Saoirse took a deep breath, and there was something apologetic in her gaze. "Since I told everyone you're an heir and that I'd be able to find you, and that we could win this."

"You—you what?"

Saoirse pressed her hands over her face. "It wasn't supposed to happen like this. So *fast*. But after we made it to the mountains, everyone decided enough is enough. They want to fight back *now*. Which is *good*—we've waited long enough—but you were supposed to be with us, and you were supposed to have the stone, and you were supposed to know exactly what you need to do." She lowered her hands and looked at Ridley. "But they'd already decided. They didn't want to wait even a day. So I told them about you, and then I went ahead of everyone and caught up with Nathan and Maverick. They told me about you taking off and how they were so worried about you. Nathan couldn't sense you anymore. But now I've found you. You're okay, and we can still do this without the stone. We just need to get outside the city and join everyone else."

Archer was standing now too. "Why didn't you tell us this the moment you got here?"

"Perhaps because I saw *you*," Saoirse retorted. "And because I'd just discovered your affiliation to the Shadow Society. And because I knew Ridley had found out the truth about her parents, and I didn't know what kind of mental state she was in. We needed to *talk* before I mentioned that oh, by the way, we're doing this *now*. And because—" she dug her fingers into her hair and sucked in another deep breath "—because they were supposed to wait. Nathan was supposed to *wait*. He was supposed to trust that I would find Ridley and not begin any of this without us. But none of us could sense her anymore, and he thought that meant she might be dead, and—"

"So let's go," Ridley said. "Now. We can be outside the city walls in less than—"

"No." Mrs. Adams stood in the doorway. "You're not going anywhere until you tell me exactly what's happening."

"I'm guessing you haven't been in the kitchen this whole time making tea," Archer said.

"What were you saying about elementals destroying the arxium around the city? Do you mean all the arxium that's protecting us? Because that sounds insane. You can't—"

Saoirse launched toward Ridley and vanished. A rush of air swept around Ridley, and an instant later, she was invisible too. She had never done this before—disappeared because of someone else's magic and not her own—but she let Saoirse's elemental form whisk her away. Out of the room, through an air vent, into an air duct, racing along pipes, up and up and up, until eventually they shot out above the building.

# CHAPTER 17

THEY FLEW BETWEEN THE skyscrapers, over the poorer districts, and beyond the wall. Saoirse's magic lowered them both to the ground where the ruins of the wastelands began. "I'm sorry," she said as they reappeared, her voice barely audible above the storm. The ground shuddered beneath them, and they were drenched within seconds from the pelting rain. "I should have gotten you out of there the moment I found you. It's just ... all of this—attacks and search-and-rescue missions—it's way outside my comfort zone." She dropped her bag to the ground beside her feet. "I don't know what I'm doing half the time."

"We ... we left Archer," Ridley said, her mind still racing to catch up.

"I thought you didn't trust him anymore?"

"I ... yes. You're right. I don't. He'll be fine." She shook her head. She wasn't supposed to care anymore whether Archer was fine or not. "Okay, so—Whoa!" She ducked as the front half of a truck soared overhead and crashed into the ground nearby. "Holy freaking—"

"It's fine," Saoirse assured her. "We'll be fine. Magic knows us. It's not going to hurt us."

Ridley remembered the first time she'd ended up out here, when magic had whipped her up and flung her back and forth before returning her, unharmed, to the ground. It had figured out then that she was no threat. She sincerely hoped it hadn't forgotten her.

"Um, okay." She tried to gather her scattered thoughts. "Just ... just hang on." Her skin glowed and her magic rose to the surface, and in the next moment she was air, picturing those she knew—Dad, Nathan, Callie, Malachi—and pushing her questioning thoughts out to the magic around her. The answers came back instantly, from every direction. Elementals were all around her, mostly in the ground. Not Callie, which made sense—she had always seemed too nervous to take part in all of this—but everyone else was nearby. Except Dad. It took Ridley longer to sense him, and when she did, she felt herself drawn toward the city, somewhere on the other side of the wall.

"My dad—he's in the city," she said the moment she resumed her human shape. "That's where he's supposed to be, right? That was part of the plan?"

"Yes. Along with everyone else who isn't elemental. They'll use conjurations to protect people, if necessary."

"Risking getting caught," Ridley said, "and unable to get away like one of us." Why hadn't that occurred to her before, when they were going over these plans?

"Possibly, but once this is all over and magic isn't forbidden anymore, they'll be freed. And that's *if* they're caught. There'll probably be too much chaos for that." They were both shouting now to be heard over the storm, but the wind still seemed to sweep their words away almost the moment they'd been formed.

"Okay, but also ..." Ridley wrung her hands together. "He doesn't know I'm all right. I just—I just *left* yesterday. I was angry with him. And when you last saw him, you said you couldn't sense me anywhere, so he's probably worried, and he probably thinks I hate him now, and—and what if he's looking for me instead of—"

"That's fine, Ridley. He's in the city, which is safer for him than if he was out here. I'll find him and let him know you're okay. Right now, you need to focus." Saoirse gripped Ridley's shoulders as the earth trembled again. "Are you ready?"

"I—I ..." Ridley shook her head, though she didn't mean 'no.' She wanted more than ever to rid the world of all its smothering arxium and the Shadow Society's influence, but, as Saoirse had said only minutes ago, everything was happening faster than anyone expected. "Just tell me exactly what's happening right now. Is this—is this the part where everyone's in the ground doing the earthquakes to break those arxium gas machines?"

"Yes. I assume that's why the storm is so bad now. If the machines are broken, all the arxium gas is probably escaping into the air." Saoirse looked behind her. "If we were a little further into the wastelands, or up there—" she turned her gaze to the sky "—I don't think we'd be able to change form without gas masks on."

"They know where the bunker is, right? They know which section of the wall to avoid?"

"Yes, Malachi told Nathan exactly where it is."

"So we wait for the storm to calm down—so it won't damage the city—and then we burn through all the arxium protection?" Ridley asked.

"Yes. You go up to the panels, and you do exactly as we practiced. Just on a bigger scale. You were already more powerful than everyone else the last time we practiced this. I know you saw that. Now you know why. Now you know you can push yourself even further."

"Okay, but ..." Ridley wiped a hand across her eyes, clearing them of the raindrops that stuck her lashes together. A futile exercise, since more rain streamed down her brow and into her eyes within seconds. "Archer mentioned there are arxium panels in the ground around all the cities. They were put there before the Cataclysm. We never knew about those, so we didn't plan—"

"That's fine. The others will sense any additional arxium down there. It'll crack because of the earthquakes, and then they'll burn through it. They'll move on to burning the wall, and if they're not done by the time you're finished with all the panels, you can take down the rest of the wall." She squeezed Ridley's shoulders again. "It's happening, Ridley. We have *you*, and this is finally, really happening."

The knot of anxiety that had begun to form in Ridley's chest jerked a little tighter at the reminder of the responsibility that rested on her. "But ... what about the rest of the details? We haven't done that video recording Nathan wanted to broadcast across the city to explain everything. And what about all the other cities across the world? I thought we wanted this to be a synchronized event. Happening everywhere at the same time, so the Shadow Society chapters everywhere else don't have a chance to fight back. It's not that I don't want to do this. I really, really do. I just don't want us to end up failing."

Saoirse paused, then said, "Change has to begin somewhere, Ridley. There are others ready to act. When they see that the revolution has begun, they'll follow suit. The Shadow Society won't have time to stop anything."

A shiver crept across Ridley's skin at the word 'revolution.' It was so huge, so dramatic, so ... *historical*. The kind of event that belonged in textbooks, not in everyday life. But that's exactly what this was, wasn't it? They were overthrowing the current order of things. Ridley had just never put the label 'revolution' onto it before.

"And Nathan's probably done the recording by now," Saoirse added. "I know we mentioned in passing that perhaps Archer should do it, but we can't trust him with anything anymore. I'm sure Nathan's already sent whatever he's recorded to various news networks. He would have done that once he was close enough to the city to get signal. Hopefully someone will be brave enough to broadcast it once this is all done and everyone wants to know what's happening. They'll be scared at first, but Nathan's message will help everyone understand."

A bolt of magic zigzagged down from the sky and struck somewhere in the distance. "And the Shadow Society?" Ridley asked. "You never came to an agreement on that particular detail, and it's kind of a major one. We'll never be safe as long as they're around."

"We know who the director is now. We also know the mayor is one of them. Nathan can name them in his recording and the proper authorities will take care of them."

Ridley frowned. "The authorities that are probably under the Shadow Society's thumb and have been stuck there ever since the Cataclysm? Have you actually spoken to Nathan about this recording? Do you know for sure what he's telling everyone? A moment ago you said he's probably done it already."

"Ridley, just—" Another tremor shook the earth, and Saoirse threw her hand out to grab Ridley's arm. "I don't know, okay? The only thing I know is that we all have our part to play in this. Yours is to burn through as much arxium as you possibly can. You need to leave the rest to other people. I don't know the details, but Nathan's been planning this for a long time. I'm sure he'll do whatever's necessary to make the world a safer place for all of us."

"So ... he's going to kill them."

Saoirse wiped rain from her face. She looked past Ridley toward the city. "I don't know what Nathan's going to do. But at some point, you have to trust everyone else involved in this." She fixed her green gaze on Ridley once more. Firm and steady, yet still ... gentle. "I know you're used to acting on your own, relying only on yourself, but you're not alone anymore. We're all in this together."

"I—I know I'm not alone—"

"Do you? Several days ago you took off on your own to find Archer."

"Because nobody else wanted to help!"

"That's not true. If you'd had a little more patience, you—" Saoirse cut herself off, shaking her head. "*Trust*, Ridley. That's my point. The responsibility of this operation isn't *entirely* on your shoulders. Yes, you can probably do all the arxium burning on your own, but there are other parts to this equation, and it's okay for you to not be in control of all of them."

Ridley blinked at Saoirse through the relentless rain—which was beginning to slow from deluge level to shower proportions. She couldn't deny that her anxiety level was pretty high not knowing exactly what Nathan had said on his recording or what the plan was for the Shadow Society or where Dad was and whether he would stay safe. But Saoirse was right. They each had their own role to play and, just like with her magic, she had to let go of the control she so badly wanted to hang onto. *It's not my plan*, she reminded herself as she wiped rain from her eyes yet again. *I don't* have *to know everything about it.*

"Okay," she said eventually. "I focus on my part, you focus on your part."

"Exactly."

"I'll wait for the storm to calm—which might actually be starting to happen—then head up there and burn as fast and far as possible."

"Yes. It would be better if you had your mother's stone—I think magic would understand you more clearly if you did—but you still have plenty of power without it. You can fragment and send your fire self as far as possible, but it'll be a bit wild and all over the place, and I don't know if you'll be able to control where all the burning arxium ends up."

"Which is why my dad and the others will be waiting down below."

"Yes. And I'll find Maverick and tell him you're okay before I join the others."

Ridley turned her gaze to the sky again, blinking through the rain that was no longer falling as fast. Magic and lightning flickered intermittently in the clouds, which were a lighter gray now and even allowed a streak of sunlight to crack through every now and then. "It's definitely starting to quieten. Probably almost time for me to head up there."

"Put this on," Saoirse said, crouching down and opening her bag. She straightened and handed Ridley a gas mask.

"What about you?"

"I brought two. I was hoping to find you, remember?"

"Right. Thanks." Ridley pulled the mask on and secured the straps behind her head. "Okay, I think I've—" The earth heaved beneath her feet, throwing her entirely off balance. She tumbled backward, shoving her magic outward a second before she would have hit the ground. She splashed onto the rocky earth as water, then returned to human form and sat up. She sucked in a breath at the sight of the jagged rift racing through the ground toward Lumina City's wall. It struck—Ridley tensed—and a crack splintered its way up the wall.

"Crap, this is really happening." She reached for Saoirse's hand as they both stood. "Right now. On a random Sunday morning. We're ..." She looked at Saoirse through the mask. "We're changing the world."

Saoirse held her gaze. "We're changing the world."

Ridley looked up again as a larger gap appeared between the clouds, allowing bright sunlight to stream down. The earth shook again, and she almost lost her balance a second time. She focused forward instead, eyes pinned on Lumina City. "Time to do this," she whispered.

Then she started running. Her form melted into fire and she launched herself upward, shooting into the sky as a mass of flames. As she neared the city wall, she wondered vaguely if anyone was watching her fiery form hurtling across the sky. If so, were they afraid? Would they assume it was another manifestation of the wild wasteland magic? Whatever they believed it to be, they probably thought the shield of arxium panels above their city would protect them. She knew they'd be afraid once those began burning. Their fear would only increase when they realized their wall was burning too.

*Only for a short time*, she assured herself. *Nathan will explain everything.* If no one wanted to broadcast his message, they could put it on all the social feeds instead. Soon there would be no more fear. Only a world that was free to use magic.

She flew higher and higher. The panels grew nearer. Near enough to make out their true size. Impossibly thin, but at least the footprint of a bus, if not bigger. Squarer. Even as a magic-powered fireball, Ridley felt tiny in comparison. She imagined a deep breath, urged her magic faster, and slammed into the first panel.

She half expected to be instantly and violently repelled by the arxium, but Nathan was right: elemental fire ate through arxium as if it were paper. *Fragment*, she told herself, but she was still too nervous to fully let go. Her flames leaped across the panel, then across the empty space to the next one. She urged herself further and faster—as fast as she could go without fragmenting.

*It isn't about control*, she reminded herself. *It's about* trust. *Trust everyone else. Trust yourself. Trust the magic around you.*

She felt her elemental form relax and begin to—

Something hit her. Not a panel, not the gusting wind. Something ... else. Something invisible. Some ... *one*. She could sense an elemental form in the air around her, and for a second she thought of—but that definitely wasn't possible. The someone wrapped around Ridley's fire form, and for a moment she blazed even brighter. Then everything went instantly dark. Solid, earthy, suffocating. The flames were gone. She couldn't move. Panic choked her.

Then the world reappeared and she was human again, falling down, down, down, hurtling toward glinting skyscrapers and a maze of criss-crossing streets. Terror stole her breath. She pushed her magic outward—or tried to, but someone else wrapped air around her a second before she could access her own magic. Together, they spiraled down between two buildings, the ground rushing dizzyingly toward them until—

They halted barely an inch from the road. Whiplash probably would have killed them if they'd been in human form. Then Ridley was dropped. She landed face down, her gas mask banging on the tarred surface of the road. She groaned and rolled over, her magic already pulsing beneath her skin and rising into the air to—

She froze at the sight of the girl standing in front of her. Yellow magic—*yellow?*—flickered beneath her skin. Ridley's eyes rose, and the familiar face was as much a shock as the unnatural color of magic.

Lilah pulled her arm back before throwing it forward, releasing a mass of sparking yellow magic. "Payback," she said, before pain radiated across Ridley's head and everything vanished.

# CHAPTER 18

RIDLEY BLINKED SLOWLY and squinted against harsh, white light as the sound of arguing voices settled into her consciousness.

"... what you've done," the male voice said.

"I know exactly what I've done," a female voice snapped in return. "I made the rest of your man-made superheroes look like idiots hunting down regular old elementals while I found the one you really want. I found the *heir*. Now you can stop treating me like a child and consider taking me seriously."

"I'm talking about the *serum*!" the male voice yelled, and though Ridley's muddled, throbbing head couldn't quite place it yet, the instinctive chill it sent down her spine was familiar. She blinked again, trying to bring the blurred shapes above her into focus. "What possessed you to use it *on yourself*?" the man demanded.

"Oh, jeez, I don't know, Dad. Maybe so you'll finally—"

*"You don't know what it does to people, Lilah!"*

Lilah. Of course. Ridley knew she recognized the female voice as well. And Lilah was the last person she'd seen before ...

Holy crap.

Yellow magic. Beneath Lilah's skin. Everything was rushing back to the surface of Ridley's thoughts now.

"I would if you'd just *tell me*," Lilah said. "Instead I have to snoop around and discover all your secrets and experiments for myself. I have to make friends with your precious *Doc*. You've left me out of things long enough, Dad, so I used his access card to get the serum and—"

"It *kills* people, Lilah!"

Silence.

Ridley blinked again.

Lilah's voice was small when she asked, "What?"

"Everyone who's taken it has died within a day. Our human bodies can't handle the magic."

"But ... I ... this is the latest version. The one with *her* blood." Lilah's voice was shaking now. "I heard Doc saying it was different. And it's—it's been over a day since I took it. I feel fine."

"This one hasn't been tested yet. Maybe it takes two days, three days, to kill someone. Or maybe—*hopefully*—we've finally got it right and you won't have to die for your stupidity."

"My *stupidity*?" Lilah's voice was hard again, all emotion gone. "Because it never crossed my mind that you were *killing your own friends* in this crazy pursuit of yours to become the very thing you hate?"

"And this, Lilah, is why snooping around is so dangerous. You don't get all the facts, you draw the wrong conclusions, and you end up sentencing yourself to death. I don't want to become an *elemental*, the thing I hate. I want to use their own power against them to finally get rid of them all. And all my 'friends,' as you call them, are willing volunteers. They know we haven't perfected this serum yet. But they want to keep our city, our world, safe. They're willing to be the test subjects in order to achieve that end."

Ridley's fuzzy brain followed the conversation as closely as possible, horror growing alongside the nausea as her eyes slowly grew accustomed to the harsh light. She could make out ceiling panels, a fluorescent tube light, and—in her peripheral vision—a narrow piece of something curved and metallic.

"Well," she heard Lilah say, "then I guess I'm willing too."

"You were never supposed to have the option to be willing!" her father fumed.

"And that's exactly the problem, Dad. You don't want me to make my own choices. You don't want to tell me what's really going on."

Ridley turned her head to the side. She looked past the metal contraption—a stand from which a bag of IV fluid hung—and saw Lilah and her father on the other side of an open doorway.

"I do not have time for your teenage drama," Alastair Davenport snapped. "The city wall is barely standing, I need to make sure an appropriate story is fed to the media, I need to find out how many of my people I've lost today, and I *cannot* put off that meeting with the president of the Arxium Mining Association any longer. Now, in addition to everything else, I have to worry about the possibility of my daughter dying in the next few days."

"Thanks, Dad," Lilah said drily. "I'm going to tell myself that your anger is a sign of how much you care about me."

"Of course I care. I *love* you, Lilah. Which is why I've always tried to keep you out of this. Magic and everything that goes along with it is dangerous. You think I'm trying to control you, but I'm only trying to—"

"Tell me about the Cataclysm, Dad."

Alastair barely missed a beat before replying. "The Cataclysm? What could I possibly have to tell you about that?"

"I don't know. Apparently it's another one of your secrets."

"Is that what Archer told you? Another one of your brother's lies? Of course he wants you to believe Cataclysm conspiracies. Like I said, I don't have time for any of this. You need to see Doc. Urgently. Tell him to do anything and everything possible to make sure you don't—Oh, wonderful." Alastair's dark eyes landed on Ridley's, sending another shiver coursing through her. "She's awake. Can someone please sedate this girl again!" he shouted.

Ridley moved to sit—and realized then what she'd missed while listening so intently to Lilah and her father's conversation: her arms were strapped to the bed. She tried to move her legs, but her ankles were secured too. She also appeared to be dressed in one of those attractive hospital gowns.

Though she knew it was probably useless, she pushed her magic to the surface of her skin. It glowed weakly, but wouldn't rise any further than that. She was too weak, too sick. Her stomach threatened to turn itself inside out, and the room seemed to spin around her.

A woman was in the room now, injecting something into the IV bag. Ridley struggled and screamed, but it was pointless. Her surroundings began to blur as her head became unbearably heavy, until slowly, slowly everything ... was ... gone.

# CHAPTER 19

THE NEXT TIME RIDLEY woke, the harsh lighting was gone. The fluorescent bulb above her head was off, and dim light illuminated the room from somewhere behind her head. No one was arguing nearby. There wasn't much sound at all except for her breathing and something that may have been the faint whirring of machinery.

Trying not to move too much—she didn't want to alert anyone that she was awake—she shifted her fingers. Then her feet. Yep, still strapped down. Still attached to an IV bag. That sucked. Aside from it being a violation of her freedom, she also badly wanted to stretch out her stiff, aching body.

She breathed through the urge to vomit—a feeling that was almost a constant state of being for her these days—as everything she'd overheard earlier spun repeatedly through her mind, shocking her again and again.

Alastair Davenport had manufactured his own elementals. *This* was the experimentation he was doing. Well, among other unpleasant things, no doubt. But this—this was insane. Never in her wildest imaginings would Ridley have come up with this. He was *giving people magic*—and they were dying because of it. *Lilah* was going to die because of it, she remembered with an icy jolt.

Lilah was the one who'd found Ridley burning the panels. It was Lilah's face that had come to mind when Ridley tried to figure out who was attacking her. She'd dismissed it instantly, and yet she'd been right. Lilah had elemental magic. And now she was going to die.

With a confusing mix of emotions jostling for her attention, Ridley couldn't figure out how she felt about that. It certainly wasn't a *good* feeling. The other feeling that wasn't a particularly good one was the feeling that surfaced when she realized that Lilah, who'd been in possession of elemental magic for little more than a day, had overpowered *her*, a supposedly super powerful elemental heir. How had that happened? Had Saoirse and Nathan been wrong about her?

She cast her mind back to exactly what had happened above the city's arxium panels. No ... It probably wasn't that they were wrong. It was Ridley's fear of earth—the element Lilah had wrapped around her to snuff out Ridley's flames—plus pure surprise that had given Lilah an advantage. Of all the threats Ridley might have expected to face above Lumina City, another elemental was not one of them. *Lilah* was not one of them. Perhaps if Ridley had had another few moments to get over her shock—and to get over her suffocating fear of being momentarily trapped inside a piece of earth—she could have thrown off Lilah's magic and escaped.

Or perhaps Lilah was also super powerful because her

man-made magic came from Ridley. If that were so, maybe it would keep her alive. Unlike everyone else who'd gone after Ridley's elemental friends. By now they were probably either dead or about to die.

As for those elemental friends ... how many had survived? It seemed silly to think that people who were as invisible as air couldn't whisk themselves away to safety. They had magic and gas masks. They were all but invincible. But if they were taken by surprise as Ridley was ... if they ended up in human form, even if only for a few moments ... they could be shot or knocked unconscious or hurt.

And what about Dad? He was inside the city walls, nowhere near any of the elementals. And there had barely been any falling arxium to worry about, so there was no reason for him to have used a conjuration in public and landed himself in jail. *He's fine*, Ridley told herself. *I'm sure he's fine.*

Like a pinball, her thoughts zigzagged every which way, striking each major revelation from the past few days and bouncing immediately to the next.

Archer's betrayal.

An orchestrated Cataclysm.

A father who wasn't her father.

A best friend who couldn't be there for her.

Manufactured elementals.

Yellow magic.

A failed revolution.

*Yellow magic.* Her mind circled back to this detail again and again. So small, but so ... unnatural. Magic was supposed to be blue. It had only ever been blue.

A recent memory surfaced of Ridley hastily sitting up on the couch in her home as magic warned her someone was coming. Now that she thought about it, a flickering yellow light had illuminated the near darkness in the moments before she was knocked out. It wasn't a detail she'd considered before, but now she realized it probably came from one of these unnatural elementals.

Her brain continued cycling endlessly through everything that had happened, exhausting her, bringing her closer and closer to despair. Was this how it would end? She would die as part of some secret, illegal experiment. Dad would never know what happened. Elementals would never free the world from all its arxium. The Shadow Society would remain in control of everything.

She was roused from her fog of depressing thoughts by the sound of a door opening. Was it Alastair Davenport, back to interrogate her again? Someone in a lab coat, ready to stick more needles into her? She squinted as the door swung shut behind her visitor and the lock clicked. He was young, dressed in a button-up shirt and jeans. He flipped a switch. Bright light pierced Ridley's eyes. She squeezed them shut, then blinked a few times.

"Ah, good morning, good morning," the man said. "You are awake." His voice was bright, energetic, and slightly accented. Ridley lifted her head to get a better look at him.

"Are you the guy people keep referring to as 'Doc'?"

"I am, yes."

Ridley's eyes narrowed as they traveled over him. He was lean, tanned, and entirely too good-looking for someone who spent their days carrying out evil experiments on innocent people strapped to hospital beds. "Where are we?"

"Well, thanks to you," he said as he crossed the room, rubbing his hands together, "we are no longer out in the wastelands in the state-of-the-art facility Mr. Davenport promised me when I came to work for him."

"You mean that crappy building I burned to the ground?"

Doc paused. "He warned me you would be difficult to work with. Fortunately, I like a challenge." Indeed, the smile he fixed on Ridley suggested he was genuinely enjoying their interaction so far.

"So ... we're in the city somewhere?"

"All I will say is that it's fortunate we have a small backup facility, and it's fortunate I kept duplicates of many of the samples I've taken and serum versions I've been working on over the past few years. As for specifics ... well, no, I won't be confirming exactly where we are."

Ridley dropped her head back down with a groan. "Fine. It doesn't matter where we are. Just ... please tell me what's going on in Lumina City. And *around* Lumina City. The wall, the other elementals. What's happening?"

He pressed a button somewhere on the side of the bed and Ridley felt the top half of her body slowly rising until she was half sitting instead of lying flat. "I don't think I should be telling you anything about that either," he said.

"*Please.* It's not as though I can do anything with the information. I just can't stand not knowing." She lifted her head again. "It will help my mental health. That's important, right?"

"I suppose so." He moved to a counter that ran the length of one side of the room and picked up a commpad. "There isn't much to tell, though," he continued absently, tapping at the screen a few times. "The wall is fine. Or it will be, after some repairs. And the other elementals ... it is my understanding that some were killed, while others got away. They don't appear to have returned—at least not to strike the wall. Things are mostly back to normal."

Any remaining hope that Ridley may have had vanished. 'Back to normal' was the last thing she wanted to hear. "So you didn't capture any of them? You know, so you can force them to be lab rats and test out all your horrible arxium weapons and who knows what else on them?"

"Oh, no, that is not my focus at the moment." He turned to face her, the commpad still in hand. "Replicating elemental magic is what Mr. Davenport has had me working on for some time now. I have already interviewed a number of elementals, so it was not necessary to capture any more of them. *You* are the only one we were hoping to find—or someone just like you."

"You *interviewed* elementals," Ridley repeated with skepticism. "Are you sure 'interrogate' isn't the word you're looking for? 'Torture,' perhaps?"

"It has been most fascinating," Doc said, sidestepping Ridley's question, "discovering exactly how they use their magic. How they change instantly to other forms, how they communicate with the magic that exists naturally in all the elements, and how it responds instantly."

Ridley was quickly figuring out that as long as Doc focused on his research, he would keep talking. He didn't seem to have the same fear or hatred of magic that other members of the Shadow Society possessed. He had the curiosity of a scientist. Perhaps, if he kept talking, he might reveal something useful. She breathed in deeply, feeling a fraction less ill now that she had a sliver of hope to cling to. "And you were actually able to take all that information and create something that could give regular people magic?" she asked.

"After several years of experimentation, yes. However, regular people—as you refer to them—are not always able to do much with their power once they have it. Some of them die before figuring anything out. Others, after being told how it works, seem to get the hang of it immediately."

"Yay for them," Ridley muttered with some bitterness. She'd spent so many years being afraid of her magic, doing as little with it as possible, that she'd only recently figured out she could use it to actually commune with the magic in the elements. "I guess Lilah is one of those who got the hang of it immediately."

"Ah, yes, Delilah Davenport. Quite the natural, from what I've heard."

"So ... she's still okay?"

"Yes, yes. Still healthy. Which is excellent news for us. Your blood has made all the difference to this latest version of the serum."

Ridley gave Doc her best deadpan stare. "Excellent news for *Lilah* too. You know, not dying and all that."

"Of course, yes. Her father was ... not happy. If there was someone else who knew all the things I know, I think he would have fired me." Doc spread his arms wide, palms up, and shrugged. "Not my fault, what she did, but still. Mr. Davenport blamed me."

"Lucky you that she's not dead, I guess." *Especially since 'fired' probably means 'killed,'* Ridley added silently.

"Lucky indeed."

"So all the other people you gave magic to—before you had a sample of my blood—they all died?"

Doc nodded, his bright expression turning serious. "It is unfortunate. None of them lasted long. That is why the attack on your people—and the other groups the mayor was told about—was not successful. The mayor convinced Mr. Davenport that his elementals would be able to follow anyone who got away, but I warned him that they would not survive the journey if it took more than a day. Sadly, I was right." He placed his commpad on the counter and removed what looked like a ring box from his pocket.

"Hey, uh, can I get out of these restraints?" Ridley asked as casually as possible. Maybe Doc would release her before he remembered he was talking to a prisoner and not discussing work with a colleague. Unfortunately, he wasn't quite as distractible as Ridley hoped. He gave her a look that clearly said, *You're joking, right?* "I just ... I need to move," she moaned. "I'm so stiff and uncomfortable. And it's not like I'm a threat to you. There's definitely still arxium in my system." Her stomach churned as if to remind her that this was true. "If there wasn't, I could turn to air right now and these straps would mean nothing."

Doc nodded. "True, but it would be a bit complicated to free you from the IV and the catheter."

"Catheter," Ridley repeated. "Are you kidding?" She wasn't her normal self, but was she really so out of it that she hadn't noticed that bit?

"I'd like you to turn your attention to this," Doc said, changing the subject. He stepped closer to the bed and raised the box, which, now that it was closer, Ridley could see was larger than a ring box. He opened it to reveal her family heirloom stone. "Tell me everything you can about it. How does it enhance your power? How does the use of your magic *feel* different when you're wearing it? Does it have any limitations, or is it like a battery that never runs out?"

Ridley considered attempting to bargain with him: Answers in exchange for him removing her restraints. She wasn't trying to trick him. She was aware that she currently had no way to get herself out of this room. She really did just want to stretch her aching body. But he'd been through this 'interview' process with other elementals, and something told her he had ways of extracting answers, whether she was willing to give them or not. Probably better to just be honest.

"I wish I knew," she admitted, "but I haven't had the stone for very long. I only just found out I'm an heir. I didn't even know elementals like me existed until ... yesterday? I don't know, my days are all mixed up. Anyway, I know it's supposed to help me focus my power so I'm even stronger. Something like that. But I'd already lost the stone when I was told that, so I haven't had a chance to test it. I mean, I knew it had *some* magic in it because of the way it lit up when I touched it, but I guess I never noticed that it didn't do that for other people, so I thought it was just some old—"

"It lit up?" Doc's wide eyes sparkled, betraying his excitement.

"Um, yeah." She almost asked if she could show him, but he might be suspicious if she offered. If she waited, letting the idea simply hang there, his curiosity would probably get the better of him and he'd—

"Show me," he instructed.

She almost smiled in triumph, but her stomach chose that moment to turn itself upside down again, reminding her not to get too excited while there was still arxium being pumped continually into her system.

Doc held the stone near Ridley's right hand and she raised a finger to touch it. The silver veins running across its smooth, gray surface glowed magic blue. A sense of relief seeped slowly through her body. She watched Doc's delighted smile stretch even wider. "What else do you know about it?"

"Um ..." She was about to say 'Nothing' when she realized the relief she felt was due to the never-ending nausea finally easing up. She remembered Saoirse saying that her mother had been able to draw power from the stone in order to heal herself. Was that what had just happened? She ran her finger along the stone's surface again, imagining pulling magic from it. *Get rid of the arxium,* she thought. *Please, please heal me of all the side effects of this horrible arxium poisoning.* Incredibly, her stomach felt like it was almost back to normal. Gone was the sense that the room was rocking ever so slightly from side to side. She swallowed, hoping Doc hadn't noticed any change. "Honestly," she said, her finger still resting on the stone, "it sounds like you know more about it than I do. How did you learn what you know? Did someone tell you? Or do you have, like, some old forbidden text or something?"

Doc pulled the box away and snapped it shut. He gave Ridley a knowing smile and wagged a forefinger at her, which made him seem about fifty years older than he probably was. "Fishing for information, are you?"

"No, I'm honestly curious." Honestly curious and honestly exhilarated. The stone would be her way out of here. She just had to convince Doc to let her use it. "I never got a chance to experiment," she said, infusing her voice with the kind of sad weakness she imagined it must have had when she was feeling ill and hopeless. "I have no idea what I'm capable of with this stone, and now we'll never know."

Now *we'll* never know. She tried not to emphasize the 'we' too much, but she wanted Doc to be aware that he was missing out on groundbreaking discoveries just as much as she was. Not knowing or understanding something was probably an intolerable concept for someone like him.

"Do not say 'never,'" Doc said with a grin, shoving the box into his jeans pocket. "I will find a safe environment in

which we can experiment. Perhaps the new containment—"
He paused as someone knocked on the door. Ridley looked
over as it opened, revealing a woman in a lab coat—and a gas
mask similar to the ones Ridley had used recently.

Doc let out a hoot of laughter. "Amateurs," he said to
Ridley as he waved the woman in. "Always funny to see how
scared they are of elementals when they are in the same room
with one for the first time. As if a mask could protect her from
you if you decided to become air. He shook his head, still grinning. "Now, one more thing, Ridley." While the woman fid-
dled with the IV bag, Doc asked, "Are there others like you?"

"I—oh. No." His expression, while still keen, had become
suddenly serious. Clearly he'd been hoping to catch her off
guard. "I mean, I suppose there must be," she added, "but I
don't know any of them."

He nodded slowly. "No siblings?"

"No," she answered immediately. Neither Dad nor Saoirse
had mentioned other children, so she was fairly certain this
was true.

"Hmm." Doc rubbed his chin. "I see we may have to use
other methods to ensure we get the truth out of you."

"I am being truthful," Ridley insisted.

"Of course, of course. Well, we are done for now."

"Really? That's all? Didn't you want me to try experimenting with the ..." She trailed off as sleep tugged irresist-
ibly at her head, her body, her eyelids. A pull too strong to be
natural. She turned her swimming head toward the woman
on the other side of her bed—but she was gone. The IV bag

swung gently bag and forth. Ridley managed to raise a finger and point at it. "Did she ... is there ..." The world began to slip away. "Ah, seriously?" she moaned.

"Seriously," Doc said as Ridley's eyelids became too heavy to hold open. "Mr. Davenport is taking no chances this time."

# CHAPTER 20

RIDLEY DRAGGED HER eyelids open.

Then again.

Again.

This happened several times as she struggled to recall what had happened. Doc was questioning her ... the stone seemed to heal her ... she'd finally had some hope! Then a woman sedated her again ... And now she just could. Not. Wake. Up. Why was it so much harder this time? Had she been given drugs that were too strong? Something different? And *crap*, what was that sudden stinging in her cheek?

She forced her eyelids apart again. This time, her blurry gaze landed on Lilah. "You're alive," Ridley murmured.

"You don't have to sound so happy about it," Lilah said.

"I am happy. I don't ... want you ... to die." Ridley's head lolled to the other side and then back. For another few blinks, Lilah seemed to be gone, but then she was there again. Closer now. Whispering. Ridley's cheek was stinging again, and she couldn't really hear what Lilah was—

"Ridley, are you listening?" Lilah hissed. "Why did Archer

mention the Cataclysm when we were talking about my father's secrets?"

"Cata ... clysm." Ridley's tongue felt thick and useless as she tried to wrap it around the word. Her mind was just as useless as it tried to wrap itself around the actual question. "He ... did it," she managed to say. Was that right? Was that what she meant to say?

Lilah's face shifted in and out of focus. "What do you mean? What do you *mean*? Ridley, what do you mean?" Lilah was saying the same words over and over. Or perhaps Ridley's brain was repeating them over and over. She couldn't tell the difference. "I think I'm dying, Ridley. What if I die? What if I *die*? Your magic was supposed to be stronger, *better*, but what if it kills me?" Lilah's voice shook. Her eyes were large and desperate. "Doc says there's nothing that can heal me if it turns out my body can't handle the magic."

"Heal ... healing ... The stone has healing properties." The words were Ridley's, but she imagined she could see Saoirse standing next to Lilah, the words coming from her lips instead. Ridley needed to get Doc to give her the stone again. She needed to draw enough magic from it to heal herself of this horrid, sickening, head-spinning confusion. Then she could understand what the heck was going on and get herself out of here.

There was a bang, and the squeak of chair wheels, and Lilah's face was gone, replaced by Doc's face. No, Lilah wasn't gone. She was next to him. They were talking. And then Doc was leaning over Ridley, and everything was fading to darkness again.

# CHAPTER 21

WHEN RIDLEY WOKE AGAIN, there was no needle in her arm. The metal stand with the IV bag had been pushed away from the bed. "Ah, good morning," Doc's bright voice said, startling her. She turned her head to the other side and found him standing there, tapping away on the commpad again. "I did not expect you to be awake for another hour or two. Well, this means we can get on with the fun earlier rather than later."

"The ... fun?" Ridley blinked a few times. Her head didn't feel nearly as muddled as the last time she'd woken, when Lilah was in here. Unless ... had she dreamed that?

"I have good news and bad news."

"Um, okay ..."

"The good news is that I have been granted permission to stop sedating you," Doc said. "I will also stop administering arxium. A new containment chamber has been under construction and was completed yesterday. You will be free to experiment with your power and the heirloom stone to see what more we can learn from you."

"Oh. Great." Silently, Ridley added, *I've always wanted to be able to teach people things so they can use them to kill the rest of my kind.* Out loud, she asked, "What's the bad news?"

"Well, at this point it seems you are unfortunately no different from the other elementals. Your magic is no different, even though you are an heir. So there is no sense in keeping you around. Mr. Davenport has allowed me to run a few more experiments, mostly involving the heirloom stone, but if there is nothing to be gained, then we will dispose of you. He says you are more trouble than you're worth."

"Dispose of me." Fear dragged an icy finger up Ridley's spine. "Yeah, that—that is bad news. But ... how do you know I'm no different? Does that mean ..." Ridley shook her head. "Wait, is Lilah—did she ..."

"Lilah Davenport is dying," Doc said.

An odd ache sucked Ridley's breath away. She and Lilah may have disliked one another for many years—even hated each other at times—but Ridley had never wanted her *dead*. She repeated the words in her head—*Lilah Davenport is dying*—but they sounded a little ridiculous. Lilah wasn't the sort of person to simply ... die. None of the Davenports were. If there was an obstacle in their way, it had no choice but to move. Plain and simple. It seemed as though death shouldn't be any different.

"But she was fine last night," Ridley argued.

Doc frowned. "Last night?"

"Yes, she ... she was here, wasn't she? You were here too. Or ... did I dream that?"

Doc's frown remained in place. "The sedative is strong.

She should not have been able to wake you, and you should not remember if she did." He shook his head. "Not that it matters. She may have seemed fine last night, but she is dying now. Slower than the others, but the same symptoms. The magic is visible just beneath her skin. She cannot pull it back within herself. Soon it will consume her."

Ridley stared at him. The detached manner in which he listed Lilah's symptoms made her shiver. "Can ... can I see her?"

"No. You cannot see her. One of my colleagues will bring you some food soon and move you to the containment chamber. You will wait there until the arxium is gone from your system, and then you can begin experimenting."

Lilah was dying. She was *dying*. Ridley couldn't quite wrap her mind around the concept. Guilt crept in at the edge of her mind. It was *her* magic that was killing Lilah. It wasn't her fault Lilah had used the serum on herself, but she still felt some sense of responsibility.

She thought of Archer, and the ache in her chest intensified. He loved his sister. Though his family wanted nothing to do with him now, he would hear of Lilah's death soon enough. Would he ever know what had really killed her? If Ridley ever saw him again—if she ever managed to get herself out of here—would she be able to tell him? *My magic killed your sister.* Even in her head, the words were difficult to formulate.

Doc turned and strode toward the door, commpad in hand.

"Oh, wait," Ridley said. "What about the stone? I need it

so I can test things out."

He let out a single laugh through his nose. "I'm not going to leave it with you *now*. It will remain locked up with all our important samples until you're safely within the containment chamber and ready to use it." He shook his head, laughing to himself as he left the room.

Well. So much for ending up alone with her mother's stone so she could heal herself and get out of here. She'd have to figure something out once she was inside the containment chamber. Doc would probably flood it with arxium gas once he decided they were finished experimenting, forcing her to return to human form. She would have until then to figure out just how powerful she could be. She would explode her way out of there if she had to. Or burn the place down like she did last time. She had no idea how this containment chamber was supposed to be able to *contain* her—presumably Alastair Davenport would have put every possible precaution in place—but she would test it to its absolute limits.

Doc's colleague, the woman in the lab coat and gas mask, walked into the room—minus the mask this time. Except ... it wasn't the same woman. It was—

"Christa," Ridley said, so shocked to see the woman who'd given her up to the Shadow Society that her voice lacked all emotion. A moment later, an appropriate amount of rage boiled its way to the surface. "You!" she hissed as Christa disappeared from view behind the bed. "Wow. You know what? I'm not surprised. You were happy to leave us for dead, so I should have guessed you'd be happy to experiment on us as well."

"Yep," Christa said quietly. "That's exactly right." Something clicked loudly behind the bed, and then Christa wheeled it toward the door.

"You are one serious piece of work," Ridley told her as she strained against the straps securing her wrists to the bed. She wasn't sure what she wanted to do with her fists, exactly, but she couldn't stand being so helpless while Christa wheeled her toward her fate. Everything inside her screamed to fight back. "You pretend to help people who just want to live a quiet life the way they used to before magic was banned, and all the while you're secretly in league with the Shadow Society."

"Will you shut the hell up?" Christa whispered. They were out in the hallway now. "I'm trying to get you out of here."

"Oh, sure you are."

"You know, Ridley, your survival instinct is impressive. I have to admit, I was surprised to see you alive."

"No thanks to you."

Christa steered the bed around a corner. "It wasn't personal," she said quietly.

"It sure felt personal when I woke up on the wrong side of the wall with a bunch of Shadow Society members trying to kill me."

"I did what I had to do to protect the people in my bunker."

"*I* was one of those people, Christa. As were Callie and Malachi and my dad. And however many other people you've handed over to the Shadow Society."

The bed stopped in front of an elevator. Christa stepped around it and jabbed the button on the wall. She crossed her arms, saying nothing.

"So you're ignoring me now?" Ridley demanded. Christa looked up toward a corner of the ceiling. Ridley followed her gaze. Was that a camera? Christa's eyes slid to Ridley, then returned to the elevator doors. She continued staring in silence. Ridley continued seething.

*Ping.* The elevator opened. Christa pushed the bed inside, then squeezed around it to press the button for the fifth floor. The doors slid shut. Christa turned immediately to face Ridley. "Can you at least *try* to imagine the impossible situation I found myself in before you judge me too harshly?" she snapped. "Alastair Davenport discovered the bunker. He threatened to reveal us all unless I swore to hand over any elementals who happened to cross my path. So yes, I gave up a few to save the rest of us. There aren't that many of you elementals, so I knew I wouldn't be sentencing *too* many to their deaths. I know that doesn't make it any better, but that's how I managed to sleep at night: Knowing I was responsible for the death of only a handful of people instead of the dozens and dozens who just wanted to live in peace beneath the city, using magic the way we should all be allowed to use it. Right and wrong isn't always as easy as black and white, Ridley. Sometimes there's no right answer, just two wrongs with you stuck in the middle trying to choose the wrong that sucks less."

Ridley stared at her. She was seething less now. In fact, the seething was almost gone, replaced by a hollow hopelessness. She could never condone the choice Christa had made, but the alternative was unimaginable too. If Alastair Davenport had revealed the bunker, everyone living within it would have been sentenced to death. It was indeed an impossible choice. "I guess that does suck," she said quietly.

*Ping.* The elevator doors reopened. Christa pushed the bed into the corridor.

"Are you really getting me out of here?" Ridley asked.

"That's the plan. Couldn't very well leave you to die a third time."

"Thanks. I'm feeling the love."

"Look, you probably find this difficult to believe, but I do actually care. I gave you as little sedative and arxium as I could without that monster of a doctor figuring out I was messing with things, and now—"

"You did? When? Oh, wait, was that *you* in the gas mask? Doc was laughing at you because he thought you were afraid of me."

"I was wearing the mask," Christa grumbled, "so you wouldn't recognize me and reveal that we knew each other. I was hoping to avoid you altogether until breaking you out, but Doctor Schulze asked me to come in and change the IV bag. I was aware I looked like an utter idiot, but I figured it was necessary." She rammed the bed into a door, which swung open to reveal a storeroom. Shelves on either side were lined with lab equipment and jars and bottles of whatever reagents were necessary for Doc's research. Between the shelves was a gap *just* wide enough to accommodate the bed. The door swung shut behind them.

"Are you sure there's no camera watching us right now?"

Ridley asked as Christa began to undo the buckles that secured the straps around her wrists.

"There's one at the other end of the corridor out there," Christa said, "but it's angled so it can't quite see this door. We should be fine. And there aren't that many people who work here anyway." She moved to the straps around Ridley's ankles.

With her arms free, Ridley was finally, *finally* able to sit up properly and twist her upper body from side to side. She stretched her arms above her and asked, "How'd you end up here?"

"Well, as you might be aware because you're probably the one responsible for this, I was thrown out of my own home by my own friends. I didn't have much left to lose, so I figured it was time to get rid of Alastair Davenport and his Shadow Society friends for good." Christa tugged the straps away from Ridley's feet, and Ridley pulled her knees up to her chest, still turning her body this way and that to relieve the stiffness in her muscles. "Here, put this on." Christa tossed a lab coat at her. "Once you've changed into your clothes, I mean." She retrieved a pile of neatly folded clothes from the back of a shelf, and Ridley recognized the jacket Dad had conjured. Her sneakers sat on top.

"I managed to get some information from one of the lab techs who escaped their last experimentation facility," Christa continued. "A building in the wastelands that was burned down."

"Oh, yeah, that was me."

Christa gave Ridley an appraising look. "Nice. Well done."

Ridley eased herself off the bed, unsure if she could trust her legs to properly hold her up. Turned out it was her head she should have been worried about. Everything went white for several moments. She blinked, holding tightly to the edge of the bed. "Definitely been lying down for too long," she muttered.

"Oh, this is also for you," Christa said. As Ridley's vision cleared, she saw Christa lifting a tray from one of the shelves and placing it on the bed. On it sat a sandwich, an apple, and a glass of juice.

"Real fruit?" Ridley said. "They treat their prisoners well here."

"I may have swiped the apple from Doc's section of the fridge in the tea room," Christa admitted with a self-satisfied smile. "We'll be gone by the time he notices."

"Thanks." Ridley took a large bite of the sandwich and reached for the pile of clothes. Christa turned her back as Ridley began changing.

"Anyway, the lab tech lady was too frightened to continue working for Davenport," Christa continued, "but he wasn't about to give her the option to step away. Not after everything she'd seen. I offered to help her disappear—something I've helped numerous people with over the years—in exchange for information. You may have burned down one building, but I knew they'd just set up shop somewhere else. I figured if I could get myself on the inside, I could learn as many names as possible and start picking them off one by one. I managed to convince Doc that his other lab technician had run away and that I already knew everything she'd been working on and was just as excited about it as he was. He's so damn besotted with his research. Not to mention egotistical. I basically *begged* for the honor of working alongside him as he makes groundbreaking discoveries that will change the world, blah blah blah. It was easy after that. I've been here a week now. Just have to make sure to avoid Davenport when he visits."

"And have you discovered anything useful?" Ridley asked. "Learned any names?" She finished pulling her shoes on and took another bite of the sandwich. Her stomach protested— *thanks, arxium*—and she almost gagged. But a deep breath helped her recover, and she forced herself to keep chewing. She'd been fed through a needle in her arm for days now, and she wasn't sure how long that would keep her going once she got out of here.

"A few," Christa answered. "I'm hatching plans to deal with those people. Hey, are you okay? Sounds like you're about to lose your lunch."

Ridley forced herself to swallow. "Yeah. All good."

"Ready to go then?" She turned back to face Ridley.

"Yes, but there's something I need to get before we leave."

Christa's eyebrows climbed. "Don't be stupid. We need to get out of here before someone discovers what I've done and kills us both."

"There's a magical item—a stone—that is extremely important. I *need* it."

"The heirloom thing?"

"Yes. Right, sorry, you know all about Doc's research so

obviously you know about this."

"I do, but I don't know where he's keeping it, and it's too dangerous to try to find it."

"But it could change everything! Seriously, Christa. If there are even fewer elementals than there were before, then I need as much power as I can get to burn through all the arxium protecting this city." She reached for the glass of juice and added, "That stone will make a difference. You know it will."

"You're going to try that stunt again?" Christa asked doubtfully. "It already failed once."

Ridley took a swig of the juice and shuddered at the sweetness. She swallowed and said, "It's not a stunt. It's a revolution. We're changing the world."

"Look, I don't know anything about this 'revolution' other than what happened two days ago when there was that huge storm and all the earthquakes and you were brought here, but I don't think the heirloom stone is going to help you."

"Christa, it doesn't matter what you think." Ridley forced herself to take another few sips of juice before returning the glass to the tray. "There are way bigger things going on than you know about, and I need that stone to be able to do my part."

"Fine. *Fine.*" Christa took a deep breath. "Doc's busy in the basement lab for at least another hour because he expects it'll be that long before the arxium's out of your system. So I guess we can take a few minutes to try to find this thing."

"Great. He said something about it being locked up with the other important samples. Do you know where that might be?"

"Fortunately this is a small facility, so there's only one place where samples are stored. I'll need to get Doc's spare access card from his office. I'll find the stone and then return here. If I'm not back in ten minutes, stay hidden until you can use your magic and then get the hell out of here."

"But I'll still need to get the—"

"Seriously, Ridley!" Christa hissed furiously. "If I blow my cover for you *and* you wind up dead, I will be extremely pissed off. So many people have died because of me. I will not let you add yourself to that number. You *will* get out here alive, so sit back down and don't do anything stupid."

Ridley leaned back against the edge of the bed, too surprised to say a word.

"Thank you," Christa finished. She squeezed around the other side of the bed, almost knocking a few glass beakers off the shelf. She opened the door.

And there stood Doc, his hand outstretched as if he'd been reaching for the handle. He looked up from the commscreen in his other hand. The device slipped from his fingers and hit the floor with a *thwack*.

"Crap," Ridley said.

# CHAPTER 22

DOC STEPPED BACKWARD, grabbing what looked like a two-way radio device from his pocket. "I need backup on the—"

Christa swiped the nearest object—a brown glass jar full of a powdered substance—and hurled it at Doc's face before he could finish speaking. He cried out as his head jerked backward. The jar hit the floor and shattered as Doc staggered to the side and fell. He groaned and cursed as he slowly found his way onto his hands and knees. Christa kicked him, and Ridley, who couldn't figure out why Christa wasn't using magic, pulled shakily at the air. She rolled the wisps of magic into a ball between her palms.

"Christa, get back!" she shouted. Christa gave Doc one more good kick before stumbling out of the way. As Ridley pulled her hands back, magic glowing between them, Doc sat up with another groan. His eyes met hers for an instant. Then she threw the magic. It struck his forehead, knocking him out instantly. She stared at him, breathing heavily.

"Thanks," Christa gasped. "I can't pull magic. Had to get an AI2 under my skin before coming to work here. I knew he'd check." She crouched down, stuck her hand into Doc's shirt pocket, and removed a slim, silver card with his face on it. Then she patted his remaining pockets. "Just checking he doesn't have it on him." She straightened. "Come on, let's find this stupid stone and get out of here."

"Sounds like he called security or something before we knocked him out," Ridley said as they hurried along the corridor.

"Yep. Part of me was hoping I might actually break you out of here without anyone knowing it was me, but that plan's gone down the drain now."

"Sorry, but I don't think that was ever likely to work out."

"Yeah, you're probably right."

They took the stairs back down one floor and stopped in front of a door with a silver panel secured to the wall beside it. Christa slapped Doc's access card over the panel, and with a beep, the door opened. Ridley peered inside at the rows of fridges, chest freezers, and more shelves. "You stay here," Christa said, "just inside the doorway. Pull some magic so you're ready in case someone shows up. I'll find the stone."

Ridley leaned her shaky body against the doorframe as her fingers scraped at the air, pulling magic from it. She wished she'd swallowed a little more of that sugary drink. She could do with the energy boost. Once she had her mother's stone, though, she could draw power from it and—

"It's not here," Christa said, startling her.

Ridley pushed away from the doorframe. "Are—are you sure? It's in—"

"This box?" Christa held the familiar box up. "I know. It's empty."

Ridley cursed. "Maybe it's ... um ... what lab did you say Doc was in? The basement?"

"Ridley." Christa dropped the box and shook Ridley's shoulders. "You can't currently use your own magic to disappear, and there are people with weapons on their way up here right now. Are you willing to die to get hold of this magical stone? Because that's what's going to happen. They will catch you, and after Doc's finished all his experiments and fun, he will kill you. And since I'll be dead too, I won't be able to get rid of any Shadow Society assholes. All of this will be a big waste."

Ridley shoved Christa's arms away. "If you don't stop shaking me I'm going to throw up on you. And how about—"

A loud spraying sound came from somewhere above her head. Ridley's gaze shot up. Equally spaced along the length of the corridor ceiling were what looked like water sprinkler heads, the type generally attached to a fire alarm system. Except there was no fire, and it wasn't water that accompanied the spraying sound.

Ridley sucked in a breath and held it as Christa groaned. "*That's* what I forgot to grab from the storeroom after Doc found us. A gas mask for you." She gripped Ridley's arm and pulled her sideways and around a corner. "We don't have time for a traditional exit. This place will be flooded with arxium gas within minutes."

They turned into yet another passageway, and straight

ahead was the answer to one of the questions Doc had refused to entertain. Through a window, Ridley could see rows and rows of fruit tress, and beyond that, buildings and skyscrapers. They were at the very edge of the city.

"Break it," Christa said as they ran toward the window, which Ridley could already see wasn't the type that was meant to be opened. With her lungs beginning to beg for oxygen, she hastily grabbed magic from the air. A conjuration wasn't necessary. The force of raw magic would do the trick, just as it had knocked out Doc. She threw it forward—and it shattered the entire window pane.

They stopped right in front of it, and Ridley stuck her head out to take a deep lungful of fresh air. She looked down—and gulped another breath of surprise. "This facility is inside the *wall*? Like, the actual city wall?"

"Yes. Okay, now I have a two conjurations in mind that can get us down to the ground without broken necks. First, you'll need to create—"

She swung her head back around at the sound of footsteps. Ridley did the same, coughing as she breathed in some of the arxium filling up the interior space. "No time," she wheezed.

A man in a lab coat rounded the corner and shouted, "I found them!" just as Ridley forced her magic outward. It was almost impossible, and the few bites of sandwich sitting in her stomach *definitely* wanted to make a reappearance, but she managed to become air and wrap herself around Christa. She almost lost hold of the form—she even saw herself flicker in and out of view—but they were up and over the jagged edge of the broken window—then falling and visible with Christa letting out a yelp—then soaring on the breeze again—then dropping, dropping—

Ridley landed with an *oomph* that knocked all the air from her chest and sent pain radiating along one side of her body. Beside her, Christa groaned and coughed. "Need to move," Ridley gasped. They were far too close to the wall and the broken window and whoever might be leaning out of it, possibly aiming a weapon at them. She didn't bother rolling over to take a look, struggling instead to use her magic again. *Come on, I'm supposed to be super powerful! I'm a freaking* heir, *for goodness' sake!*

Then she was invisible again, wrapping around Christa and speeding away, silently screaming at herself to go, go go, *just a little further, just a little further*, until she absolutely could not anymore.

She found herself on the ground surrounded by trees, and this time, she did throw up. Christa crawled a few feet away and leaned against a tree trunk as Ridley's stomach emptied itself. When there was nothing left, she wiped the lab coat sleeve across her mouth, then shuffled on hands and knees to the tree across from the one Christa sat beneath.

"Thanks," Christa said. "I was a little afraid we might break our necks after all, but you did well, given the circumstances."

Ridley nodded slowly. "Wasn't much other option. Figured we were dead if we stayed there. My dad taught me some conjurations that could have shielded us from their attack, but it would have taken too long to pull magic and then do them.

It was better to just get out."

"I agree."

Ridley filled her lungs with air, then exhaled slowly. She looked through the trees back the way they'd come. "How exactly was that special containment chamber supposed to keep me from getting out? Doc had to know that once I could use my own magic—and if I had the stone as well—I would eventually burn or break my way out."

Christa sighed. "The containment chamber is underground, beneath the city wall. It's reinforced with multiple layers of arxium and concrete. Doc figured you'd attempt to burn your way out, but he hoped that before you managed to get through all the layers, you'd either run out of power, or his arxium gas would incapacitate you."

Ridley shut her eyes for a moment, exhaustion washing over her at the mere thought of battling her way out of something like that. She was relieved she hadn't been forced to try. She looked up at the leafy branches that formed a canopy overhead. Whatever fruit grew on these trees had already been picked this season and had probably found its way by now into Lumina City's wealthiest homes and most expensive restaurants. "Do you think they'll search the area for us?" she asked.

"As far as they know, you're able to use your magic and we could be anywhere by now, so they probably won't bother. They wouldn't know where to start." Christa straightened and looked around. "I suppose Davenport might insist they search nearby, just in case you weren't able to get far, so we should keep an eye out. But I think we're probably okay."

Ridley tilted her head back against the tree. "It shouldn't be too long before my system is arxium-free. Then I can get us away from here. I can take you to … I don't know, wherever it is you're living these days. Not the bunker, I assume."

"Not the bunker," Christa answered shortly. She didn't add 'Thanks to you,' which was probably what she was thinking.

"It's still a secret, right?" Ridley asked, only thinking now of the implications of the deal Christa had struck with Alastair Davenport. If Christa was no longer there to notify him of any elementals who crossed her path, he had no reason to keep the bunker's existence hidden.

"I haven't seen anything about it in the news," Christa said, "so I assume it's still a secret. I'm willing to bet Davenport has made himself known to whoever's in charge now, and that unlucky person is stuck with the same bargain I was stuck with." She looked at Ridley. "We should stick together. Help me get rid of them. I know some of the members now, and we can—"

Ridley cut Christa off with a weak laugh. "Are you serious? You handed me over to them. *Twice.* And now you want me to trust you and work with you?"

Christa heaved a sigh. "You know I had no choice. I never *wanted* to give you to them."

"I suppose you did do me the courtesy of dressing my unconscious body in a jacket," Ridley added with sarcasm. "All should be forgiven, right?"

"Yes, well," Christa said stiffly. "You seemed a little … *in-*

*decent* lying in that hotel corridor in nothing but your pajamas. I know it doesn't make up for anything, but I figured I'd at lease cover you in a jacket."

"Thanks. Much appreciated."

"Look, Ridley, we're on the same side. We want the same thing: to get rid of the Shadow Society. We can go our separate ways, which means we probably have less chance of succeeding, or we can work together. I'm not an elemental, so I can't do all the things you can do, but I've discovered things that can help."

"Such as?"

"Well, for a start, Alastair Davenport never goes anywhere unprotected. And I don't mean bodyguards—although he does often have several of those hanging around. I mean clothing with arxium cufflinks and buttons, and tiny little devices sewn into collars that he can press to release small amounts of arxium gas."

It took Ridley a moment to figure out that Christa wasn't joking. "Are you serious? He's that paranoid?"

"Yes. So if you're planning to swoop down and wrap an element around him, like a solid chunk of earth to suffocate him, that won't work."

Ridley frowned. "That hadn't even crossed my mind. Perhaps because my mind doesn't generally lean toward killing people." Her frown deepened. "But now that you mention it, I wonder why another elemental hasn't tried that already."

"Perhaps they have. Sadly, they would have failed. Or perhaps because, if elementals are even aware of the Shadow

Society, they don't know who's in it. You didn't know any of the members until recently, did you? I assume not, since you appeared to trust Archer Davenport."

Ridley examined Christa, her frown still in place. "So Archer came to you, proclaiming to be on our side, and all the while you knew his father headed up the Shadow Society. You knew Archer was also one of them."

"Well, Archer always seemed genuine, from what I could tell, so I never questioned him about the Shadow Society. It was possible he didn't know what his father was involved in. Unlikely, but possible. And I didn't want him asking how *I* knew about it, so ... saying nothing seemed easier."

"Of course. Let everyone keep their own secrets." Ridley sighed, knowing she was including herself in her next statement. "That's the way we do things."

"That's the way we've *done* things," Christa said, "but we both know where we stand now, so why not stick together?"

Ridley shook her head. "I'm grateful for your help. I honestly am. But I have friends in this city I trust far more than you. That's where I'm going when I'm ready to leave here."

# CHAPTER 23

RIDLEY FELT TRULY AWFUL by the time she arrived at the Lins' place. It was directly across the road from Kayne's Antiques, so she made sure not to reveal herself anywhere outside the building, just in case someone was monitoring her old home for any sign of her. After drifting past the Chinese takeout shop below the Lins' apartment—where Mr. Lin was behind the counter, taking an order—she floated up to one of the windows on the floor above and slipped inside.

Remembering what she'd told Saoirse about randomly showing up in people's homes, she moved through the apartment to the front door and released her magic. She slumped against the door and raised one fist to knock against it. Sure, it wasn't as polite as waiting on the *outside* of the door and knocking, but the Lins were like family. They would understand.

Her eyes slid shut as she waited. On the way here, she'd pushed her questioning thoughts out to the magic around her, but so far she'd found no one. She tried to keep her panic at bay. They couldn't *all* be dead, could they? No. Dad was somewhere in the city, and the city was full of arxium structures, so magic would have a hard time getting around everything to find him. That had to be the reason.

And Saorise, Nathan and all the others ... perhaps they were back at their mountain home by now, packing up and moving somewhere else. Maybe they were planning a second attempt at their revolution. Or maybe they'd given up. But they couldn't all be ... dead.

"Oh, Ridley!" Ridley's eyes sprang open as Mrs. Lin rushed out of the kitchen. She wrapped her skinny arms around Ridley. "Your father will be so relieved."

Ridley's heart leaped wildly. "Is he here?"

"He ... unfortunately not." Mrs. Lin stepped back. "He was, but he left."

"When?" Ridley swayed and put a hand out against the door to steady herself. "Why did he leave?"

"You look like you need to sit," Mrs. Lin said, taking Ridley's arm and guiding her into the kitchen and onto one of the chairs that sat around the small table. "Your father arrived late on Sunday afternoon, sometime after the shudders ended." She took a glass from the drying rack and filled it with cold water from the fridge. "By Monday morning—yesterday—he was gone. We assume he's looking for you."

Ridley accepted the glass of water. She took a sip, which turned into a gulp, and then another several gulps until the glass was almost empty. She hadn't realized how thirsty she was. "But," she said, taking a deep breath as she lowered the glass, "where would he go? How would he know where to begin looking for me?"

"He thinks the Shadow Society has you." Mrs. Lin took the glass and refilled it. "It's possible he's gone to confront Alastair Davenport, now that we're aware he's the director."

"He wouldn't be that stupid. He can't possibly think that would end well."

Mrs. Lin shook her head. "We don't know what he's thinking. He's desperate, Ridley. He said ... well, that the two of you didn't part on good terms the last time he saw you. He can't bear to think that those moments may be the last he ever shares with you."

Ridley placed the glass on the table and buried her face in her hands. "This is my fault. I was so upset. But ... I couldn't *not* be upset. And now ... ugh, what a mess."

"He told us about everything. The big plan to change our world. How something must have gone wrong, because everything suddenly stopped. But he couldn't contact anyone, so he couldn't find out what happened."

"So he has a commscreen with him? Do you have the number?"

"Yes, but I've tried contacting him and there's no response."

"Maybe ... maybe the battery died?" Ridley suggested, trying to keep her hopes up.

Mrs. Lin looked doubtful, but she said, "That could be it. Your father is a little on the scatterbrained side. He probably wouldn't notice if the device turned itself off unless he needed to use it himself."

"Yes, exactly." Ridley appreciated Mrs. Lin playing along,

even though she was fairly certain this was *not* the reason Dad wasn't replying.

"Can I get you anything else? Some food? I have a little more time before I need to join Bo downstairs. And I should probably tell you that—"

"Ridley?" The familiar voice sent Ridley's blood rushing through her veins. Without thinking about it, she was suddenly standing, looking toward the kitchen doorway.

"I should probably tell you that Shen returned," Mrs. Lin finished quietly.

Ridley was so surprised that all she could do was stare at him. It was Shen who moved first, striding toward her on long legs and wrapping her in a tight hug. Still, Ridley couldn't bring herself to unfreeze. Shen had lied. He'd murdered. He'd chased after her with a gun through the Wallace Academy library. Well, not *her* specifically, but that's what it had felt like. And yet ... he was so achingly familiar that she wanted to cry. He had been her friend for so long that this moment— him hugging her in his kitchen—was like coming home and finding that nothing had changed.

Except that things had changed. *Everything* had changed.

"I'm so sorry," Shen said, stepping back before Ridley managed to return the hug. "About everything. And I'm so happy you're safe. I wanted to tell you about all of this so many times. *So* many times, Rid. You're my oldest friend, and it was so, so hard having to keep it all from you."

She nodded, unable to meet his eyes now. Unable to find the right words to say. "I ... I understand."

"Do you?"

"I ... it's just ... so much has happened. So much is different now."

"I know." He let out a long sigh. "I know I couldn't explain things, but I wish you'd listened to me about Archer Davenport. You never should have trusted him."

Ridley's eyes shot up, ice freezing her veins in an instant. "Yeah? Well you never should have murdered an elemental."

The look on his face told her she may as well have slapped him. She wasn't even sure where the words had come from. They'd risen to her tongue without thought. Probably from that deep well of hurt buried within her. She shook her head, feeling sick and guilty. "I'm sorry. I'm so sorry. I didn't mean that."

"No, it's ... I deserved that. I ..." Shen turned away, pushing a hand through his straight, sticking-up hair. "I didn't know who it was. I didn't know he was an elemental. I mean, he was talking to *Archer Davenport*. And why was he visible? I was on that roof the whole time Archer and his sister were in your store, and that man was totally visible walking down the street, into the alley, peering through the window by your back door. If he was an elemental sneaking around, he should have been using his magic to make himself invisible. Why didn't he do that?"

Ridley frowned. She hadn't considered that before. Perhaps the man had traveled far using his magic and was tired, the way she used to be after too much magic use, before she'd learned to properly let go. It didn't matter. The fact that he was elemental didn't matter. It would have been just as much of a tragedy if Shen had killed a non-elemental man.

"I guess it makes no difference," Shen muttered, probably coming to the same conclusion as Ridley. "I've asked myself these questions over and over, but it doesn't change anything. I'm still left with all this guilt. I tried to outrun it, but it turns out that's not possible. I just have to live with it instead."

"And keep doing what you can to help us," Ridley said quietly. "Our revolution attempt failed, but that doesn't mean we won't try again. At least, I hope that's not what it means. I don't want our world to stay the way it is."

"Neither do I."

"Shen," Mrs. Lin said, removing a pile of containers from the fridge. "Please organize some lunch for Ridley and yourself. You can use up these leftovers from last night. I'm going downstairs. Stay out of trouble."

Shen's serious expression became a fraction less serious. "She says that every time now."

"For obvious reasons." Mrs. Lin pinned her stern gaze on him. Then she moved it to Ridley. "And Ridley," she added, "I know you're worried about your father, but please don't rush off on your own and do something silly. He wouldn't want that."

Ridley nodded. The last proper meal she'd had was at Mrs. Adams' place, and she couldn't remember the last sleep she'd had that wasn't drug-induced. She was feeling horrible enough that it didn't take much convincing to be responsible instead of reckless.

"Good," Mrs. Lin said, patting Shen's shoulder before she left the kitchen.

"Are your brothers around?" Ridley asked Shen. Based on how quiet the apartment was, she guessed the answer would be no.

"They're at school," Shen said. He opened one of the containers and investigated the contents.

"Oh, right. I'm having difficulty keeping up with the days of the week." Ridley lowered herself to the chair again. This was a little weird, she decided. Sitting in a kitchen having an everyday conversation with Shen, given everything that had happened recently and everything that was still unknown. Despite feeling crappy, there was definitely a part of her that wanted to race off and do ... *something*. "Um, when did you get back?" she asked. "Have you seen Meera?"

"Only a few days ago. And yes, I have seen Meera, although only from a distance. At the indoor rock wall, of all places."

"Oh, really?"

"I went by the sports center yesterday. Just to kind of ... watch from a distance. See who's still there." Shen removed two bowls from a cupboard. "Anyway, I saw Meera on the wall. Looks like she continued lessons without us."

"That's ... kind of funny," Ridley said with a small smile. "I didn't think she liked it that much."

"Yeah. I think ... maybe she's doing it because she misses us?"

"Maybe." Guilt added itself to the sick feeling in Ridley's stomach. "So you didn't speak to her?"

"No. I haven't figured out yet what to say."

"I, uh ... I tried to tell her everything."

Shen looked around at her, eyebrows climbing. "Everything?"

"Well, about me, at least. Although ... I think I mentioned you at one point. I was blurting out a lot of stuff, and I think one of the things I said was that you had to leave because of people like me. And then I showed her my magic."

"You *what*?"

"But she didn't give me a chance to say much after that. She didn't *want* to know any of it. Told me she wanted to stay out of it all, for her family's safety. Which I understand. Looking back ... I don't know. I thought telling her the truth was the right thing to do, but maybe it was just selfish."

"Okay, that's ..." Shen leaned against the counter. "Now I really don't know what to say to her."

Ridley pulled her shoulders up toward her ears, indicating she didn't really know either. "Maybe just acknowledge that you have secrets and ask if she wants to know them?"

"Yeah. Maybe."

Shen continued dishing food into two bowls. Ridley leaned her elbows on the table and asked, "Hey, uh, do you have an old commscreen or commpad I can use? Just to see if my dad will reply if I send him a message. I know it's unlikely, since he didn't respond to your mom, but I just want to try."

"We have all your old devices, remember? I think we have at least one commscreen that hasn't even been switched on since you gave it to us."

Ridley smiled. "Thank goodness for Wallace Academy

and their insistence on handing out new devices every year to us poor scholarship students."

They ate lunch together, Ridley trying to keep the conversation topics light, and Shen following her lead. They didn't mention the elemental man Shen had killed, or Lawrence Madson, or the Shadow Society, or Archer. They didn't speak of justice and whether Shen should have remained imprisoned for what he'd done. Mostly, they reminisced about old times, because that was easier.

Afterward, before Ridley fell asleep on the couch, she switched on the old commscreen Shen pulled out of a cupboard and sent a message to her father.

Dad, this is Ridley. Please let me know where you are.

# CHAPTER 24

RIDLEY BARELY STIRRED the entire afternoon. When she did wake up, the first thing she reached for was the commscreen. But there was no reply from her father.

"Feeling any better?" Shen asked as he walked into the living room with a pair of shoes in one hand.

"Much better. Thanks." Except for the fact that she could now clearly feel that sense of urgency again. That quiet insistence that she should be doing *something* instead of just sitting here.

"I'm heading out to do some food deliveries for my parents," Shen said. He sat on the end of the couch and pulled his shoes on. "Mom said you can go downstairs and get some dinner there. My brothers are already down there, doing homework. Or you can wait for me to get back and we can down together?"

"I'll wait for you." Ridley stood and stretched her arms up above her head. "I'm going out for a little bit too."

Shen paused while lacing one shoe and looked up with a frown. "You're doing what my mother asked you not to do?"

"No. I'm not rushing off to do something silly. I'm just going up into the air above your building to see if I can sense anyone. Dad or any other elementals. I think all the arxium in the city makes it difficult, but if someone's nearby, I might be able to find them. If I can't, then I'll come straight back inside."

"And if you do sense someone? Like, captured or something? Will you do something silly then?"

Ridley inhaled slowly before answering. "No. I'll come back for help. Someone reminded me recently that I don't have to do everything on my own. That I should trust others to help me."

"Sounds like a sensible someone."

"She is," Ridley said, her heart squeezing painfully at the reminder that she had no idea where Saoirse was or if she was okay.

"Okay, well I'll see you a bit later then." Shen gave her a casual wave before standing and moving to the door. It was such a familiar line, such a familiar gesture, that it felt for a moment as if the past few weeks had never happened. It was Shen's smile though, before he turned away, that reminded Ridley of everything that had changed. It was tight, strained, not the easy grin he'd so often given her in the past.

She pushed aside thoughts of Shen and the things he'd done that had wiped away that easy grin. There was nothing she could do to change any of it. She looked down at her hands as her magic become visible beneath her skin, pulsing through her veins before drifting upward in wisps. *I'm made of air*, she thought, and then she was invisible.

Within seconds, she was out of the window and soaring high above Shen's building, watching the city lights wink on as evening approached. She wasn't sure if it made much difference being up here as opposed to inside his apartment, but it *felt* different. She felt freer.

Her thoughts bounced in quick succession from one person to the next. No Dad, no Saoirse, no—Wait. Was that Malachi? She whirled around in the direction she'd felt his presence. Nathan too. *They're coming*, magic seemed to tell her. *They sense you too.*

She drifted downward, hope expanding inside her as she returned to Shen's living room. Nathan and Malachi were close enough now to follow. They would find her. It was safer in here than out on the roof where nosy neighbors or drones— or someone spying on Ridley's home across the street—might see them.

She resumed human form. She held her breath, looking around the room, hoping she hadn't imagined that Nathan and Malachi were nearby. After another few heartbeats, they stepped out of the air.

"Ridley!" Malachi embraced her immediately. Behind him, Nathan's eyes took in the room before settling on Ridley.

"Are we safe here? Is this your home? If Archer knows where you live, then the Shadow Society probably knows—"

"This place belongs to friends. *Trusted* friends. They've known about elementals far longer than I have." Ridley stepped out of Malachi's embrace. "Where are the others?

What happened out there?"

"What happened to *you*?" Nathan asked, moving closer. Ridley was relieved he didn't try to hug her as well. She didn't feel they were quite on hugging terms.

"I—it doesn't matter now. I was caught and then freed, and then I tried burning the panels after you started the earthquakes, but I was caught again and now I'm free again. But what about you? Where's everyone else? Please don't tell me they're all ..."

"Dead? Not all of them." Nathan's brow creased. "We started this with almost three dozen, and now eleven are missing. We don't know for sure who's dead or who ... I don't know, maybe got swept away and injured or something. The rest of us managed to sense one another and congregate further out. Then we traveled even further away. But Malachi and I decided to come back." He scrubbed his hands through his hair. "We're not done with this, even though everyone else is too scared. They don't want to try again. They're convinced we'll fail. There was ... I don't know what to call it, Ridley. *Something.* Some strange magical force. It just ... it didn't make sense. Something I've never experienced before."

"Man-made elementals," Ridley said. "I guess you wouldn't have figured that out if you only felt the effects of their magic and didn't see them change form."

For several moments, Nathan and Malachi simply started at her. Then Malachi said, "Wait ... did you say *man-made elementals*?"

Ridley told them everything she'd learned since waking

up strapped to a hospital bed in a secret research facility. "So Alastair Davenport must have given this serum to a bunch of people and sent them out to find us and fight us off—"

"Knowing they'd all die because of it," Malachi muttered with a shake of his head. "I mean, it's great that there are less of them now, but what kind of person does that?"

"The kind of person who's been killing our kind for years," Nathan said quietly. He slowly lowered himself to the couch, his head in his hands. "This is crazy. He *made* his own elementals. I never would have thought it possible."

"He was hoping my blood would make a difference to the serum he's concocted, since I'm supposed to be different and super-powered and all of that, but it didn't really. It makes his man-made elementals last several days before dying instead of one day, that's all."

Nathan rubbed his hands over his face. "I don't know what this means for us. If we try again, will we fail in the same way? Surely he's going to run out of people to send after us if they keep dying."

"He called them 'willing volunteers,'" Ridley said. "If that's true, then I'm sure he's going to run out of them quickly."

Nathan nodded. "Yes. Hopefully. I don't know. We just need to think. There has to be a way for us to do this and succeed. Magic isn't bad, and it doesn't want to be smothered and riled up. It's on our side. I know we can do this."

"If it's on our side," Ridley said slowly, frowning as something occurred to her, "then why did it help them? They're not real elementals. They don't want to preserve magic or make the world a better place. Magic *knows* that. But they must have reached out with their thoughts in order to find all of you, right? And magic must have responded."

"I thought we could only do that with people we already know," Malachi said. "Otherwise how do you communicate to the magic who you're looking for? You said the person who found you is someone you already know, so that makes sense."

"So then ... they couldn't have asked magic where you were?"

"They probably didn't have to," Nathan said. "We were attacking the wall and the ground just outside the wall. They already knew roughly where we were."

Ridley nodded. "Oh, I should have asked as soon as you got here: Is Saoirse with the group you left out in the wastelands?"

Nathan looked up. "No. I thought she might be with you."

Ridley shook her head. "She was, but we separated before I went up to start burning the panels. She was planning to go into the city to find my dad—to tell him I was okay—and then she was going to join the rest of you outside."

Nathan's expression grew troubled. "I haven't seen her since she left us to go and find you."

They were all quiet for a moment as the possibility that Saoirse hadn't made it sunk in.

"And your dad?" Malachi asked quietly.

Ridley shook her head again. "I don't know where he is. Somewhere within the city, I think, but I can't sense him. I'm, uh ..." She swallowed. "Getting really worried."

"Planning to take off on your own again to find him?" Nathan asked, a hard edge to his tone.

Indignation burned immediately through Ridley's veins. "Planning to *forbid* me again?"

Silence filled the room for several moments. Malachi looked back and forth between the two of them. Then Nathan responded, his voice gentler now. "You can understand why I said that, can't you? I knew how important you were—still are—to our cause. I didn't want to lose you."

Ridley looked away, the heat of her anger vanishing as quickly as it had appeared. "Yes. I guess so. But I can't do *nothing*. Will you help me? Maybe we need to spread out across the city. Just ... I don't know, fly around until one of us gets close enough to sense him?"

"We could try that," Malachi said.

"Still might not work if he's being contained within arxium walls," Nathan said, "but yeah, we can try."

"Does now work for you?" Ridley asked. She felt she was being remarkably diplomatic when what she really wanted to do was shout, *Can we go right now PLEASE?*

Nathan stood. "It's not as though I've figured out how we're going to recruit a bunch more elementals to help us, so yes. Now works. Which part of the city—"

The front door flew open midway through Nathan's sentence. Shen stopped in the doorway, eyes widening at the sight of two strangers in his home. "They're friends!" Ridley said hastily. "Elementals."

"Uh, okay."

"You weren't gone very long," Ridley added. "Is something wrong?"

"Not *wrong*, exactly." Shen shut the door and strode toward her, his commscreen in one hand. "I just wanted to make sure you saw this." He thrust the device in front of her. On the screen, a video had been paused. She tapped to play it, watching the words scrolling on a red banner across the bottom of the screen: 'Breaking News: Linevale city wall destroyed by magical earthquake and fire originating in wastelands.'

"Holy freaking crap," Ridley whispered, vaguely aware that Nathan and Malachi were standing behind her, peering over her shoulders. On the screen, shaky footage taken from inside a building right on the edge of a city showed great cracks splitting their way through a wall. The video shook again as the earth shuddered. The wall began to come apart. Flames raced across the giant pieces of the wall as they fell, eating through them. Smoke filled the sky.

"This is Linevale," Shen said. "It happened this morning. Looks like most of their wall is gone."

Nathan swore quietly. "Linevale," Ridley repeated. It was one of the surviving cities on the west coast. She turned to face Nathan. "It's happening. They've done it. They've got rid of their arxium." The urgency that had been coursing through her since she woke up increased in intensity. Her magic felt restless, eager to act.

"We need to try again," Nathan said, voicing Ridley's thoughts. "As soon as possible. Before the Shadow Society does something to make it even harder. We need to get everyone back here. Hopefully the fact that another city has suc-ceeded will boost everyone's confidence."

"You think?" Malachi said doubtfully. "They were pretty damn terrified by the time we all found each other and start-ed counting the number of people we lost. They won't easily change their minds. We'll be lucky if a handful of them decide to come back with us."

"I can convince them," Nathan insisted. "Show them that it's possible. Last time, they didn't know whether it could be done. And they didn't know we had Ridley." He gave Ridley an apologetic look. "I ... I should have waited for Saoirse to return with you. I shouldn't have given up on you. I was ... too eager. I'm sorry."

Ridley's eyebrows climbed. Was Nathan actually apolo-gizing for something? She wasn't sure what to say to that, ex-cept perhaps apologize for sneaking off to find Archer.

"We have to try," Nathan said to Malachi before Ridley could formulate any words. "We need as many people as we can get."

"Yeah, Lumina City is like double the size of Linevale," Shen pointed out. "And you don't know how many elementals they had, but it was probably more than three."

"If we leave now," Nathan said, "we can probably be back here by morning. By that time, another city's wall may have fallen. We need to join the revolution. That story ..." He ges-tured at Shen's commscreen. "They're blaming this on the wild magic in the wastelands. But as we free more and more cities, it'll become obvious that this isn't a freak storm or a coincidence. Hopefully some small news channel will finally be brave enough to share the video I recorded and sent out."

"Honestly?" Malachi said. "You should just upload that thing to the social feeds right now and let it go viral."

Nathan hesitated. "I suppose I could ... But I'm not on any of those social things."

"And you can't just *let* something go viral," Ridley added. "We have no control over that."

"I'll post it," Malachi said with a shrug. "You can share it," he told Ridley. "Oh, wait, we can ask Callie to share it. She must have a large following from back when she used to make music. That should get things going."

"It'll take a hundred years to get a message to Callie out in the middle of nowhere," Ridley argued, "and then for her to get close enough to a signal to log into her social accounts." She looked at Nathan. "Sorry, but that recorded video thing was probably never a good idea. We need to just *do this*, and by the time it's over and all the arxium's burned and the wild magic finally calms down and the sun comes out—like *really* out, the way we haven't seen it in years—everyone will have their commscreens out, recording what's going on. And they'll probably be doing live video, not just recording. So that's when you stand up in the middle of a busy square somewhere and tell everyone what's going on. It'll be *everywhere* within minutes."

Nathan looked doubtful. "Everywhere? Really?"

"Ridley's right," Shen said. "Waiting to see something on the news is old school. People check social before they check anything else."

"That video we just watched about Linevale was on the news," Nathan pointed out.

"Yeah, and I saw it because someone shared it on one of the social feeds."

Malachi gave Nathan's shoulder a light punch and grinned. "Come on, man. You're not that old. Don't tell me you've forgotten how this stuff works."

Nathan narrowed his eyes. "Okay, fine. That's what we'll plan to do. And if I don't survive, then it'll be one of you who has to stand up in the middle of a busy square to tell everyone the truth."

The possibility of Nathan not surviving—of any of them not surviving—was enough to wipe the grin from Malachi's face.

"Well, we should get going," Nathan said to Malachi. "Ridley ..." he added, looking at her.

"My dad," she said quietly. She hadn't forgotten that they'd been about to go out and search the city for him when Shen showed up.

"Please don't try to find him on your own," Nathan said.

"What if I just do what we were going to do? It'll take me longer to cover the whole city on my own, but that's fine. I'll stay above the buildings and—"

"Above the buildings is where you were caught before," Nathan reminded her. "If Davenport is still creating elementals, you could be caught again."

Ridley paused, chewing on her lip. Nathan had a point. "So ... you want me to just wait?"

"We need you, Ridley. You know that. You can't risk yourself. And you never know, Maverick might be back here by the time we return. If he's looking for you, and if Saoirse is with him, they'll probably find their way here."

Ridley nodded, though she felt that was probably too much to hope for. "Okay. I'll wait."

Nathan looked at Malachi. "Time to go."

They disappeared, and Shen slipped his commscreen into his jeans pocket. "I need to go. I'm probably late for those deliveries now. We're still on for dinner when I get back?"

Ridley nodded, pasting on a smile that was far brighter than anything she felt inside. "Yes, definitely."

Shen pulled the door open, then hesitated and looked back. "You will be here when I get back, right?"

"I will," Ridley said. And she meant it.

But the door shut, and she was left alone in the semi-darkness with that sense of urgency nipping at her, and the prospect of sticking to her word seemed almost impossible. She switched on a lamp, sat on the couch, and reached for the old commscreen she'd been using earlier. With her knees pulled up to her chest, she scrolled through the social feeds, looking for any news of other cities' walls coming down. *We can do this*, she kept telling herself. *We can free Lumina City. We can change the world. We don't have to hide forever.*

But if anything had happened elsewhere in the world, it hadn't been shared online yet. Trying not to be discouraged, she tapped her way over to Meera's profile to see if her best friend had posted anything recently. Nothing except a link to a fundraiser event happening at the indoor sports center Meera was apparently a frequent visitor at these days.

Ridley looked at Lilah's profile next, but nothing had been posted in days. Was Lilah ... gone? Was there now a gaping hole in the universe where Delilah Davenport had once been? Guilt squeezed Ridley's insides tighter. *It's not my fault*, she tried to tell herself. She tried over and over, but the guilt wouldn't loosen its grip.

She was about to toss the commscreen across the couch when a notification popped up in the corner of the screen, sending her heart tripping over itself: *Archer Davenport is live now.*

# CHAPTER 25

RIDLEY'S GRIP TIGHTENED on the commscreen. "Archer Davenport is *what*?" she whispered, tapping on the notification before it disappeared. A moment later, Archer's face filled the screen. Ridley's heart jolted, then took off at a gallop. She almost dropped the device before reminding herself that he couldn't see her. This wasn't a video call. He didn't know she was watching. Well ... she didn't *think* he knew. Archer Davenport had so many followers and 'friends,' there were probably a hundred other people who'd tapped on that notification at the same moment she did—and more joining every second. There was no way he could keep track of everyone watching.

The video background was a plain cream wall, giving Ridley no clue as to where Archer was. He cleared his throat. Pushed his shoulders back. Swallowed. If not for everything that had happened in recent days, Ridley would have smiled. "You look far more confident when you don't even try," she would have told him. Except ... confident Archer was the one who could tell a great story. She didn't trust confident Archer. But this Archer? It was possible he might say something she actually wanted to hear.

"Hi," he said, then cleared his throat again. "My name is Archer Davenport. Some of you know me; some of you don't. I've never done anything particularly amazing, but people know who I am because I had the fortune—or misfortune, depending on how you look at things—of being born into an obscenely wealthy family. We throw lavish parties, we buy yachts and planes and private islands—or we did, before the Cataclysm—and we socialize with actors and singers and politicians. Apparently all these things make us celebrities too, though it really shouldn't." He let out a long, slow breath, beginning to look a little more relaxed now.

"The reason I mention this," he continued, "is because I'm hoping that by the time I'm finished talking, thousands of you will be watching. Thousands of you will know the truth. And you'll tell everyone you know, and they'll tell everyone they know, and soon the truth will be everywhere."

He paused, looked down, then focused on the camera again. "Our world is not what you think it is. You don't know that the magic outside our walls isn't the deadly power the government wants you to believe it is. You don't know that they're trying to keep you afraid, contained. You don't know about the machines buried in the ground outside every city, routinely spraying arxium gas into the air to stir up the magic in the wastelands. And you don't know about the people who are different from you." He took a deep breath just as Ridley held onto hers. "The people who are born with magic coursing through their bodies."

Ridley released her breath in a rush. He'd done it. He'd actually said it. Her gaze flicked to the bottom of the screen, where the number of viewers was going up and up and up.

"Let me say that again," Archer said, "just in case you missed it. *There are people in this world who are born with magic rushing through their veins.* They're called elementals. You don't know about them because they've lived in hiding for a very long time. Why? Because there is an organization of people known as the Shadow Society dedicated to wiping them out. They have always believed magic is unpredictable and deadly, and that a world with elementals is a dangerous one.

"It sounds crazy, I know," he added with a brief laugh and that half-smile she'd fallen in love with. "Like I'm telling you the plot of a superhero movie." His expression grew serious once more. "But this is all too real. And the reason I know this is because I've been on the inside. The *wrong* side. That secret organization of people who murder elementals and then tell themselves they're just doing their bit to keep the world safe?" He inhaled deeply. Ridley's arms tightened around her knees. "I was part of it."

Ridley's eyes ached with unshed tears. The pain hit her all over again. The pain of losing Mom. The pain of knowing that Archer had been involved, even in a small way. Her hand shook ever so slightly as she squeezed the commscreen a little tighter.

"I ... I've been responsible for people's deaths," Archer continued. "Not directly, but I was involved in—in devastating events, and that means my hands are just as blood-stained as everyone else's." There was the slightest tremor in his voice, and he had to swallow before continuing. "I'm sorry." He looked directly at the camera, and Ridley felt that he was looking at her. "I'm so, so sorry." She sucked in a trembling breath as the tears she could no longer hold back spilled onto her cheeks.

"I've lied," Archer said. "I've betrayed the trust that was given to me. I have deeply hurt people I care about. And I've learned that I was wrong. I've spent time with elementals over the past year. They're not dangerous or evil or soulless. No more than any other person who has the free will to choose the way they want to live their life and treat others. Their magic is ..." He stared past the camera, shaking his head a little as if he couldn't find the right words. "It's *right*. It's beautiful. It's the most natural thing in the world for them to interact with the elements. To commune with magic. It's ..." He let out another breath of a laugh. "To be honest, I wish I was like them instead of like me. But I'm not. I've done terrible things, and I will never stop trying to make up for all the pain I've caused." He looked straight through the camera and into Ridley's soul. "I will never stop hoping for forgiveness."

Ridley unwrapped one arm from around her knees and wiped the tears from her cheeks. Within seconds, more tears fell to take their place.

"Why am I telling you all of this now?" Archer asked. "Because the world is about to change, and you need to know why. You deserve to know the truth. Others will tell you a different story. I know the people behind all this secrecy, and I know they'll try to keep controlling you with their lies. They'll try to keep you afraid. Of magic, of elementals, of *change*.

"So here's the truth of what's happening: Elementals want to return the world to the way it used to be, and they want to be able to safely live in it." Archer shrugged and smiled. "That isn't too much to ask for, is it? That isn't something to be *afraid* of. Remember when magic was part of our daily lives? Remember when it helped out with everyday tasks, and when certain medical procedures were quick and easy, and when art and dance and food were *literally* magical experiences? Remember when we didn't have to be afraid to leave our own city, and when we didn't have drones constantly flying overhead? Remember when a magical storm was a spectacular light show in the sky, and not something angry enough to rip through vehicles and buildings?"

Archer leaned forward, getting even closer to the camera. "Don't you want to live in that kind of world again? I do. Maybe it seems impossible to you, but it's not. We just have to get rid of our walls, our panel shields, our AI2s. And that stupid law that forbids us from using magic. Just think about that one for a moment. How can it be a *law* that we can't pull magic and use it when some people are *born* with magic inside them already? We've been told over and over that magic is too wild now, that it will kill us if we try to use it. And that's simply not true." Archer sat back and lifted one hand. Nerves tightened Ridley's stomach again. Was he really about to film himself performing a crime in front of thousands of—

Yes. Yes he was. Archer curled his fingers and dragged

them through the air, pulling bright, glowing wisps of magic from it. Soft blue light illuminated his face. He cupped both hands around the magic and did a quick conjuration, fingers flicking apart and then touching lightly together. His thumbs circled around one another to end the conjuration, and the magic fell from the air as droplets of water.

"See?" Archer said, looking at the camera again. "Not dead. Except for the fact that I just broke a death sentence-worthy law, so someone in authority will make sure I end up dead for what I just did." He shook his head. "Messed up world, right? That's why it needs to change. That's why it's *already* changing. You saw what happened in Linevale this morning, right? Same thing happened just an hour or two ago in a city on the other side of the world. It wasn't a freak storm or angry magic. It was intentional. It's the start of a new world."

He sucked in a deep breath and let it out in a rush. "So I guess that's it. I just wanted to make sure someone told you the truth before all the lies start spreading their way through the media." He leaned forward again, his hand reaching for the screen. Then he paused, and Ridley knew he was speaking to her when he said, "Be brave. This is the future we dreamed about. You're strong enough to make it happen." Then he tapped the screen and the video ended.

Ridley stared blankly at the device in her hand. Her mind was a jumbled confusion of emotions. The truth of her existence was out there. Thousands of people were aware of elementals now. Soon thousands more would know. Her immediate instinctive response was fear. But beneath that was relief. She had never wanted to hide forever. Hopefully now she wouldn't have to.

Well ... unless the Shadow Society remained intact. Archer hadn't mentioned any names. Ridley didn't think she could really blame him for that. The director was his father, after all, and she didn't think she could give up her own father, even if she knew he'd done terrible things. But if no one knew who was part of this secret organization, they would probably—as Tanika had said—continue to quietly get rid of elementals.

*One step at a time,* Ridley reminded herself. *Free the cities first. Then worry about the Shadow Society.* Archer had done a great job at making sure everyone would understand what was going on when all the arxium protection came down. Now Ridley had to focus on making sure it actually happened and that his father didn't somehow put a stop to it.

She switched the lamp off, lay down on the couch, and pulled the blanket she'd used earlier up to her chin. With her face turned away from the door, Shen would hopefully think she was asleep when he got back. Perhaps she *would* be asleep. Either way, she didn't really want to talk to him. Her mind was full of everything Archer had said, and that was the way she wanted to keep things: inside her head and wrapped around her heart.

He'd spoken to the public, but so much of it had been for her. She didn't want to rehash it out loud with Shen. She didn't want to argue about whether she'd been right to trust Archer or not. She *had* been right. She knew it with everything inside her. He shouldn't have kept so many things from her, but he'd apologized again and again, and she believed every word he'd said tonight.

She wished he was here.

She squeezed her eyes shut, trying to deny the ache in her heart for him, but there it was. She desperately wished he was here. She wanted to feel his arms around her as she curled up against his chest and told him how sorry she was for not believing him sooner. How sorry she was for holding her mother's death against him. From the moment he'd admitted the truth about the Cataclysm, she had held him partly responsible. How grossly unfair of her. All he had done was trust his father and then live with the crushing guilt ever since. How cruel of her to make him feel even worse.

Perhaps she was tired out from all her tears, but it didn't take too many replays of Archer's speech before Ridley drifted off to sleep. She didn't hear Shen or the rest of his family come home. She slept solidly until the noise of Shen's brothers getting ready for school the next morning reached into her dreams and pulled her out. She rubbed her eyes and focused on the window where weak morning light was trying to filter through the curtain.

She reached for the commscreen on the coffee table and turned it over. Adrenaline jolted her awake at the sight of a message from Dad.

Or at least ... from the number Dad was using.

Ridley, this is Alastair Davenport. I have your father. And your grandfather. If Lumina City falls to the elementals, they're both dead. Let me know when you've made your choice.

Ridley sat up, staring at the message, breathing hard. She read it several times, but that didn't make the contents any better. If anything, she felt sicker each time she read it. How did he have Grandpa as well? What was Grandpa even doing here? He was supposed to be far from Lumina City. In fact, as far as Alastair Davenport and most other people were concerned, Grandpa was already dead.

*Let me know when you've made your choice.*

Her family or her city. That's what it came down to. If she didn't make sure her elemental friends backed off and left Lumina City alone, Alastair Davenport would kill Dad and Grandpa.

Ridley lowered the commscreen to the table and pushed both hands through her tangled hair. If she hadn't realized it before, it would have hit her squarely in the chest now: Dad and Grandpa were absolutely, one thousand percent her family. It made zero difference that she wasn't related to them by blood. She would do anything—*anything*—for them.

And Alastair Davenport knew that. He knew what her choice would be, just as Ridley had known since the moment she read the message. She squeezed her eyes shut against the dark, ugly picture of herself that took shape in her mind. She had raged across the wastelands after she'd learned her true heritage, her storm self coming apart as she realized she had no idea who she truly was. But the answer was right here: She wasn't good or selfless. She didn't really want to help other people. All the tutoring and extramural activities she'd done so she could one day join The Rosman Foundation were for nothing. When it came down to it, she chose the small circle of people she loved over everyone else.

Lumina City's residents would remain afraid of the magic beyond their wall. Those living in the bunker would have to stay hidden. Any elementals living in the city would have to continue hiding who they were. *Nothing* would change for these people the way Archer had said it would. Even if the world changed everywhere else, Alastair Davenport would make sure his city remained firmly in his control. Because Ridley couldn't bear to give up the people she loved.

*Sometimes there's no right answer*, Christa had said. *Just two wrongs with you stuck in the middle trying to choose the wrong that sucks less.* Ridley dropped her head into her hands. She wished she'd never judged Christa for the impossible decision she'd had to make. Of course she chose the people she knew and cared about—the bunker's residents—over all the unknown elementals she was yet to meet. She had to live with her guilt, and now Ridley would—

She lowered her hands quickly as a swishing sound caught her attention. On the other side of the living room, the curtain stirred as a breeze moved through the open crack at the top of the window. "Nathan?" Ridley whispered.

He appeared a moment later, breathing heavily as if from

exertion. He leaned on the back of an armchair. "Okay, we did it. Got back here faster than I expected. Man, I'm tired. But we can rest when this is done." He sucked in a deep breath and let it out with a whoosh. "Only managed to convince six people to come back with us. Not a lot, I know, and on our own, we wouldn't stand a chance. But with you, I think we can do it. And we've already taken care of the arxium machines. There's no way they'll have rebuilt those yet. I don't know if you've noticed, but there's been no storm since we destroyed those machines. Yes, there are some unhappy looking clouds swirling around the panels over the city, but out there beyond the wall, things are starting to clear up. We've made a difference already, Ridley. Now we just need to finish what we ..." He trailed off, seeming to finally notice that something wasn't quite right. "Are you okay? Is something wrong?"

Ridley's insides had been winding tighter and tighter with every word Nathan spoke. *Don't tell him*, warned a tiny voice. *He'll make you choose the city over your family.* But she wasn't supposed to be acting on her own anymore. She was supposed to be *trusting* people to help her. At the very least, she had to tell Nathan she could no longer be part of his big plan.

"What is it?" Nathan asked.

*Tell him. Don't tell him.*

*Ask for help. Act alone.*

*Save the city. Save your family. If you don't, who will?*

Ridley pressed her eyelids shut. She saw Dad removing his wedding ring to show her that his AI2 was fused to it. She didn't know that he'd removed it from beneath his skin years ago. "I needed to know I could protect you if something ever happened," he'd told her. "So yes, I know how to use certain offensive conjurations." She saw him fighting on the balcony of a Lumina City skyscraper. She saw him hurling fireballs of magic at Shadow Society pursuers on the edge of the wastelands. She saw Grandpa sitting on the couch in their old apartment saying, "There are things I know. Certain conjurations. Old, dangerous ones that most historians believe were forgotten centuries ago." She saw Saoirse sitting on a couch in Mrs. Adams' apartment. "You can just about have a *conversation* with magic if that's what you want. You can ask it for things and it will understand you in a way it will never understand the rest of us."

"Ridley?" Nathan asked. Ridley opened her eyes as he stepped around the chair, concern growing on his face.

She stood, her hands clenched at her sides, her decision made.

# CHAPTER 26

RIDLEY STOOD AT THE VERY edge of Lumina City and craned her neck as she stared up at the interior surface of the arxium-reinforced wall. At least ten stories high, she'd thought most of it was solid, aside from the security infrastructure set up at certain points. However, as she'd recently discovered, the windows in this particular section of the wall belonged to Alastair Davenport's secret research facility. Ridley never would have guessed she'd be back so soon.

She tilted her head back even further and looked at the sky. The unhappy clouds Nathan had mentioned darkened and tumbled over one another and began to cry. Ridley opened her palm as rain showered over her. *Please don't leave me while I'm in there*, she begged. *Listen to me. There are windows and cracks and gaps. You'll find a way in and out.* A bolt of magic flashed straight down, struck the earth beside her, then rebounded and whizzed around her outstretched hand before vanishing. "Thanks," she whispered out loud, her chest swelling with gratitude. She wasn't alone. She felt it now as surely as she had when she'd been broken-hearted in the dark of her old home above Kayne's Antiques.

She faced forward, fitted a gas mask onto her wet face, and walked toward the door she'd been told to come to. Yes, there was an actual front door. She'd missed that when she and Christa tumbled out of a fourth floor window. Though her presence was no doubt already known by whoever was on the other side of that door, Ridley raised her fist and banged on the metal surface anyway.

Surprisingly, it was Alastair Davenport himself who opened the door. Ridley would have assumed he had security people or Mr. Knockoffs or other minions for things like that. No doubt they were lurking nearby, just in case Mr. Davenport needed something urgently. "Well," he said to Ridley. "I'm mildly disappointed. I thought you would at least attempt to sneak in using magic and try to get your family out of here before I could stop you."

Ridley glared at him, an expression he probably couldn't see but which made her feel slightly better. "This is what you asked for. You assured me they'd be dead if I tried something like that."

"True. But you don't have a particularly good track record of doing what I or my subordinates ask."

"I guess if you'd *started* by threatening my family, things might have worked out well for you sooner."

Alastair sighed. "Such a cliché. And yet it almost always has the desired effect." He tilted his head to the side. "I'm not sure why you bothered with the mask. You won't be leaving here unless you're happy for me to dispose of your father and grandfather—who, by the way, I was surprised to discover is still alive. I assume the story behind his fake death is an interesting one."

It was, but if Alastair didn't know it already, Ridley wasn't about to enlighten him. "I'm not taking the mask off," she told him.

"Then you're not coming inside. If you're keeping a gas mask on, then you're clearly not willing to hand yourself over, so there's no point. Our negotiation ends here."

"And if you're lying about having my father and grandfather?"

"You heard their voices when we spoke earlier. I have the commscreen your father was using. And clearly he's been missing long enough for you to be concerned about him, since you're here. But you're right. I could be lying. Your father could be ..." Alastair shrugged. "Missing somewhere else."

Ridley exhaled slowly. She knew this was probably how things were going to go down. But she'd figured she should at least show *some* resistance before walking straight inside. Grudgingly, she reached up and pulled the mask off her head, then dropped it on the ground at her feet. She hated how weak this simple action made her look.

"Good girl," Alastair said. He stood back and gestured politely for Ridley to come in. This time, the glare she gave him was entirely visible.

Almost drenched now from the rain, she stepped inside. The door creaked as it eased shut behind her. The entrance to this place was simply a hallway with a solid metal, full height turnstile up ahead. "How welcoming," Ridley muttered.

"As you're aware," Alastair said, placing his forefinger against the fingerprint scanner beside the turnstile, "this place isn't meant to be welcoming." He pushed Ridley ahead of him. She stumbled forward, catching hold of one of the metal bars as the turnstile swung forward, then clanged to a halt with her on the other side. A minion stood in front of her. He tapped a code onto the screen beside the fingerprint reader on this side. After a beep, Alastair scanned his fingerprint a second time and walked through. "This way," he said.

Another three muscular minions materialized from the shadows. Two fell into step ahead of Alastair, while two strode behind Ridley. "I hope we're on our way to your fabulous new containment chamber," Ridley said, "since that's where you're apparently keeping my father and grandfather."

"Think I was lying about that too?"

"There's a good chance you're lying about everything," Ridley said as they turned a corner and continued along the next passageway, "so I'd like to see for myself that they're okay, and then I'd like to see you let them go."

"It's touching that you have such strong feelings for people you're not even related to."

"Yeah, well, I think it's been established that I'm capable of far more *feelings* than you are. Your level of concern when you realized your own daughter had taken that useless serum of yours and was probably going to die wasn't exactly—"

"Do not talk to me about Lilah!" Alastair shouted, startling Ridley as he whirled around to face her, all composure shattered in a second. His dark eyes bored into hers. No one moved. Ridley held her breath, not daring to ask whether Lilah was dead yet or not. Her galloping heart pumped adrenaline through her body. She was prepared to let go of her magic and change to an elemental form at a second's notice.

Alastair inhaled, turned around, and continued forward. When he spoke again, it was in a level tone. "You are a menace. You and the rest of your kind. You have the sort of power no mortal should possess and you're using it to destroy what's left of our world. *That* is why people like you should not exist, and that is why I'm going to extraordinary means to rid the world of all of you. I may have had to make sacrifices along the way, but the final outcome will be worth it for everyone left behind."

"We're destroying the *arxium*," Ridley corrected, "not the world. Destroying the world is what *you* did."

Alastair stopped in front of a door and turned to face her. There was something like disbelief on his face and amazement in his voice when he said, "You still think you have the right to life."

Ridley almost said 'Of course I have that right,' but she figured that part was obvious. The part that confused her was that this man seemed to genuinely believe the opposite. It hurt in a way that didn't make sense, given how little she cared about his opinion. "Why shouldn't I?" she asked.

"I've known for some time that elemental fire burns through arxium, but I had no idea until you destroyed an entire building in the wastelands just how easy it was for you.

How effortlessly a single elemental could bring about such destruction. I thought our arxium provided us with a decent level of protection from people like you. But even if we reinforce every wall and floor and ceiling of our homes with arxium, you can still burn your way through and then vanish afterwards. Doesn't that seem wrong to you?"

"You can kill someone and then pay people to cover it up. Doesn't *that* seem wrong to you?" Ridley countered. "We all have a responsibility to be decent human beings, no matter what kind of power we have."

Alastair shook his head. "There is such a thing as too much power, Ridley, and I'm not the one who has it." He opened the door to reveal a room full of screens. Images across the wall displayed numerous scenes: the grassy area outside the entrance where Ridley had ben standing minutes ago, the wastelands on the other side of the wall, various laboratories and passageways, several rooms like the one Ridley had been kept in.

Alastair gestured for Ridley to walk in ahead of him. Her feet carried her forward as her eyes scanned every screen until she found the one showing two male figures. She rushed toward it, leaning closer to be sure the two figures were Dad and Grandpa. Relief flooded her body. Grandpa sat on a bench, while Dad paced back and forth in front of him. Even from the limited view the screen provided, Ridley could tell the room they were in was sizable. "So that's your containment chamber?"

"Yes." Alastair and two of his minions followed Ridley into the room. The other two remained outside. "They're both capable of pulling magic, given they don't have their AI2s anymore. The containment chamber seemed the safest place to put them."

"You think it will hold them?"

Alastair laughed. "It was built to contain someone like *you*. I think it can handle a couple of regular people. I thought they might have tried something by now, but clearly they've noticed the walls are made of arxium. They're sensible enough to know that any conjurations they throw around will rebound back on them."

"I want to talk to them," Ridley said immediately. "I want to know they're alive, and that this isn't some recording you're showing me."

"Of course. We'll be heading down there soon, since the containment chamber will become your new home once they're out. You and I just need to get a few details ironed out first."

"No. I want to speak to them first. You must have set things up so you can communicate with people in the chamber."

Alastair frowned. "You're not in a position to make demands, Ridley. You don't have the upper hand here. Stray from our agreement, and your father and grandfather will pay for it with their lives."

Ridley pressed her lips together, considering what to say next. "I believe you. And can you imagine the devastation my broken-hearted elemental self will wreak upon this place before you manage to restrain me? That's *if* you can restrain me. You might save your city by getting rid of me, but you won't be around to see it. You'll be dead too."

Alastair appeared to consider this. Then he approached the long, blank screen that ran the length of the wall beneath all the other screens. He touched it. It lit up, displaying numerous buttons and dials. He tapped one and said, "Maverick, I have someone here who'd like to speak to you."

Ridley's eyes shot immediately to the screen that showed Dad and Grandpa. Dad turned on the spot, looking up and around. "Who?" he asked, his voice issuing from somewhere above the screens.

Though Ridley's insides remained tightly wound, a weight lifted from her shoulders. Dad and Grandpa were okay. They would get out of here. They would survive. "It's me, Dad," she said, stepping closer.

On the screen, she watched Dad ball his hands into fists. "Ridley, dammit, you're not supposed to be here. What are you thinking? You should be—"

"Dad, I trust you," Ridley interrupted. "I trust you and Grandpa to take care of yourselves. You have to trust me too."

"I can't if you're—"

Alastair tapped the control screen again, cutting Dad off mid-sentence. "Well, there you have it. They're alive. Now, let's get a few things clear. If you haven't already told your elemental friends that Lumina City is not to be harmed, you'll have to get back out there and do that."

As Alastair detailed the time frame in which Ridley would need to make this happen, she looked down and did her best to block his voice out. Her fingers spread out at her sides. She didn't push her own magic outward—the minions would probably tackle her in an instant if she did—but she tried to sense the magic that existed in the air in this room. In the materials in between all the arxium in the walls. It didn't have to carry her message far. It just needed to be able to slip through the gaps beneath doors and around windows and get outside.

*Send the signal now*, she told magic. *So bright and big they can't possibly miss it.*

"What are you doing?" Alastair asked. "If you—"

"Nothing." Ridley relaxed her hands and looked up. Two of the screens—the one showing the entrance area and the one showing the wasteland side of the wall—flashed for a moment. A second later, thunder boomed overhead.

Alastair narrowed his eyes. "What did you do?"

"Me?" Ridley asked innocently. "You're aware there's still bad weather out there because of the panels over the city, right? Lightning and thunder are normal around here."

Alastair crossed his arms. "Have you told the rest of your accomplices that Lumina City is off limits?"

"Do you really think any of this is going to work?" Ridley asked. "So what if you lock me up and manage to keep my friends from attacking your wall? It's too late now. Cities are already being freed. Archer has told the world the truth. At some point, even if I'm not the one to do it, Lumina City will be free."

"That isn't going to make any difference," Alastair scoffed. "People don't want to know the truth, Ridley. It's too ... inconvenient. They've become used to the way we live now. They don't want to change."

"People like *you*, perhaps. The rest of us are certainly not happy with the way things are."

"And a small city here and there?" Alastair continued as if she hadn't interjected. "Ha. That means nothing. We'll get our arxium protection back in place soon enough, and the world will return to the way it should be. If not, then I suppose a particularly nasty storm or two might just have to wipe out those cities that no longer have any arxium protection. It'll be a good demonstration for the rest of the world. Show them Archer Davenport is a deluded brat and it's not safe out there after all. We have mobile arxium machines, so it won't be too hard to bring a number of them together and arrange a magical lashing out of the elements the likes of which have not been seen since the early days following the Cataclysm."

Ridley let out a disgusted huff of breath. "You would destroy whole cities all over again? You would kill thousands more people just to keep the rest under control?"

"To keep the rest *safe*, yes. I think you're already aware of the lengths I'll—"

A tremor shuddered through the floor and shook the screens on the wall. Ridley raised her arms to steady herself, her eyes flying to the screens again. Specifically, the one showing the wasteland side of the wall. Not one, but two great cracks raced through the ground toward them. The room shuddered again—more violently this time—and the screen blinked before going blank.

"What have you done?" Alastair demanded as he skidded sideways. He slapped a hand against the wall to stop himself from ramming into it.

"I guess I can't control my friends after all," Ridley said, excitement lighting her nerves on fire. So far, everything was happening the way it was supposed to. As crazy as it had all sounded when she and Nathan had put the plan together, it seemed it may actually be working.

"How disappointing," Alastair growled. "I honestly thought you'd choose your family, Ridley."

The two minions gripped her arms, and Ridley was impressed to see that one of them had produced a syringe already. She pushed her magic outward—*right* out—and it shoved them away from her. "I did choose my family," she said. "But then I remembered they're both far more badass than I am, and they don't actually need much help from me."

Her magic hadn't done as much as it would have if she'd had the time to roll it into a more concentrated ball, so the two men were up again already. *Air*, Ridley thought as her magic swirled around her, and she vanished in less than a heartbeat.

"Activate the standby subjects," Alastair was saying into his commscreen as one of the minions launched toward a button beside the door and slammed his palm over it. Nothing happened. "Why isn't it working?" Alastair barked at the minion. Ridley assumed there was supposed to be arxium gas filling the room now, but she wasn't about to stick around to see if the malfunction corrected itself. She soared toward the gap beneath the door—

—just as two gunshots sounded somewhere out in the passageway. Ridley hesitated, which was silly because, in her current form, arxium was far more of a threat to her than a gun.

The door flew open.

*Crack!* Down went the first minion. *Crack!* The second. And then *crack*! Alastair Davenport jerked backward, hit the wall, then slid to the floor.

# CHAPTER 27

RIDLEY WAS SO SHOCKED she didn't make a move to slip out of the doorway. A figure stood there, gas mask concealing his or her face, arms raised, a small, black gun gripped between hands that shook ever so slightly.

Ridley's first thought was Nathan. He was the one who'd spoken about getting rid of the director and the rest of the Shadow Society leaders. He knew where Alastair Davenport was right now. But that thought was replaced almost instantly by another when Ridley noticed the knitted, rainbow-striped sweater.

"Saoirse," she gasped. Shock had forced her back into human form. Startled, Saoirse swung the gun toward her. Ridley ducked, but Saoirse stumbled backward and lowered the gun, stuttering something Ridley couldn't make out behind the gas mask. "What the *hell*, Saoirse? Seriously, what the ..." She gestured at the three bodies. "What did you just *do*?"

Saoirse tugged the gas mask off. "I ... I did what had to be done. You weren't ... I didn't know you were here. I didn't know where anyone was after our attack on the wall failed. So

I ... I ..." The floor shook again and something rattled above the ceiling. Saoirse grabbed hold of the doorframe as Ridley reached one hand toward the wall.

"It was you," a strained voice said from across the room. "You were Jude's informant." Saoirse swung the gun back up to point at Alastair, who was slowly pushing himself up to sit against the wall. He had one hand pressed against the area just below his left shoulder. Blood seeped into his clothing.

"No," Ridley said, launching herself forward and tugging Saoirse's arm down. Another gunshot pierced the air, and she gasped in fright. But the bullet had gone through the floor. "Saoirse!" she exclaimed, squeezing Saoirse's wrist until the gun clattered to the floor. "What are you doing? You're not a killer!"

"He's the director, Ridley. He wants to kill *you*!"

"I know." A small part of Ridley was thinking she should just let Saoirse do it. Why was she trying to *save* the man who'd killed so many of her kind? But she'd decided this already, when they were first discussing all the details of this revolution. There would be casualties, and Ridley had accepted that, but she wasn't okay with standing face to face with someone and ending his or her life.

"I thought Jude got rid of you," Alastair said between labored breaths.

Ridley looked at him, his words only now beginning to sink in. *You were Jude's informant. I thought Jude got rid of you.* "Wait," Ridley said, releasing Saoirse's wrist and stepping away from her. "You ... you were the one who ..." She shook her head and swallowed, but there was no denying the puzzle piece that had just slipped into place. "You told the Shadow Society about us? About the reserve. And all those other communities that were attacked."

Saoirse pulled herself a little straighter and lifted her chin. "Because they needed a push," she insisted. "They needed a reason to act. We couldn't keep living like that, in our perfect little sanctuary out in the wastelands. It wouldn't have lasted."

"Are you ... are you *kidding*?" Ridley's hands were clammy, her skin hot and then cold and then hot again. "How could you do that? You got the reserve destroyed—you got people *killed*—because you wanted action? You wanted change?"

"We *needed* change. The society would eventually have found us and destroyed the reserve anyway."

"You don't know that."

"I do know that. I've lived through this before, Ridley. So did you, though you don't remember it. You don't remember the way everyone else was—was *slaughtered*." Her voice hitched, and she took a deep breath before continuing. "At least this way, we were able to save almost everyone. I sent anonymous messages to the other communities, and I warned ours as well. I was already there, ringing the bell, when you arrived. It wasn't like before. Last time, when your parents were killed, we were taken completely by surprise. And that's what would have happened again one day if I didn't act."

"You *warned* us?" Ridley repeated. "Are you joking? You gave us like five seconds warning. You were at the bell at the same time I was. In fact, if I'd listened clearly to what magic was trying to tell me earlier in the day, I would have warned everyone *before* you did. Your warning barely gave us a head start."

"Because they were faster than I realized! I was listening carefully all night, sending out my intention to magic and trying to get an idea of exactly where they were. But I couldn't sense anything until it was almost too late." She shook her head. "I told you before, Ridley. I can't communicate with it the way you do. Even after years of meditation and listening and trying to converse with magic ... it'll never be easy for me the way it is for you." The envy in her tone was unmistakable.

Ridley let out a shaky breath. "When did you do it? When did you tell them where to find us?"

Saoirse was quiet a moment. Then she sighed. "A day or two after you arrived at the reserve. I knew what kind of power you could wield, and I knew then that we had a real chance. We couldn't continue hiding. We *had* to act. I had to make sure of it."

Ridley's mouth fell open. "*That long?* You knew for that long that the Shadow Society would be coming? You could have warned us *days* before the actual attack. Why did you wait?"

Saoirse pushed her hands through her hair. "Because it ... it needed to be real. The fear. We had to be running from *them*, not just the idea of them, otherwise nothing would change."

"You're unbelievable."

"You can judge me, Ridley, but I don't regret what I did. I've been living the fugitive life far longer than you have. It was time for change. Time to get rid of *them*—" she jerked her head toward Alastair "—and time to change the world."

"You're the one who tried to get me a few days ago," Alastair said, struggling to sit a little straighter. "Outside Aura Tower."

"Yes. That was me. We never knew who the director was before, otherwise I probably would have come for you sooner. But Ridley learned the truth from your son, and I knew then that I'd be getting rid of you myself."

"This is crazy," Ridley murmured. "How did I not know this about you? I thought you were so ... peaceful. Instead you've been running around with firearms for *days*, trying multiple times to kill someone."

"I am a peaceful person," Saoirse said, her eyes pleading with Ridley to understand. "That's all I've ever wanted for us. I've never used a gun before. I didn't *want* to use one now. During the attack, after I left you outside the city, I went looking for him. I waited until I could sense him. I was going to fly down, grab him, whisk him away as air, and then drop him from a great height. But something ... repelled me. There was arxium all over him. I realized I wouldn't be able to get close. So I went back to your friend's apartment and stole her gun. Then I started watching and following and trying to work up the nerve to use the darn thing. I discovered this place. I got inside easily enough and shut down the arxium gas system. Magic told me exactly which room to find the director in, and now ... here we are."

"So you never went looking for my dad like you said you

would," Ridley said. "And you never joined the others while they were trying to break through the wall. You just went off on your own little murderous mission."

"Ridley—"

"After your whole speech to me about not acting alone, about *trusting* everyone else." The world shuddered beneath her feet again. A horrible, shiver-inducing sound, like the screech of metal against metal, reached her ears.

"I told you to trust everyone to do their part," Saoirse said. "This is *my* part. This is for the good of all elementals. I—I'm not a killer, Ridley, but someone has to do this. Someone has to—What is *happening* out there? Are we trying to break through the wall again?"

"*We're* not doing anything," Ridley told her, "since you're apparently acting on your own now. But Nathan and the others are—Hey!" She shoved away from the wall as Alastair launched himself across the floor toward the fallen gun. She kicked it aside, which meant he grabbed her leg instead and tugged her down. She splashed to the floor in the form of water, slid away from him, and became human again near the bank of screens, at least half of which no longer displayed an image. Alastair scrambled for the gun again, but his fingers had barely scraped the edge of it when a piece of the ceiling fell and hit the edge of his head.

"Get out of here now," Saoirse said, and then she vanished. Ridley knew she should follow. Saoirse clearly assumed she *would* follow.

There was a bang and a screech overhead, and another

part of the ceiling began to crack. "Dammit," Ridley muttered. This room was on the ground floor, and approximately ten stories worth of city wall and illegal research facility were about to cave in on her. Her magic pulsed beneath her skin, ready to transform her in an instant.

But she hesitated. Was Alastair dead? No. Ridley's gaze caught on the slow rise and fall of his chest. She should go. She should leave him here. She wouldn't have to kill him, but he would die anyway, and that was a win, right? But this was Archer's father. His *father*. It was possible Archer and Alastair hated one another by now, but Ridley had lost a parent, and there was something inside her that couldn't simply leave him here to die.

Her magic transformed her to air in a second. A crack split the ceiling from one side of the room to the other. She swooped forward—

—and someone raced into the room, hands raised, fingers splayed, magic forming a hemisphere shape in the air. Archer lifted his hands, and the shield of magic rose toward the ceiling, expanding to fill the room. The shield sparked where pieces of concrete, brick and metal struck it before being blown aside by the magic. But the pieces were growing larger, falling faster, as the facility collapsed on top of them. Archer let out a guttural cry, his arms shaking beneath the strain of holding the shield in place.

Ridley's air self slipped past the shield and into the mass of falling rubble. *Tornado*, she whispered to the magic. *Hurricane. Whatever you have to do, just throw this all AWAY!*

There was a moment—less than a moment—when everything seemed to freeze. And then the chaos of falling concrete, metal, beds, computers, laboratory equipment, arxium, torture instruments, and everything else that made up this horrible place was hurled violently outward. Exposed now, Ridley watched the debris spill across the ground on the wasteland side of the wall.

She dropped back down. In the single, non-demolished room, Archer released the shield of magic and leaned over, shoulders heaving as he breathed heavily. There was nothing above them now but a sky full of tumbling dark clouds. Rain pattered down. The earth continued to shudder around them.

"Archer," Ridley said once she'd pulled her magic back inside herself.

He straightened quickly, turning to face her, surprise clearing the exhaustion from his face. "Rid."

Raindrops trickled down her face. The space between them swelled with every secret, every past mistake, every moment of hurt and betrayal. But the rain kept falling, and it seemed to Ridley that it was washing everything away, leaving behind only the desire to fall into Archer's arms and never leave his embrace.

"I ... I want to talk," she said. "About everything. But—"

"But you have to go save the world?"

Ridley almost found it in her to laugh. "Well, I need to check first that my dad and grandfather got out from under all of this. I asked Nathan and Malachi and the others to focus all their earthquakes on this section of the wall to try to break through the—"

"I saw them," Archer interrupted. "I was looking for the entrance to this place—I only just found out about it—and there was a tremor. I thought it was another earthquake, but then the ground exploded, like someone set off dynamite underneath it. This great big hole appeared and then out climbed Mr. Kayne and another Mr. Kayne."

Ridley smiled. Her chest swelled with something like pride. "I told your dad they were badass." The smile slipped away and she wiped rain from her eyes as she looked down at Alastair Davenport. "He's still alive. But I don't know if he's … okay. Saoirse shot him and the others, and she was going to finish him off, but—"

"Saoirse?" Archer repeated in surprise.

"Yes. That's another long story, but—"

"—you should go. Sounds like the others are attempting to break through the wall again. They probably need your help. I'll get my father out of here as quickly as possible and then you're free to go wild."

Ridley nodded. Her magic drifted around her. She was about to vanish when instead she stepped forward, grasped Archer's T-shirt, and pulled him closer. She pressed her lips against his. For several heartbeats, the rain-drenched kiss was the only thing that mattered, and Ridley wished she could climb inside this moment and hide here forever.

But another shudder of the ground reminded her that none of this was over yet. "I'll find you afterwards," she told Archer. Then she disappeared.

# CHAPTER 28

THIS REVOLUTION WAS PRETTY much all on Ridley now. There were eight other elementals involved, and they were doing what they could—they'd broken apart the section of the wall that housed the research facility, along with a decent portion on either side—but everyone was aware that they would fail again if Ridley didn't have the kind of power that an heir with *two* super-powered parents should supposedly have.

They'd agreed that after freeing Ridley's father and grandfather, Nathan and the others would send earthquakes through the ground around the rest of the wall, cracking and breaking it apart as much as possible. The earthquakes were supposed to be controlled enough that the rubble fell toward the wastelands and not toward the city. Which basically meant they would be begging the elemental magic around them to help make that happen.

Ridley would then follow and burn through everything that fell. She could, of course, burn the wall while it was still standing, but that had never been part of the plan in case enormous, fiery pieces of arxium fell toward the city instead of away from it. That certainly wouldn't leave anyone feeling favorably disposed toward the elementals who'd just revealed themselves to everyone.

She soared above the demolished research facility, waiting until she could no longer sense Archer or his father nearby. Then she shot down, transforming into a blazing ball of fire. She struck the rubble and fragmented, sending flames racing across the ruin to consume all the arxium. *Further, faster, hotter. Burning, burning, burning.* Barely a minute had passed when she pulled herself back together and spun upward as air to see her progress. An inferno blazed across the entire ruined section, leaping up toward the intact parts of the wall on either side.

There were more cracks further along, and other colossal sections of wall screeching and groaning and toppling to the ground. Ridley raced toward them, ready to burn—then slammed up against an invisible force and went tumbling backward on the wind. She held her elemental form this time, recognizing the odd magical force she'd knocked into as another elemental. An *unnatural* elemental.

*Dammit.* Alastair was knocked out and his lab was gone. Doc was probably gone too. They couldn't possibly have injected new volunteers in the time since this attack began. And it couldn't be Lilah, because if so, Ridley would have been able to sense her.

*Lilah's dead*, she reminded herself with a pang.

So maybe Alastair had been constantly making new elementals, losing them every few days as they died and then making more—

No. Ridley remembered him barking an order into his commscreen just before Saoirse showed up and shot him. Something about standby subjects ... and she was pretty sure he'd used the word 'activate.'

*Doesn't matter*, she told herself. There was definitely a man-made elemental somewhere close by, and she had to get past him or her and continue burning. She whirled up and then around, hoping to avoid whoever was in her path. But there was another—she changed direction to avoid the presence—and then another.

Furious, Ridley summoned a cyclone wind and sped away from the city, tossing her thoughts out to the magic around her. *How many? Where are they? How do I get past them? I thought I was supposed to be incredibly powerful?*

The answers came in flashes of knowledge, one tumbling over the next over the next as they filled her mind. *There are others, more, everywhere, more, you're stronger, focus, the stone, alone now but not alone.*

Alone now but not alone. It was the sense of comfort Ridley had received from magic before, but it was also telling her ... she was alone? *What about the others?* she asked. She pictured Nathan and Malachi, reaching out for them with her thoughts. They should be nearby, in the ground, forcing cracks through the earth. Her mind filled with the answer, images of their solid earth forms ramming up against other solid earth forms, pushing their way up to the surface, transforming to air, elemental and fake elemental tangling together like two interlocking vortexes.

*You have to do it*, magic whispered to her, and she understood that it meant she had to do *everything*. She had to be the earth and cause the quakes and break the wall and burn the panels. Fear filled her at the idea of earth, but at the same time, she understood that she *could* do everything. That's what it felt like she was being told. She just needed that darn stone. She needed an extra boost, extra focus, extra strength.

*Where is my mother's stone?* she asked, wondering if it might possibly be that easy and if she should have asked days ago. She sensed magic drawing her in a certain direction. Like a game of hot or cold, she followed as best she could, dodging the man-made elementals when she sensed them nearby. At times, the trail seemed to disappear. Or perhaps magic didn't actually know where the stone was and it was searching, listening, feeling just as intently as Ridley was searching, listening and feeling.

She soared over the city, this way and that, responding to the tug when she felt it, until finally, she figured out where magic was leading her: Aura Tower. The penthouse. Which made sense. Alastair Davenport must have hidden the stone somewhere in his home. Ridley just had to find it.

She swooped down until she found a floor that was low enough to have windows that actually opened. Up at the penthouse, where storm clouds swirled dangerously close and deadly winds sometimes rocketed past, not a single gap could be found anywhere. Ridley made her way swiftly up through the skyscraper until she conjured a hole in the penthouse floor and drifted up through it as air.

Once again, she was in the Davenports' vast, flawless, magazine-worthy home. Exotic artwork, vases of fresh flowers, glass boxes on marble pedestals displaying priceless artifacts. It was becoming quite familiar to Ridley these days. She moved forward, then stopped, her heart squeezing at the sight of a familiar antique music box. It was made of wood with a flower-shaped mother-of-pearl inlay decorating the lid. She had sold this to Archer and Lilah the evening they'd come looking for a last-minute birthday gift for their mother. It was so soon after Archer had returned to the city that Ridley didn't even know yet that he was back. The other thing she didn't know at the time was that he'd come to Kayne's Antiques that evening specifically to see *her*.

She took a moment to slow her racing, invisible heart, then continued past the music box. She floated through the open-plan living space, turning a corner to where the grand piano sat in front of floor-to-ceiling windows. Rain pattered quietly against the glass. Her gaze skimmed across statues and painted bowls and furniture she doubted anyone ever sat on, hoping she might spot a large stone pendant on a chain. She couldn't help feeling a little as if she'd come full circle. The threads of her life had begun to unravel the night she crept in here to steal a gold figurine, and now here she was again, hunting down another ancient artifact inside the Davenports' home.

"Ridley."

Ridley spun around at the sound of her name, her heart

almost jumping clear of her chest. She vanished a split second later—more of an instinct than anything else—then reappeared, recognizing Lilah's voice at the same moment her eyes fell on the dark haired girl standing by the piano.

Lilah. Who wasn't dead.

The last time the two of them had been inside this home, Lilah had filled the place with arxium gas and told Ridley she would be caught. This time, when Lilah's hand moved, it was to touch the chain that hung around her neck. "You're looking for this, aren't you." She lifted the chain and pulled a large pendant free from beneath her sweater. It was Ridley's family heirloom stone.

# CHAPTER 29

"YOU'RE ALIVE," RIDLEY breathed. Immense relief seeped through her body, leaving her feeling weak and exhausted and oddly happy, given how cruel Lilah had been to her at times over the past ten years. Ridley found herself almost smiling— and then almost laughing. Hadn't she thought to herself that it should be impossible for anything to wipe out a force like Delilah Davenport? Turned out she was right.

Lilah took a deep breath and let the pendant rest against her chest. "I was out there," she said, gesturing vaguely to one of the windows, "just flying aimlessly around, trying to figure out ... some things. And I sensed you. I couldn't tell if you were searching for me, or if you just happened to be nearby. I returned to the top of Aura Tower, and you came inside. I came in through the air cooling ducts from the roof. I sensed you floating around here, and I realized you must be looking for this."

"Yes. Are you the one who took it? From that store room of samples at the research place. I looked for it when I escaped, but it wasn't there."

Lilah nodded. "You told me it would heal me. You were right."

"I—I did? I was?"

"You may not remember. You were drugged. I struggled to wake you. I think I slapped you a few times. Sorry about that," she added, sounding genuinely remorseful. "You mumbled something about a stone with healing properties, and even though no one ever told me about this heirloom thing, I'd overheard enough conversations and hacked enough of Doc's notes to know what you were talking about. Didn't take me too long to find it."

"And it actually worked," Ridley said in amazement. "It healed you."

"Yes. Well ... sort of. Not permanently."

"What do you mean?"

Lilah's dark eyes, so similar to Archer's, traveled Ridley's face. There was something different about her. This was not the same Lilah who'd hoped Ridley would be caught. This was not the person who'd pointed a shotgun at her own brother and accused him of betraying their family. "If I take it off," Lilah said carefully, "the symptoms come back. When I put it back on, the symptoms go away. So if I want to keep living, I'm guessing I have to keep wearing it. But ..." She paused and bit her lip. "You need it." She looked toward the window as a faint shudder reverberated through the building. "You're trying to do what Archer was talking about on his live video. Getting rid of the arxium and returning our world to the way it used to be. And this stone will help you."

"Yes," Ridley said simply, a crack slowly splitting her heart. She *did* need it, but she didn't want Lilah to die. She knew what she had to do—take the stone by force, if Lilah wouldn't give it to her—but that didn't mean she wanted to do it.

"I know my father caused the Cataclysm," Lilah said, changing the subject out of the blue. "He didn't tell me—obviously—but thanks to a conversation you recently had with him, and an archive of surveillance footage, I now know what he did. I know that he's lied to me for years and that he's the reason magic retaliated and billions of people died." She walked closer, pulling the chain up and over her head. Her voice shook when she said, "It's the most horrifying of all the secrets I've ever discovered, and it makes me sick—so, so sick—to think that I firmly believed he was right about magic and elementals all these years." She shook her head and sucked in a deep breath. "My life always felt so trivial, Rid. I wanted so badly to be part of everything my father was doing. To be part of something *bigger*. I just didn't realize until now that we were on the wrong side of that something. Archer did, and I wish he'd told me sooner. I wish he'd *made* me listen to him." She held the pendant out toward Ridley. "I hope you can change the world."

Slowly, some part of her wondering if this was a horrible prank, Ridley reached for the necklace. Lilah let her take it. She exhaled slowly and lowered her hand. Ridley's gaze traveled down as a yellow-gold glow began to pulse through Lilah's veins, visible just beneath the surface of her skin. Looking up again, she saw the same glow fading in and out of the veins that coursed across Lilah's face. The same glow in her eyes.

"Don't look at me like that," Lilah said, rolling those oddly golden eyes and sounding more like herself. "Like you're terrified I'm about to drop dead on the spot. I'm not going die *immediately*. I think it'll take a bit of time."

Hope surged in Ridley's chest. "How long?"

"I don't know. Just hurry. If you can. I know I'm a grade A bitch who doesn't actually deserve to survive any of this, but I don't particularly want to die."

Ridley managed a small smile. "That's funny. I kind of feel the same way about you." She looped the chain over her head. "I'll get back here as quickly as I can."

"No. Meet me on top of the Boards24 Building. The building with the rooftop garden. There's something else I need to do ASAP. In case I don't ..." In case she didn't make it.

"You'll be fine," Ridley insisted. "I'll be there as soon as possible."

"Thanks." Lilah took a few steps back, the golden glow intensifying as wisps of yellow magic rose away from her skin. "In case I don't get to tell you later, this magic thing is actually really cool."

Ridley grinned. "I know."

"And Rid? I'm really sorry. About everything." Then Lilah shut her eyes and disappeared.

Ridley's next breath left her in a rush of air. She could barely believe any of that had just happened. She looked down at the pendant and pressed one hand over it. "Time to end this," she whispered.

And that was when she heard a scuffle of footsteps and a grunt. She shifted to air immediately. Spinning away from the piano, she saw Archer dragging his father toward a couch. Alastair's jacket was off, rolled into a bundle and pressed against the gunshot wound below his shoulder. "Stop fighting me," Archer groaned. "I'm trying to help you."

Ridley soared past them. She must have missed the sound of the front door opening while Lilah was talking. The door was still open, in fact. Archer was probably planning to leave soon.

"Get *off*!" Alastair shouted. "I don't need your help." Ridley twisted around near the front door, looking back as Alastair shoved Archer so hard he stumbled into a small table, knocked it over, and sent a giant wooden egg rolling toward the window. It came to rest against the glass surface. "Doctor Manly is on his way over. He'll be far more help than you. Now get out of here. Your mother never wants to see you again and neither do I."

"Great," Archer said flatly. "The feeling is mutual. In fact, I should have let you die earlier. You'd probably prefer that over knowing I used *magic* to keep your torture facility from collapsing on you."

Alastair, who'd been leaning on the edge of the couch, launched forward and struck Archer across the face. Archer stumbled backward another few feet, then tripped over the fallen table and landed near the wooden egg. Ridley rushed back across the room. "What disgusts me just as much is that you used magic to get us back here," Alastair said. "What the hell was that? Some primitive transport conjuration?"

As Ridley hovered anxiously nearby, torn between grabbing Archer and leaving versus letting him have it out with his father, Archer climbed to his feet. He scraped at the air, pulling handfuls of magic from it within seconds. "This is not disgusting, Dad!" he yelled, pulling more and more magic. "Look at it. *Look at it!*" He stepped aside, letting the glowing mass hang between them. "This has *never* been disgusting!"

Alastair grabbed his jacket from where it had fallen onto the couch. He swung it at the crackling, sparking magic.

*There's arxium in the jacket*, Ridley thought the instant before the jacket swiped the magic. She hurled her air form at Archer, becoming a waterfall of water at the same moment the magic exploded outward in a blazing flash, reacting to whatever arxium had touched it.

Ridley's ears rang, which made her realize she *had* ears, which made her realize she was in human form again. Lying on a hard floor. Beside a dripping wet Archer who was struggling to sit up. The howl of a gale joined the ringing in her ears. Icy air tore across her wet skin. Not wet from the water form she'd been in moments before. Wet from rain. Rain pelting her skin. Rain gusting in through the enormous hole that had been blasted through the penthouse windows.

"What have you *done*?" Alastair bellowed. He was across the room on the other side of multiple upturned items of furniture. Not to mention multiple shattered glass boxes, fallen statues, broken vases, and probably a great many priceless artifacts. Perhaps because he'd been the one wielding the arxium jacket—or perhaps because he had other forms of protective clothing—he appeared to have survived the magical blast. "*You.*" His eyes locked onto Ridley.

Archer was up already. In one swift motion, he tugged Ridley to her feet. Without another thought, she launched toward the gaping hole, taking Archer with her. Together, they fell.

Even with the knowledge that she could shift to air—which she did about a second later—it was terrifying. She thought she heard the wind scream in her ears before she shifted form, but it was probably her own voice.

Ridley sped toward the Boards24 Building and deposited Archer in the middle of the rooftop garden with zero explanation. She'd wasted enough time already. Were Nathan and Malachi still trying to dodge fake elementals? Had they given up? Had they been hurt or ... worse?

As she passed the wall and soared over the wastelands, she reached out for Nathan. She found him, further out, and her instinctive question—*Is he okay?*—was answered immediately: *Yes.* She could tell Malachi was with him, and along with the vague sense of their location, she felt a hint of ... playfulness? No, that wasn't quite right. But the idea trying to take form in her mind was definitely of some sort of game. She strained harder to understand, and the answer finally hit her in a single thought.

*Distraction.*

They were drawing the man-made elementals further

out, giving Ridley a chance to get close to the wall. They were trusting that she could do it all without them as long as they kept the threat at bay.

Again, like earlier, she felt magic telling her, *You have to do it*. Meaning: You have to do *everything*.

*I know*, she answered. But the idea of diving into solid earth still scared her. Then her fear seemed to drift away as hope swelled inside her and around her. It wasn't her own. Well, some of it was, but mostly it was the magic out here, taking her tiny kernel of hope and amplifying it and adding its own. She felt encouraged and ... lifted. Almost literally. Buoyed up by the currents in the air. And then ...

She was catapulted down toward the earth. Fear and determination and excitement collided in every particle of her being as the ground rushed toward her. *I can do this*. A conversation that seemed like a lifetime ago came to mind. *Fall into it*, Grandpa had said. So she did. She fell *into* the earth.

It was utterly dark. Terrifying and exhilarating. She hurtled forward the same way she would as air or water or fire, but somehow as a continually moving *solid* being. She didn't know how and she didn't try to direct it. She fragmented and all she knew was *crack, shudder, smash, demolish*. Except ... that wasn't all she knew. She was scattered, but somehow ... focused. Her magic stretched through the ground, reaching further and further, but she was precisely aware of every inch of it.

*Break the city wall*, she thought. *Break. The. Entire. Wall.*

Power erupted through the earth and past what remained

of the broken, burned arxium machines, and though Ridley couldn't *see* it, she knew where it went. It rushed through the ground, circled the city, and struck the entire wall at once. Cracks fractured their way through the structure. *Fall outward*, she thought as she burst from the ground and became air. Like a shock wave radiating out from a central point, hurricane-speed wind rushed away from the city in all directions, and colossal pieces of the wall fell with it.

Ridley shot downward, shifting to fire, and struck the rubble. With a deep, imaginary exhale, she let herself come apart, sending flames rushing across the ruins. They licked, raced, leaped, blazed, and soon the whole of Lumina City was encircled by flame. Pulling herself back to her contained elemental form, Ridley glided overhead. She couldn't help imagining someone sitting inside their home staring out at this, possibly thinking the end of the world had come. *I'm sorry*, she thought. *It'll be over soon. All the arxium will be consumed and then this will be over.*

She directed her attention upward to the arxium panels that hovered above the city, unable to help herself from feeling a touch of doubt. There were thousands of panels. The area was *so* much bigger than the area she and the others had practiced in near the reserve. Lumina City was enormous. And though Ridley was an heir, she was also just one elemental—and she was starting to tire. Could she really burn through everything? Fling all those thousands of burning panels beyond what remained of the wall?

*The rest of us could probably sit back and watch while you burn through all the arxium around Lumina City on your own.*

That's what Saoirse had said. But did she really *know*? She didn't. She'd been guessing. Hoping.

*You can*, magic said, and there was that feeling that had pervaded Ridley's being after she'd burned through the Shadow Society building in the wastelands. The sense that magic was pleased with her.

Without giving her doubt another moment to strengthen its hold on her, she shot toward the panels. She fragmented before reaching them, racing through the air on the wind, spreading out further and further until her air self felt as if it encompassed the entire dome of panels. Then, with a single explosive thought, she let go entirely.

*BURN.*

An inferno of apocalyptic proportions erupted instantly across the sky, igniting every arxium panel in a second. The fiery mass blotted out the sky for barely a moment, and then the force of the magic hurled every burning panel outward and away from the city.

It felt to Ridley as if a tiny piece of herself was launched into the wastelands along with each of those panels. If not for the pendant she wore, she might have been so far-flung that it could have taken hours, days for her to pull herself back together. But she retained enough focus to snap herself back into a single ball of flames. Then into a gust of air.

She remained high up, watching as the broken pieces of Lumina City's wall slowly burned themselves down to nothing. Further out in the wastelands, the fiery specks that were the burning arxium panels blinked out one by one until none were left. Finally, Ridley watched as the clouds that had been rolling overhead all morning drifted apart just enough for sunlight to stream through, lighting up several gleaming glass skyscrapers.

Exhausted, relieved, amazed—an overwhelming combination that mostly just made her want to cry—Ridley swooped over the buildings of the Opal Quarter, looking out for one in particular. A building with a rooftop garden. A building where Archer was waiting for her.

# CHAPTER 30

RIDLEY FOUND ARCHER holding onto the railing that encircled the edge of the Boards24 Building's rooftop garden,
staring up at the blue sky that was visible in a gap between the
clouds. She stepped out of the air and brushed aside a palm
frond.

"Archer," she said quietly, not wanting to startle him. He
turned immediately. His expression mirrored the mix of emotions she was feeling, but there was also a question in his gaze.
An uncertainty.

Right. That probably had something to do with the kiss
Ridley had left him with earlier. After telling him she would
never trust him again, a kiss was understandably confusing.
She wanted to explain that she'd heard everything he said on
the video he'd broadcast to the world and that she forgave him
for all that was in the past, but words seemed like they required a lot of effort right now, and actions were simpler.

She walked to him, slid her arms around his waist, and
pressed herself against his chest. His arms came up around
her back, holding her tightly to him. His cheek rested against
her head. "You did it," he said.

She nodded, but didn't answer.

"Are you okay?"

"I'm ... tired." Tired was an understatement. She was utterly spent. She wasn't sure if she could change form now if she tried. Now that everything was over, she wanted to hold onto Archer and never let go. She wanted to ask a dozen questions—how was he able to use magic again after Saoirse had done that conjuration on him? Where did he go after Ridley left him at Mrs. Adams' place? What was he doing at his father's research facility when the wall began collapsing? She wanted to find Lilah and give her the stone before it was too late. She wanted to hug Dad tighter than she'd ever hugged him before and tell him he would never, *ever* stop being her father. Mostly, she wanted to lie down and sleep for days.

But her mother's stone was heavy around her neck, reminding her that finding Lilah was the priority now. She stepped out of Archer's embrace just far enough to be able to twist her head around and look behind her. "Have you seen Lilah?"

"Here?" Archer asked. "No, why would she be here?"

"She told me to meet her here. I need to give her ..." Ridley trailed off, realizing that Archer might not be up to date on this particular piece of news. "Do you know about her? About ... her magic?"

Archer's eyebrows almost vanished into his hairline. "Her *what*?"

A shrill siren pierced the air, and both Ridley and Archer turned toward the sound. It wasn't the fact that it was a siren that caught their attention. Sirens and alarms had been blaring since Nathan and the others had first begun breaking the wall apart. It was the *type* of siren that made Ridley's nerves jump. The single, high-pitched wail followed by a short, upbeat jingle. It meant there was an important announcement about to be broadcast onto the billboard screens across the city.

She and Archer leaned on the railing and peered down. Ridley's eyes sought out the nearest billboard and found it just as the current advertisement—a woman with impossibly shiny hair holding a shampoo bottle—was replaced by an image of Mayor Madson sitting behind a desk. He greeted the public as Archer swore quietly. "This can't be good."

"... address the devastation that has been brought upon our city by a group of radicals," the mayor was saying. "But first I must urge you all to remain calm. The city wall and arxium panels may be gone, but we are extremely fortunate that the wasteland magic is currently experiencing what scientists term a 'rest phase.'"

"Rest phase, my ass," Ridley snorted.

"I assure you that the appropriate emergency protocol has already been initiated," the mayor continued, "and we will be erecting interim protection while new arxium infrastructure is built."

Ridley shook her head. "Right. 'Interim protection.' He means mobile arxium gas machines that will cause new magical storms and remind everyone they should be afraid after all."

"... gone viral on all the social feeds," the mayor was now saying, and Ridley pressed a fist against her lips as her heart thudded with anxiety. "A video of a very unstable young man spreading lies and attempting to delude the rest of the world. Many of you know Archer Davenport. You know about his problems with alcohol and drugs. He spent many months in a private facility recently, and his family believed he was ready to rejoin society. Unfortunately, his delusions have only grown worse."

"Unbelievable," Archer muttered beside Ridley. He shook his head and gripped the railing harder, his knuckles turning white. Ridley placed a hand gently over one of his.

"The sad truth is that this unstable young man uncovered a secret—a secret we have tried to keep safe for years for fear of causing further panic after the Cataclysm—and he has concocted wild tales around this secret. He has left me with no choice but to reveal a dangerous truth to you: The beings known as elementals are real. They are the ones who have attacked our city and exposed us to the harsh and deadly elemental magic of the wastelands. They are the ones—" he paused and let out a heavy sigh "—who are responsible for the Cataclysm."

"*What?*" Ridley shrieked. "How dare he! *They* ruined the world, and now he's blaming it on *us*?" She'd thought she had no energy left for anything, but it turned out fury was enough to wake her exhausted mind and body.

"I urge you to disregard the lies Archer Davenport is trying to spread. His past record of delinquent behavior and—"

The screen flickered. The image of Mayor Madson disappeared. Suddenly, eerily, it was Ridley's own voice that she could hear ringing out from the billboard's speakers: "I know the truth about the Cataclysm. I know what you did."

Ridley's breath vanished from her lungs. Her heart hammered wildly within her chest. Her hand gripped Archer's so tightly that her fingers began to hurt. On the giant screen, she saw herself sitting on a bed, her arms and ankles bound. Alastair Davenport stood across the room from her.

"Somebody told you," he said.

"You turned the GSMC into an apocalyptic event," she accused.

Ridley's nerves were so on edge, her heart thrashing so frantically in anticipation of his next words, that she thought she might throw up.

"I did," Alastair Davenport replied, admitting to the entire world what he'd done. Ridley let out the breath she'd been holding, her body feeling weak and shaky and exhilarated all at once. "It was the perfect opportunity," Alastair continued. "We couldn't waste it. Thousands of magicists gathering together around the world. Energy conjurations plus amplification conjurations ..." The pounding in Ridley's ears drowned out the next few sentences, but it didn't matter because she already knew what he'd said. He'd mentioned the Shadow Society. He'd mentioned—Ridley almost laughed with glee when she remembered—Jude Madson. He'd even spoken about manipulating the Secretary-General himself.

Her ears tuned in again as Alastair finished with, "... and the whole world went boom. Devastating, but perfect. Overpopulation? Solved. Magic? Confined to the wastelands. And that's where it will stay for the rest of time."

The recording froze and the screen faded to ... black. Nothing. No mayor. No advertisements. No propaganda. When had there ever been *nothing* on the billboard screens? But there is was. Nothing but space and silence for people to contemplate exactly what Alastair Davenport, one of the world's wealthiest and most influential people, had just confessed. He had *planned* the Cataclysm.

"Lilah did this," Ridley murmured. "Lilah showed everyone the truth." Then she straightened, urgency rushing through her. "Where is she?" She reached out with her magic. *Where are you, Lilah?*

The answer came at the same time as the sound of a banging door. Ridley raced through the garden, pushing aside leafy branches and exotic flowers. And there, hidden behind a hedge of red roses, was a brick structure and a door. Standing wide open. A body slumped across the threshold. A body with threads of gold glowing beneath every visible inch of her skin.

"Lilah!" Archer exclaimed, rushing past Ridley. He knelt and scooped her up so she lay across his lap, while Ridley crouched beside her, tugging the necklace off. She looped the chain over Lilah's head, lowering the stone pendant to rest against the bare skin at the hollow of her neck. Lilah's eyelids fluttered open and closed, revealing her glowing eyes.

"What the actual ... Is this *magic*?" Archer asked.

"Mm hmm," Lilah mumbled. Then she managed a weak smile. "Told you I know more of Dad's secrets than you do. Also ... he's an asshole, and you were right about everything." She lifted a shaky finger and pointed it at him. "Hope you were listening closely. Not gonna say that last bit again."

Ridley almost laughed in relief—Lilah was going to be just fine—but the sound of voices sent her heart tripping over itself again. No one else should be up here. No one else should be close enough for her to hear. She rose to her feet and peered around the hedge, her eyes darting across the exquisitely expensive vegetation, her magic ready to hide her in an instant. She would take Archer and Lilah too, of course. Lilah might not be strong enough to use her own—

"Dad!" Ridley blurted out as he stepped around a tree with hundreds of tiny white blossoms. With no thought for how he could possibly be here, she launched past the roses and threw her arms around him. "Dad, I'm sorry. I'm so sorry I just left. I'm sorry I called you a coward. I was so shocked and hurt and just ... overwhelmed, but I should have stayed and talked to you. I shouldn't have left like that. When I thought I might never see you again, I—"

"Rid, it's okay. It's ... *I'm* the one who's sorry." Dad hugged her tightly. "I *am* a coward. I should have told you the truth long ago."

Ridley sucked in a shuddering breath as tears gathered in her eyes. "You'll always be my dad," she whispered. *"Always."*

Dad stepped back and took her face in his hands. "I'm so proud of you, sweetie. So, so proud of you. Look at what you've done. You always wanted to make a difference, and now you have."

Ridley blinked as the tears slipped down her cheeks. She sniffed and wiped them away. "It wasn't just me. I couldn't have done it without help." She noticed Nathan then, standing a few paces away, and suddenly she understood how Dad had come to be up here. "You're okay," she said with relief. "You got away from them. The fake elementals."

"Yes. We were surprised and confused the first time, which is how we ended up losing people. But we were prepared this time. Just had to make sure they didn't force us into human form." He walked closer. "Malachi and I came back to search for you. He's somewhere else in the city, still looking. I sensed your father before I sensed you, and he insisted I take him with me."

Ridley gave Nathan a grateful smile. "Thank you for everything today. Thank you for drawing those other elementals away from the city."

"Sure," he said with a shrug. "Thank you for taking care of everything else."

Ridley mimicked his shrug. "Easy peasy."

"Well then." He grinned. "Ready to get out there and liberate some more cities?"

# CHAPTER 31

THE TINY LIVING ROOM IN the apartment above Kayne's Antiques had always been perfectly adequate for Ridley and her father. They didn't exactly entertain much. Sometimes Meera and Shen were there too, but that was about as far as they pushed the limits of the living room's size. But that evening, as most of Lumina City tried to figure out what the heck had just happened—while also gazing in wonder at a perfectly clear, star-studded night sky for the first time in years—seven people crowded into the Kaynes' living room.

As containers of Chinese takeout from across the road were passed around the room, Ridley slowly pieced together everything that had happened over the past few days.

As she was already aware, Dad had wound up at the Lins after Revolution Attempt Number One had failed. Knowing that something had gone terribly wrong and suspecting the Shadow Society had Ridley, he'd decided he couldn't simply sit at the Lins and do nothing. Though he knew it was probably foolish, he went to Aura Tower to confront Alastair Davenport.

That, of course, hadn't gone down well. Dad figured he

could take care of himself—with no AI2 and a bunch of offensive and defensive conjurations up his sleeve—but Alastair had bench-pressing minions on his side, plus the ability to smoothly lie about taking Dad straight to Ridley—and then throwing him into an empty containment chamber instead. The next day, Grandpa had joined him there.

He hadn't received the message Dad had sent him just before the reserve was attacked. The message that said Dad and Ridley had left Lumina City and were safe. He had, however, received a message from Mei Lin informing him that Ridley had accidentally revealed her magic and she and her father were on the run. He'd received the message days after it was sent, but as soon as he knew what had happened, he began making his way back to Lumina City. He was much further away than the last time he'd returned though, and the journey took him a number of days.

After entering the city via the bunker, he'd gone to Kayne's Antiques, hoping to find a clue of Ridley or Dad's whereabouts. Unfortunately, this was just after Ridley and Christa had escaped the research facility, and Alastair Davenport had people watching the apartment in case Ridley showed up there. They took Grandpa by surprise—meaning he didn't get a chance to use any of those ancient badass conjurations he knew—and carted him off to Alastair to ask what to do with him. Alastair recognized him and figured it would be worth hanging onto him along with Ridley's father. That was when he ended up in the containment chamber with Dad.

Archer had left Mrs. Adams after Ridley and Saoirse abandoned him and tried to contact Ridley's dad. Either because of a signal problem or because Dad didn't trust Archer anymore, he didn't answer. Figuring he was on his own and should try to help in any way he could, Archer planned to look out for falling pieces of arxium and deflect them so no one got hurt. But when the fire in the clouds vanished soon after it began and the earthquakes outside the city came to an end, he realized something had gone wrong. With no one left who trusted him, he decided to go to the bunker.

Turned out Christa was gone, and since the magic users living there were just regular people—meaning most of them probably weren't even aware of elementals or the Shadow Society—there was no one there from either side reporting that Archer Davenport was a traitor. He was still there when Grandpa showed up. He told Grandpa everything that had happened since he'd fled the city with Ridley and her father—and since they'd ended up returning because of the Shadow Society's attack on the reserve. He also told Grandpa the truth about the Cataclysm and his family being part of the Shadow Society.

Grandpa left the bunker, hoping he might be able to track down Ridley or Dad, but not before performing a conjuration that reversed the effects of the one Saoirse had done on Archer. He could pull magic again.

A few hours later, Archer heard about the wall coming down in Linevale. He realized change was happening after all and decided the one thing he could do was make sure as many people as possible knew the truth. So he sat in a room near the bunker's entrance where it was possible to get a signal and did his live video recording.

Then he spent the rest of the night out of signal range, worrying about whether the Shadow Society had already come up with a way to fight back. Maybe his father had been able to get the video taken down. Maybe someone official— the Secretary-General himself, perhaps—had released an opposing story. The social feeds were global, after all, so it was possible the video had reached the SG. Would he take it seriously? Or did the man who governed the entire world have more important things to worry about?

But the following day, it seemed nothing had happened yet to Archer's video confession aside from it going viral and racking up thousands of comments he didn't even want to read let alone attempt to reply to.

Then Christa arrived at the bunker. There were more than a few people who wanted to hurt her, given that they were all now aware she'd sold out certain magic users. But she'd seen Archer's video, and since everyone now knew about elementals and the Shadow Society, she had decided to come crawling back to ask for help getting rid of the society members she knew about.

Archer hadn't given Christa the chance to explain much— he didn't, for instance, know anything about his father's synthetic elementals and the fact that his sister had turned herself into one of them—but she did tell him about the research facility and helping Ridley escape. Having no interest in working with Christa, Archer left the bunker and decided to check out this backup facility his father had failed to tell him about when they were supposedly on the same side. That was what had led him to the city wall and the surveillance room Ridley was in just as the entire place began collapsing.

He sat beside Ridley now, occasionally resting a hand on her leg, or leaning over to press a brief kiss to her temple, or rubbing his hand in gentle circles on her back. She stole glances at him every few minutes, in between shoveling food into her mouth and deconstructing the past few days with everyone else who was squashed into the living room. He kept meeting her eyes, and some unspoken understanding passed between them each time. They hadn't had a chance to properly talk yet, but the kiss earlier, and then the embrace on top of the Boards24 Building—plus all the secret glances and small smiles this evening—probably gave him a good indication of how she felt.

Lilah, who'd made a quick recovery once she was wearing the heirloom stone, sat primly on the desk chair Ridley had wheeled out of her bedroom, questioning Malachi about all things elemental-related and refraining from commenting on the worn, tattered state of pretty much everything inside the room. Her eyes had almost bulged out of her face at the sight of the loose plastic covering the gaping hole in the window but, to her credit, she'd managed to keep her lips zipped. Either that or she'd been shocked speechless.

Malachi, for his part, was playing things cool, but Ridley could tell he was a little star-struck. He'd hated the Davenports when Ridley met him—their first few minutes together had involved him attempting to beat up Archer—but Delilah Davenport was gorgeous, famous and currently directing all her attention at him. He was definitely soaking it all up.

Nathan was the one who completed the group of seven

gathered around the collection of takeout containers on the crate at the center of the living room. He kept checking his commscreen, looking out for reports about cities being liberated, important people being arrested—like Alastair Davenport—and people attempting to remove their own AI2s. In between, he kept throwing out suggestions to Ridley about which city they should tackle next. "Other elementals are getting ready to act," he kept saying. "They could use our help. There might be some other heirs out there, but probably not many. You can continue making a difference like you've done here."

"Maybe," Ridley kept answering. And she meant it. She was too exhausted and overwhelmed by everything to properly contemplate it right now, but she *did* want to keep making a difference if she could.

"And no, still haven't heard from her," Nathan added quietly after his latest city suggestion. Ridley had told him about Saoirse being the one to give up the location of the reserve and some of the other elemental communities, and then attempting to kill Alastair Davenport. Nathan said he'd sensed her out in the wastelands, helping to draw the manmade elementals away. But when he'd gathered together with everyone after it was all over, and before he and Malachi returned to the city to look for Ridley, Saoirse was gone.

"Oh, I think that's my delivery," Lilah said at the sound of a vehicle outside. She stood and squeezed around the couch to look out the window.

"Your delivery?" Ridley asked. "You don't think we have enough food here already?"

"We have plenty of food, but I figured we need some celebratory drinks to go *with* the food." Lilah peered through the window. "Yep, that's Sven. Poor guy, he looks so lost out there. Probably never been to this side of the city. I'm just gonna go downstairs and—"

"You called *Sven* to come here?" Archer asked.

"Yeah. The world may be in upheaval, but he's still employed by us, right?" Lilah maneuvered her way between chairs and knees and takeout containers. "I called him when we got here and sent him to Dad's cellar to pick up some drinks for us. What?" she added defensively. "Dad was just arrested. He's not going to need his Champagne in prison."

"You asked Sven to bring *Champagne*?"

Lilah looked around the room. "I mean ... if you guys *don't* think we have something to celebrate, I'll just keep it for another occasion."

Grandpa leaned back and attempted to stretch his legs, which resulted in the crate of food sliding across the floor a few inches. "I wouldn't mind some, especially if it's the real deal."

"Oh, it's the real deal," Lilah assured him with a grin. "Champagne with a capital C. I'll go down and get it."

Ridley looked at Dad. "Um ... I don't think we have appropriate glassware." Legitimate Champagne was worth an appalling amount of money, given the tiny section of the Champagne area that had survived the Cataclysm and how little of the alcoholic beverage was produced these days. It seemed all kinds of wrong to drink it out of a cheap wine glass, and they didn't even have enough of those for everyone.

"Actually," Dad said, "there's a set of antique champagne flutes in the store downstairs. I'll get them." Dad shuffled past Lilah's empty chair and behind Malachi and made his way downstairs, leaving Ridley lost for words. If anyone in the room was going to disapprove of opening an astronomically expensive drink that several of the room's occupants technically weren't even old enough to consume, it was going to be Dad.

"He continues to surprise me," she said with a laugh, lacing her fingers between Archer's and then lifting his hand to give it a quick kiss.

Lilah returned with two Champagne bottles, which she clutched possessively to her chest when Archer stood and offered to open them. "I don't think so," she told him. Ridley's mind flashed back to Lilah holding a shotgun while telling her brother not to patronize her. With considerable effort, she managed to keep her snort of laughter inside.

The takeout containers were moved aside, the antique glasses lined up, and Lilah popped the Champagne bottles without injuring anyone or losing a drop of the valuable contents. Then, on a cheap crate in a shabby living room on very much the wrong side of the city, one of the world's most expensive drinks was poured. They toasted—"To a new world!"—and Ridley had her first taste of real deal, capital-C Champagne. She savored every sweet, sparkling sip.

Later, when she stood and took the glasses to the kitchen, Archer gathered up the empty takeout containers and followed her. She placed the glasses carefully beside the sink before facing him. Nerves fluttered in her chest. "Do you want to get out of here? Just for a few minutes?"

"Anywhere," he answered, taking her hand.

They vanished and escaped the apartment within seconds, but Ridley didn't take them far. They reappeared on the roof of her building. She looked up at his warm eyes and that beautiful smile she'd missed so much over the past few days—and then turned away. She'd wanted to be alone with him but suddenly she felt ... awkward. She moved to the edge of the roof and looked out over the neighboring buildings. Sirens wailed in the distance. "What do you think is going to happen now? What kind of world are we going to wake up to tomorrow?"

"Honestly? Absolutely no idea." Archer took her hand and pulled her around to face him again. "Though I think you can safely assume you don't have school tomorrow."

"Probably not. And if I do, I might just have to take a mental health day instead."

"Or several," Archer said, one side of his mouth curving up.

Ridley smiled, hesitated, bit her lip. Then she finally said, "I got your message."

Confusion crossed his face. "My message?"

"The one you sent out to your bazillions of followers."

"Oh, right. The video message. Yeah, a lot of that was for you."

"I know. I ..." Ridley took a breath and let it out in a rush. "I'm sorry I reacted the way I did when you told me everything."

"I don't think there's any other way you could have reacted."

Ridley nodded. "I guess. I think I just needed ... time? To

process it all. I think I'm *still* processing everything. There's ... a lot."

"Like ... the news about your dad?"

"About him *not* being my dad? Yes. Definitely still processing that one. At the end of the day, it doesn't change anything important. He loves me and I love him and he'll always be my father. But I guess it takes a while to properly see yourself in a new light, you know?"

Archer nodded. "I do know."

Ridley bit her lip again. "Your dad was arrested tonight."

Archer nodded, but didn't say anything.

"We all kind of just stepped over that moment when Nathan mentioned it and moved onto the next takeout container, but ... it's kind of a big deal."

"It is," Archer agreed. "It's a *good* big deal. He can't get away with all the terrible things he's done."

"I know. I guess I just wanted to acknowledge it."

"Acknowledgment noted."

They stared at one another for a moment or two, and then Ridley started laughing. "Why is this weird?"

Archer's laughter joined hers for a moment, but then he sighed. "It's weird because I screwed everything up between us. I'm sorry, Rid. You'll never know how sorry I am."

At some point he had reached for her other hand, and now she slid her fingers between his, gripping both hands tighter. "I think I do. When I saw you in that Shadow Society meeting ... when I thought that everything that had happened between us was one big lie ... it felt like it broke everything inside me."

"Ridley ..." Archer's expression was pained. "I am so, so—"

"And I'm not saying this to make you feel worse. I'm saying this because the fact that it hurt so, *so* much made me realize how much you mean to me. So I do know how sorry you are, because that's how sorry—how utterly, distressingly sorry—I feel when I think about not being with you." She looked down at their joined hands, then up again. "You mean a lot to me. Like ... *a lot*, a lot. A *huge* amount of a lot, a lot. And it's kind of scary to say that out loud because what if—"

"I love you,"Archer said simply.

Ridley's stomach dipped. Her pulse rushed and her breath seemed to keep catching in her throat. There were other words that had been cued up, ready to leave her mouth, but she couldn't remember what they were.

"I'm sorry, that wasn't supposed to freak you out, and it's not like I'm expecting you to say the same thing back to me. I just wanted you to know. I wanted to tell you before, when the truth about everything else was spilling out of me, but it seemed selfish—manipulative—to throw it out there when everything else I was saying was breaking your heart, so I—"

Ridley stood on tiptoe and touched her lips to Archer's. The first kiss was soft, chaste. Then she untangled her hands from his and wove her arms around his neck, pulling herself tighter against him. His hands trailed down her spine and pressed against the small of her back as his tongue slid across hers. She kissed him harder, shivers dancing up her neck and into her hair when his fingers found their way beneath the edge of her jacket and T-shirt and skimmed across her bare skin.

She rocked back down onto her heels, breathless, happy,

exhilarated. "I love you too," she said. Archer's smile stretched wider. Ridley tried to keep hers a respectable size, but she felt like a grinning maniac so she was probably failing. "I very definitely love you too."

He kissed her again. She kissed him back. They remained entwined until Ridley could barely breathe and her skin was flushed and her heart was racing out of control. Laughing, she finally forced herself to step back. She sucked in a deep breath of cool night air and released a happy sigh, turning her face toward the sky. The stars weren't nearly as bright here as they were over the reserve, but the fact that she could see them at all was incredible. Lumina City had been covered in near-constant cloud for so long.

Her eyes lowered to Archer's again. "The stars feel close enough to touch." They didn't—not the way they did out in the wastelands—but it had been far too many days since she'd spoken those words, and it felt like they needed to be said again.

Archer's expression told her he knew exactly what she meant. "Stretch high enough," he answered immediately, "and maybe your magic *can* touch the stars."

She stood on tiptoe and stretched her arms up, fingers pointing toward the sky, reaching, reaching, reaching. Archer looped his arms around her waist, lifted her, and spun her around. She laughed, and it was one of the best feelings in the world.

"Are you touching them yet?" he asked.

"Almost!" She stretched high once more, then let herself slide back down to her feet. Her arms slipped around Archer's waist. "We should probably go back before my dad finds us missing from the kitchen and panics."

"Probably." Archer kissed her brow, then her nose, then stopped near her lips. "One more kiss?"

She smiled. "One more kiss."

# EPILOGUE

RIDLEY TOOK A STEP BACK in the living room and surveyed her handiwork. Well, her conjuration work, to be more accurate. It had been three days since the Reverse Cataclysm—a term someone had come up with that was now trending on all the social feeds—and it was technically still illegal to use magic. But everyone was doing it, no one was being arrested, and it was high time the hole in the living room window was fixed. So Grandpa showed Ridley a few conjurations, and she set about doing it herself. "Not bad," she said, tilting her head to the side and nodding at the window. "Not bad at all."

She skipped downstairs to tell Grandpa. He was behind the desk at the back of Kayne's Antiques, writing something on a notepad. Dad was talking to a customer about repairing something, from what Ridley could tell. She caught the words 'don't mind if you use magic,' and felt her eyebrows climb. Less than a week ago, people would have shamed Dad and turned him in if they'd discovered him using magic for anything. Now they didn't mind?

Before she could say anything to Grandpa, the bell above the front door jangled, announcing the arrival of another customer. "Shen," Ridley called, waving when she saw it was him. She made her way between the display tables and gestured for him to head back outside with her. No point in hanging around inside a dingy old shop if the sun was shining outside.

"How's it going?" Ridley asked, hoping her words didn't sound forced. She and Shen had seen each other a few times over the past several days, and even though things seemed normal enough on the surface, she could tell it wasn't the same as before.

"Look at that," Shen said, turning his face toward the afternoon sky and avoiding Ridley's question. "Another sunny day."

"I know. Amazing, right?" It wasn't like the sun had *never* broken through the clouds after the Cataclysm. It did occasionally, and there was often a thin layer of dull gray cloud with sunlight burning through from the other side. But clear blue skies and blazing sunlight had been exceedingly rare over the cities where there was so much arxium.

Shen pushed his hands into his pockets. "I just came from the bank. You know there's that clinic across the street?" Ridley nodded. "Almost everyone who came out of that clinic while I was waiting in line had a small bandage stuck behind their ear."

"Getting their AI2s removed?" Ridley asked.

"Yep. It's not allowed yet, but clinics seem to be doing it anyway. Probably a good thing, otherwise people are going to slice their own skin open at home to get their AI2s out and make a mess of things."

"Yeah, definitely a good thing," Ridley agreed.

"So, um ... have you seen Meera yet?" Shen asked.

"She called earlier, actually. We're meeting tomorrow." Her stomach clenched every time she thought about it. She had never before had any reason to feel anxious about seeing Meera, but now ... she had no idea what to expect from the girl who'd told her she didn't want to know anything about Ridley's magic or any of her other secrets.

"Oh yeah? That's great."

"It is." Ridley nodded, but her tone was hesitant.

"Or ... not great?"

Ridley shrugged. "It was awkward. Talking via commscreen, at least. And it'll probably be even more awkward talking in person. But it's good. We need to talk about everything." She folded her arms and leaned against the front window of Kayne's Antiques. With a smile, she added, "I could hear Anika in the background begging to come with so she could also talk to me. Meera kept shushing her."

Shen chuckled and leaned against the wall beside the window. "Anika must be overjoyed about this Reverse Cataclysm. She was always far more interested in magic than her older sister."

"Yeah, not nearly as afraid of the law as she should be, Meera always liked to say," Ridley added with a sigh. "Anyway."

"Anyway," Shen repeated. He looked away. An empty soda can tumbled across the street on a gust of air. "Um, how long is your grandfather staying?"

Ridley eyed Shen with a narrowed gaze. She got the feeling that none of these conversation points were the reason he'd come over here. "He's uncertain at this point," she answered. Technically, Grandpa was still officially dead. With no idea whether the people who'd threatened him years ago were still around, he didn't want to stay here for too long in case someone found out. But he'd agreed to stick around for a bit while everything was so chaotic and government officials had other things to worry about.

"And, uh ... no plans yet to 'liberate' any other cities?"

Ridley turned so she only had one shoulder against the window and was fully facing Shen. "You know the answer to that." She hadn't *had* to liberate any other cities because after seeing what was happening in the rest of the world—after seeing that magic *wasn't* waiting to tear down any area without protection—numerous cities had chosen to begin dismantling their own arxium infrastructure. "Shen," she said. "I feel like there's something you want to tell me, and for some reason you're too afraid to spit it out."

He shut his eyes, ran a hand over his hair, then looked at her. "I'm leaving."

Ridley blinked and unfolded her arms. She pushed away from the window. "Again? Like ... for good?"

"I don't know. I just ... I don't think I can stay here. I can't get it out of my mind. The—the terrible thing I did. I have to learn to live with myself and I don't think I can do it here. I need to start over somewhere else."

"I ..." Ridley looked past him, considering this development before voicing her thoughts. "I think you're right. Maybe it is best that you start over somewhere new. When are you planning to leave?"

"Tonight. I made the decision this morning and booked a ticket on one of the inter-city trains."

"Oh, wow. So soon." She looked around as the bell tinkled over the door and Dad's customer walked out. He nodded briefly to Ridley and Shen before striding away.

"Yeah," Shen said. "Staying here another few days isn't going to change anything. May as well leave now."

"I guess." Ridley let her gaze travel his face, wondering if today was the last day she would ever see him. "So do you want me to explain things to Meera when I see her tomorrow?"

Shen shook his head. "That would certainly be the easier way out, but I think I owe it to her to explain everything myself. We've been friends for years. I can't just disappear forever without saying goodbye in person."

Ridley nodded, relieved. She happened to agree with him.

"I, uh ..." Shen straightened. "I'm heading over to see her now actually. I just wanted to come and tell you and say goodbye in case you're out later and I miss you."

"So—so this is it? This is goodbye? I ... this ..." Ridley shook her head. How had this moment of great significance come out of nowhere? "Shen, you're my oldest friend."

"Yeah, and I turned out to be a pretty terrible one."

"No, you didn't. You just—"

"I messed up. I was so intent on protecting you and everyone else like you that I went too far and I messed up. Anyway, this probably isn't goodbye forever." He stepped closer and pulled her into a hug. "You can race across the continent on the wind if you feel like it. I'm sure we'll see each other again."

After a final goodbye, Ridley leaned against the window again, watching as Shen's long-legged lope carried him back across the street. When he was gone, she turned back to the shop's front door. She opened it, then froze as something pressed against her ankle. Looking down, she found a black cat with one white paw, four ears, and eyes that glowed magic blue. "Ember?" she said in utter astonishment. She hadn't seen the magic-mutated cat since she'd first escaped into the wastelands and Ember had helped Archer to find her.

Ridley reached down to run her knuckles across Ember's head, which Ember allowed for approximately two seconds. Then, shoulders back and tail held high, she sauntered past Ridley and into Kayne's Antiques as if she'd been here all along and had merely gone out for a brief jaunt.

"Wow, I thought that conversation was never going to end."

Ridley straightened in fright, looking around at the figure who'd suddenly appeared on the sidewalk behind her. "Lilah? How long have you been here?"

Lilah pointed a perfectly manicured fingernail at Ridley. "You're supposed to be the super powerful one. Didn't you notice I was here?"

Ridley hadn't noticed a thing outside of her oldest friend announcing he was leaving and then her peculiar pet showing up out of the blue. What she did notice, now that Lilah was standing in front of her, was that while they were similarly dressed—jeans, T-shirt, jacket—Lilah managed to look like she'd stepped off the pages of a fashion magazine, and Ridley looked ... well, average. "I was a little distracted, okay? Was that you moving the soda can? I knew that gust of air didn't seem entirely natural."

Lilah grinned, like she was proud of the fact that she could roll a piece of tin across a street without touching it. She flicked her sleek dark hair over one shoulder. "That was me."

"You're supposed to use your powers for good, not for eavesdropping."

"I didn't eavesdrop. I watched from up there." She gestured to the roof of Ridley's building. "And I *know* you've done plenty of eavesdropping in your time, so get down from that high horse of yours before you fall off."

Ridley rolled her eyes. "What are you doing here?"

"It's almost five. You're supposed to meet us, remember? Sunset drinks in the wastelands? Toasting to something epic? With wine, because you and I used to do pretend wine tasting with our kiddie grape juice pouches?"

Ridley smiled at the memory. Six-year-old Lilah and Ridley had thought they were so sophisticated copying their parents' wine tasting ways. "I haven't forgotten. But last I looked, it was barely four."

"Right, and four is almost five, and this way you get an extra hour with Archer."

Ridley had to admit, that was an appealing prospect. "Okay, either you're bored, you're overexcited by your magic again and can't wait to use it, or things with your mom are becoming too much and you had to get away."

Lilah sighed. "All of the above?" She scraped the tip of her designer tennis shoe back and forth across the sidewalk. "Okay, maybe mostly Mom. Things are ... hard. You know, because of—" she waved her hands in the air "—everything. Dad and the arrest and everything becoming public and now she's suddenly being shunned by everyone who used to suck up to her. And Archer's not around because she refuses to see him, so she takes everything out on me."

"She still doesn't know you were the one who leaked the video of the conversation your dad had with me? About the Cataclysm?"

Lilah shook her head. "No, things would be *way* worse if she knew about that. She'd probably kick me out. Anyway, let's go." She reached for Ridley's arm and tugged it. "Hanging out on the sidewalk in a dodgy neighborhood is fun, but hanging out on the remains of a ruined building in the wastelands is funner—which, by the way, is a real word."

"Oh, trust me, 'funner' is not what I was about to object to. It's the 'dodgy neighborhood' I take issue with." Ridley opened the door to Kayne's Antiques, and leaned inside. "Dad?" she called. Alone now—Grandpa must have gone back upstairs—Dad looked up from the desk. "Still okay if I go out with Lilah and Archer? I'll be back later this evening."

Dad opened his mouth, then paused. Ridley could tell it was on the tip of his tongue to say something like 'Be careful' or 'Don't stay out too late' or 'Don't take off on your own and do something crazy.' But then he smiled and said, "Have fun. I'll see you later."

Lilah grinned at Ridley. "Can we go burn something?"

Ridley laughed. "When did you turn into a pyromaniac?"

"Pyromania has nothing to do with it. I'm just a tiny bit obsessed with the fact that I have *magic*. Seriously, Ridley, this stuff is awesome."

"It is, isn't it." Ridley tilted her head as she eyed Lilah, who probably hadn't shown this much excitement about anything since they were children.

"So, lead the way," Lilah prompted.

They flew above the city, beyond the area where the wall used to be, and into the wastelands. On a buckled suburban street where nothing but rubble and overgrown vegetation remained of the homes that once filled this area, Lilah leaped from shrub to shrub, burning through the tangle of weeds and grass. Ridley dove into the earth, confronting what little remained of her fear, pushing up the foundations of ruined buildings and sending faint shudders through the ground.

As the sun inched toward the horizon, Ridley convinced Lilah to return to human form. "You can hang around here longer if you want, but I should probably go back and fetch Archer." Until Archer made a more permanent plan, he was staying at the bunker, which had survived the destruction of the city wall with barely a broken brick. Ridley liked to think she'd been super focused with her earthquakes and with asking magic not to destroy the bunker, but the fact that it had survived probably had more to do with the magic users living there who knew how to protect their home with conjurations.

"Oh, Archer's already out here," Lilah said. "I left him on top of that half-demolished cinema before coming to get you."

Ridley pinned Lilah with a glare. "You mean I could have spent all this time with him instead of supervising your pyromania?"

"Don't try to pretend this wasn't fun," Lilah argued. "You brought down that water tower like a kid knocking over a pile of blocks. Which is to say," she added, "that you did it with great delight."

Instead of arguing further, Ridley launched herself into the air and swept back toward the city, sensing Lilah close behind her. The half-demolished cinema she'd mentioned was near the edge of the wastelands. As she drew near, she spotted Archer sitting on the highest point of the remaining structure, a commscreen in one hand and his back against a curved piece of concrete that had once been part of the building's roof design.

Ridley landed a little lower down on the roof and looked up. From this angle, she could see the small line between Archer's brows and the intense focus on his face. Something about the way he sat there, one arm draped over one knee, entirely absorbed in whatever he was reading and oblivious to everything else, made her love him even more. Internally, she rolled her eyes at herself. *Everything* about him made her love him more. It was kind of ridiculous.

"Hey," Lilah said quietly, catching Ridley's arm before she could climb up to Archer. "You know that long list titled Things Lilah Was Mean To Ridley About? I, uh ..." She ran a hand through her hair, which was somehow still sleek and glossy even after all her wild elemental antics. "I need to add Archer to it. I know I said you were like all those other silly girls, falling for his charming ways and then ending up with a broken heart, and—"

"And that's exactly what happened," Ridley said. "Sort of. I mean, I *thought* that's what happened. And before you said it—before anything even happened between Archer and me—I was already thinking it. I was very much aware of that long list of girls, and I didn't want to add myself to it. You weren't doing anything more than voicing my fears out loud."

"Okay, but I still shouldn't have said it. At least, not in the *way* I said it. I was ..."

"Hurt?" Ridley asked. She'd figured out that that was where most cruel comments came from.

"Yes. My dear big brother told me I shouldn't be friends with the girl whose dad used to be a magicist, and I listened to him. So you and I spent years at odds with each other. And then he returned after being away for so long, all secretive and refusing to share anything with me, and then showed up at that party with you as his date. And it was like ..." She shook her head, her brow creasing. "I don't know, like I was losing my brother *and* my friend all over again. I just felt really ... alone."

"I'm sorry," Ridley said.

"*I'm* the one who's trying to apologize here, Rid," Lilah answered with a laugh.

"I know, but I'm sorry too. You may not have heard any of the nasty comments I made about *you* over the years, but that doesn't mean I didn't make them. So yeah, I'm sorry too."

"Well, anyway, the thing I *actually* wanted to say—since I noticed you staring so adoringly at Archer—is that I'm happy for the two of you."

"Adoringly, huh?" Archer said, and Ridley looked around to see that he'd climbed down a foot or two. He extended a hand toward her.

"Whatever," she said, her face flushing, but she reached for his hand and let him pull her up. "I was looking at—the sunset."

"Sure you were." He tugged her closer and wound both arms around her waist. "You two took your time getting here."

Ridley gave him a careless shrug and a teasing smile. "I guess we had better things to do."

Archer leaned down and pressed a long, lingering kiss to her lips. "Better than that?" he asked quietly, mouth close to hers still.

"No," she whispered, "but don't tell Lilah."

"I'm right here," Lilah announced flatly. "I can hear you both. Where's that bag with the drinks?"

"Behind that broken bit of concrete there," Archer said, removing one arm from around Ridley so he could point. He sat and pulled her down next to him, sliding his commscreen into his pocket.

"I thought we were too far from the city here to connect to any network," she said.

"We are. I was reading."

"All right, first up," Lilah said, sitting on Ridley's other side and placing a backpack in front of her, "we have another one from Alastair Davenport's private collection." She produced a bottle of red wine, followed by three plastic wine glasses. "Dad would be horrified we're drinking out of plastic."

"I doubt he knows we even own those," Archer commented.

"When you say 'first up,'" Ridley said, "are you telling me there's more inside that bag?"

"Just some sparkling water. Oh, and that coconut pineapple combo my mom loves. Plus snacks. Don't worry, Rid." She nudged Ridley's arm. "I'm not planning for us to get drunk out here. Just enjoy a good vintage, watch the sun go down, and fly back home without crashing into anything."

"Sounds perfect," Ridley said, watching as Lilah gathered

up some wisps of her own magic and began a conjuration. She wove the magic around the top of the wine bottle, and the next thing—*pop*—the corked jumped free.

"Where'd you learn that?" Archer asked.

"I looked it up."

"Where? Nothing's been legalized yet."

"I happen to be capable of accessing hidden information online," Lilah informed him. She poured wine into the plastic glasses lined up on the roof in front of her. She passed a glass to Ridley and one to Archer. Then she lifted her own, held it beneath her nose, and inhaled deeply. She breathed out of her mouth. "Mm. Cigar box."

Ridley snorted. Archer reached around her and tugged Lilah's hair. "Don't be so pretentious."

"Hey!" Lilah leaned across Ridley and punched Archer's arm.

"Woah, hey!" Ridley held both hands up, her wine sloshing dangerously close to the top of her glass. "What happened to enjoying a good vintage and a sunset?"

"I *was* enjoying a good vintage," Lilah grumbled, "before I was rudely interrupted." But she turned her face toward the city, swirled her wine, and took a sip.

Ridley met Archer's eyes, then bit her lip to keep her laughter in. She happened to agree with the 'pretentious' comment. Archer put one arm around her shoulders, and she snuggled against his side as she tasted the wine. "Better than a kiddie grape juice pouch," she said.

"Definitely," Lilah answered with a laugh. Then she sighed and added, "Doesn't this take you back in time? The three of us hanging out together, like we used to do before the Cataclysm?"

"Yeah," Ridley murmured. "Minus the wine."

"And minus us all sitting *together*," Archer said. "Back in the day, it would have been you two playing together and me very definitely *not* playing with you."

"Oh yes, you were too cool for us," Lilah said. "I remember now. You were probably stealing our unicorn cookies and running off with that jerk friend of yours. What was his name? Verne?"

"Jeez, don't hold back, Ly," Archer said. "Tell me what you really think."

Lilah smiled sweetly. "Asswipe?"

"Nice."

"It's a term of endearment."

Archer shook his head. "Sounds like you missed a lesson or two at school."

"Ugh, school," Lilah groaned. "Do you think we have to go back on Monday?"

"I hope so," Ridley said.

"Only *you* would say that," Lilah accused with a roll of her eyes.

"Look, I don't know about you, but I still plan to graduate—if at all possible." Ridley turned the stem of her wine glass, her eyes following the scratches on the plastic surface. "Hey, do you think if I let everyone know I'm an elemental I'll be seen as cool or even more of an outcast? Not that being considered cool has ever ranked particularly high on my priority list."

"Hmm, I guess things *are* going to be quite different," Lilah mused. "Even if I don't show everyone my weird yellow magic—which I'm not planning to do, by the way—there's the fact that I'm the daughter of the guy who made the Cataclysm happen." She pursed her lips, absently running one hand over the bump beneath her T-shirt, where Ridley assumed her mother's stone heirloom pendant lay. "I guess that puts me very firmly in outcast territory." She turned to Ridley. "Will you be my friend?" Her tone was light, almost teasing, but Ridley could see the plea in her eyes.

"I'm already your friend, nitwit."

"Nitwit. Wow."

"It's a term of endearment."

Lilah laughed so hard she almost choked. Eventually, after Ridley smacked her back, she calmed down and sighed. Looking out across the wastelands, she said, "The city looks so different without the wall."

"And without the storm clouds," Archer added.

"It's beautiful," Ridley murmured. The sun had disappeared on the other side of the city, lighting up the sky with an expanse of color. Bright yellow bleeding into orange-pink bleeding into purple. Ridley leaned her head on Archer's shoulder. "What about you? Any plans yet? You're still staying, right?"

"Wherever you are, that's where I'll be. Until you get tired of me."

Ridley tapped her glass against his. "Not gonna happen."

"But aside from that, I do actually have a plan. It begins with an interview."

"An interview? Where?"

"The Rosman Foundation."

Ridley straightened, her mouth falling open. "That's *my* thing! You can't take my thing!"

"Hey, I'm sure there's room there for both of us," Archer said with a laugh. "I'm not *taking* anything. I just ... I kept trying to figure out what the heck I should be doing with my life now, and I kept coming back to that. I have no idea what I'd actually do there, but they're all about creating new opportunities for people—in a whole variety of ways—and that sounds ... I don't know, really fulfilling."

"Archer Davenport," Lilah said. "I don't even know who you are anymore."

Ridley stretched up and kissed Archer's cheek. "I love you. And you're right. I'm sure there's room there for both of us." She nestled against his side again. She was about to lift her glass to her lips when she remembered something. "Hang on, weren't we supposed to toast to something?"

"Oh yes," Lilah said. "We were. To something epic."

"You pick something," Archer said to Ridley.

She looked at her glass, considering. "Well, we already toasted to a new world the other night. So ... I guess ... to the future." She lifted her plastic wine glass, remembering the last thing Archer had said to her in his live video message. "To the future we dreamed of. The future we're in now."

"To the future," they repeated. And together the three of them raised their glasses.

# Acknowledgments

This is the book I thought would never be finished. It has seen a coronavirus lockdown, Riley sick (multiple times), me sick (multiple times), Kyle in hospital (a hiking accident), teething, sleep regression, numerous changed publication dates, Riley's first birthday, and—most of all—me figuring out how to be a mom and an author at the same time.

Pretty sure I haven't got that last one down yet!

So thank you to God for getting me to the end of it. Thank you to Kyle for doing Riley night duties so I could get enough sleep for my brain to function during the day. Thank you to all those involved in getting this finished book out into the world. And thank you to you, my dear reader, for still being here!

© Gavin van Haght

Rachel Morgan spent a good deal of her childhood living in a fantasy land of her own making, crafting endless stories of make-believe and occasionally writing some of them down. After completing a degree in genetics and discovering she still wasn't grown-up enough for a 'real' job, she decided to return to those story worlds still spinning around her imagination. These days she spends much of her time immersed in fantasy land once more, writing fiction for young adults and those young at heart.

www.rachel-morgan.com

Printed in Great Britain
by Amazon